"*Lights Out* is a thriller that starts at breakneck pace and never lets up. Kate Green is a great character—you'll want her to be your best friend, but she already has one, and she has to answer the question: Is she a murderer? In this striking debut, Elise Hart Kipness writes with heart, empathy, and psychological insight into evil that exists where you least expect it. She has created a main character who is real and warm and tough and faced with the biggest mystery of all: Who in her world can she trust? You don't have to love sports to love this book, but either way, Kipness's inside knowledge will pull you right in."
—Luanne Rice, *New York Times* bestselling author of *The Shadow Box*

"When a basketball superstar is murdered in his gated home, all eyes look to his wife and circle of insiders for possible suspects. Drawing on her experience as a national sports reporter and long-time resident of suburban Connecticut, Elise Hart Kipness takes us inside both worlds in this scandalous, page-turning thriller!"
—Wendy Walker, international bestselling author

"What a fantastic debut! A unique protagonist, an interesting setting, and a story that grabs you from the beginning and keeps on building. I couldn't put this book down and read it in one sitting!"
—Chad Zunker, Amazon Charts bestselling author of *Family Money*

"Welcome to Connecticut's Gold Coast, where celebrity athletes rub shoulders with the locals and marriage can be murder. When basketball star Kurt Robbins is found dead in his palatial Greenwich home, suspicion immediately falls on his wife, and it's up to her best friend, disgraced sports reporter Kate Green, to unravel Kurt's secrets and lies. Part posh domestic suspense, part puzzle box, Elise Hart Kipness's *Lights Out* is a skillfully constructed story of female friendship, hidden truths, and the mysteries that can lurk in seemingly quiet neighborhoods. I devoured every page."

—Tessa Wegert, author of *Death in the Family*

"Elise Hart Kipness's debut novel, *Lights Out*, is the kind of gripping, tightly paced domestic suspense mystery sure to delight fans of the genre as well as general readers. Set in the high-stakes world of professional sports, the book pits an appealing female protagonist against an increasingly slippery killer who will stop at nothing to evade capture. Elise Hart Kipness is a writer we are sure to hear more from in the future!"

—Carole Lawrence, acclaimed author of *Cleopatra's Dagger*

"*Lights Out* is a seminal triumph in mystery writing, as original as it is polished. Elise Hart Kipness's sterling debut takes us inside the world of professional sports on the one hand and a female reporter cracking that particular glass ceiling on the other. A crime thriller of rare depth and societal implications, *Lights Out* shoots straight and hits the bull's-eye dead center."

—Jon Land, *USA Today* bestselling author

LIGHTS
OUT

LIGHTS OUT

ELISE HART KIPNESS

THOMAS & MERCER

Text copyright © 2023 by Elise Hart Kipness
All rights reserved.

Published by Thomas & Mercer, Seattle

www.apub.com

Amazon, the Amazon logo, and Thomas & Mercer are trademarks of Amazon.com, Inc., or its affiliates.

ISBN-13: 9781662512667 (paperback)
ISBN-13: 9781662512650 (digital)

Cover design by Caroline Johnson
Cover image: © Tetra Images, © phototropic / Getty Images; © moomsabuy / Shutterstock; © storybylindsay / Unsplash

Printed in the United States of America

My parents told me to reach for the stars.
My husband held my hand for the journey.

PROLOGUE

My face smashes against concrete. Pain erupts through my jaw. My hand hits something damp. Fallen leaves? I try to open an eye, but the throbbing in my head stops me.

I feel my body hoisted into the air, then dumped onto a hard floor. Darkness swallows me. Pain pulsates through my flesh. The bouncing makes it worse. I feel around. There's something above me. I hear a car. Where's the car? It's loud. Is it getting closer? I'm thrown forward and back. A car isn't nearby. I am *in* the car. In the trunk. Hard metal smashes against my shoulder, and I realize I'm jammed against a suitcase. I reach my hand up. The trunk inches above. I sense myself panicking.

I force my eyes open despite the pain. It's completely dark. I reach into my pocket for my phone. It's not there. The car swerves, and I'm thrown against the side, pain shooting through my back.

I feel a curved shape by my head. Space for the tire? There's a damp blanket or towel too. The liquid feels sticky. I bring the fabric closer. It smells of blood. My blood? I'm woozy and adrift. The car jolts. My head knocks against the side, and pain shoots through my brain again. There's not enough air. I'm suffocating. I clench my hand into a fist and bang against the hood. It's quiet. Too quiet. And the horrible realization rushes over me—I may not survive.

CHAPTER 1

I wanted to spend the afternoon in bed, under the covers, tuning out the world. Instead, I'm in the auxiliary gym of Greenwich Lake School setting up for a high school Halloween dance. My best friend, Yvette, insisted I come. *No sulking,* she said. *This will blow over, and you'll be back at work in no time.* Personally, I think I've earned the right to sulk. After all, I was completely humiliated on a gotcha video that just happened to go viral. I know what I said wasn't ideal. A few choice expletives: an f-bomb and an a-hole. But he goaded me, accused me of being a bad mother.

I was just doing my job—asking the tough questions after the tough NBA game. When I was a professional athlete, I fielded those questions too. But he came at me. Sneering. Provoking. I did what any other self-respecting female athlete turned sports reporter would do—I defended myself. He doesn't get to call me a bad mom. Only *I* get to call me that. Of course, his part of the conversation didn't get recorded—an apparent equipment glitch. Then he denied it. Mason Burke stared into the cameras with his angry eyes set in pasty-white skin and claimed that I'd just gone off when he'd tried to answer a question. If the whole exchange had been taped, he'd be the one suspended and I would be celebrated as a woman who stands her ground. Or, at the very least, a woman with a job.

Even worse, my boss sided with Burke. *We all know what a sexist jerk Burke can be,* my boss began. *But, Kate, it doesn't look good. You cursed at him. Take the suspension while we sort things out. I talked the brass out of firing you. Be grateful.*

Just thinking about it makes my blood boil, and now my only *real* friend in all things Greenwich-related volunteered to make the 1:40 run for coffee and supplies, leaving me to hang Halloween decorations with Christie and the rest of the judgy volunteers.

Christie tilts her head like a little bird. "You know—I worry about Yvette. How does she handle Kurt's affairs? They're so public. I feel so sorry for the poor dear. And that article today in *Star* . . ."

"Yvette doesn't need anyone's pity," I snap, aware Christie is probably saying similar things about me to other moms. *Poor Kate, did you see that video? And she's out of a job now.*

I study all five feet of Christie, who wears heavy bronzer and shoves her thin frame into tight exercise outfits that come in varying shades of pink and purple.

As a former Olympic soccer player, I boast an athletic body, lithe but strong. I have thick, long honey-colored hair, which could never conform to a bob even if I wanted that. I don't like bronzer, making do with my fair skin, and I line my blue eyes with dark pencil—more Greenwich Village than Greenwich, Connecticut. And, for the record, I never, ever wear pastels, preferring a wardrobe of blacks, browns, and grays.

Christie seems undeterred by my retort and steps so close I can smell yogurt on her breath. "Do you ever see Kurt with other women when you cover his games?"

"That's a ridiculous question." I turn from her and pick up a spiderweb to hang. Not one for lying, I have no problem deflecting or avoiding. As a reporter for TRP Sports Television, I literally have a front-row seat to Kurt's indiscretions as he goes from dancers to models to whomever catches his fancy. It's hard to separate Kurt the player from Kurt the husband of my friend. Kurt Robbins the player is a superstar forward. Not quite a LeBron James, but close. Drafted to the New York Comets out of high school, he's led the franchise to three championships and made the all-star team every year. He's also charming and polite and would never call me or another reporter a bad parent. No matter how much he didn't like the question.

Kurt also adores the spotlight. Handsome with a chiseled face, warm brown eyes, and a quick smile. He easily moves from volunteering at food pantries to partying at exclusive nightclubs. The tabloids love and hate him, jumping from singing his praise one day to completely shredding him the next. As a retired athlete, I respect Kurt the player. He's always the first one at practice and the last one to leave. Through and through he embodies a true competitor.

Kurt Robbins the husband, however? That guy sucks. A lot of people question why Yvette stays married to him. Her go-to excuse is that the cheating Kurt doesn't represent the real Kurt—that fame and money corrupted him. *He was in the church choir when we met in middle school,* she always says about their childhood in upstate New York. *He just doesn't know how to navigate stardom. I mean these women throw themselves at him.*

Yvette explained the *real* reason she stayed with a cheating husband on our first annual girls' weekend away, which must have been fifteen years ago. It was that weekend when I felt our friendship moved toward something special.

"Werewolves of London" explodes through the gym. *You hear him howling around your kitchen door . . .*

I see my seventeen-year-old son, Jackson, hoist a large bale of hay over his head. His long, thin arms shake under the weight as he plops the bundle onto the outer part of the corn-maze wall, straw dispersing in the air. My eyes linger a second too long; he sees me and scowls as I turn away.

Christie walks off to fetch another box of decorations and stops to chitchat with a few of the other moms. I feel a bit ill at ease with the parents at this private school. It's not like they're outwardly rude, but they don't open their arms in a warm welcome either. They represent generations of Greenwich. Their grandparents were all best friends, then their parents, and now them. Why we needed to send our kids to private school in a town with such great public schools is something I still can't wrap my head around. But I pick my battles with my ex-husband. And since he comes from three generations of Greenwich Lake, this was never my battle to win.

"Dad's here." Jackson meanders over to me, keeping his gaze down so I can't see his blue eyes, mirror images of mine. He runs his long fingers through unruly hair. I sense the scowl forming on his lips.

"Okay. You and your sister are staying with your father tonight. Correct?"

"That's the plan." Jackson kicks his ripped sneaker against the gym floor. "I need to go."

"Well, have a good time," I say as he walks away. What is wrong with me? Who tells their child to have a good time at court-mandated therapy? Maybe Burke is right and I am a crap parent.

Christie returns with a crate of plastic creepy-crawly critters, drops them at my feet, and then runs off to make a call. I step around the crate and text Yvette, asking her to make my coffee extra large. I need all the caffeine I can get. Yvette sends back a thumbs-up. Christie returns and informs me that she needs to leave to show a client a house. In addition to being the town gossip, she's also the top local real estate agent. Luckily, Greenwich maintains firm restrictions on broker advertisements, or I imagine Christie's face would be emblazoned on the benches and buses of our town. Christie grabs her coat, turns to the students carving jack-o'-lanterns, and yells to her stepdaughter that she's leaving. Her stepdaughter grimaces but says nothing.

The music changes to "Monster Mash." *It was a graveyard smash. They did the mash.* Some of the teens start dancing by the fake cemetery. I spot my daughter, Nikki, jumping up, a few strands of honey-colored hair falling loose from her bun and over her cheek. She tucks the pieces behind her ear, reaches out her graceful arms, and totters to the beat. Nikki reminds me of a ballerina from a child's jewelry box, all delicate legs and arms. She sees me and waves, her soft brown eyes sparkling. I can't help but marvel at how different she is from Jackson, even though they are twins.

The front door bangs open, and four teenagers tumble into the gym lugging a mannequin of Frankenstein's monster. The green monster's head hits the ground, breaks from the body, and rolls across the floor. The kids scramble after the head. A police siren sounds from outside, distant at first but growing louder. Another siren, piercing and insistent, momentarily drowning out the music. I return to my spot as the noise fades and pick up two plastic bats hanging upside down and fold them into the webbing. Before I know it, I've hung dozens of critters.

More sirens erupt, the high-low frequency echoing across the gym. A few volunteers walk to the window. I can feel tension bubbling through the room; Greenwich is a quiet community that almost never elicits a large police response.

From across the gym, I spot Yvette wrapped in a floor-length cashmere coat. She sails toward me like a model crossing the runway, both in demeanor and appearance, with bright copper eyes and a slicked-back high ponytail. Today her extensions give the illusion of full, long ashen hair.

With one hand she holds her phone pressed against her ear, a large hoop earring pushed sideways. The other hand balances a tray of coffee, which she pushes toward me.

Yvette seems agitated, eyes darting back and forth.

"What's going—" I start, but Yvette puts up a finger. I stop talking and watch as she furrows her well-plucked brows. Under her cashmere coat she's wearing trousers and a cream-colored silk top. A bit dressy to decorate a gym. But that's Yvette. In all the years I've known her, I don't think I've ever seen her in sweats. At least she's replaced her usual heels with sneakers. She shakes her long ponytail and twists red lips into a deep frown.

"Can you repeat that? I can't hear . . ." Yvette's voice sounds thin. "Hello? Hello?"

"What's going on? Who is that?" I can't help asking. She ignores me, focusing on the phone. More police sirens blast through the gym, reverberating in the open space. I check the clock above the basketball hoop—2:30 p.m. A group of kids walk outside, and I glimpse red and blue lights.

I turn back to see Yvette's phone fall onto the hardwood floor. The screen cracks. I bend down and wrap the damaged phone in my scarf. "Yvette. Calm down. What's going on?"

More sirens pierce the air, like angry, invisible jabs. Everyone stops working to peer out the windows.

Tears sprout at the corner of Yvette's eyes. "All those police cars . . . I think they're going to my house."

CHAPTER 2

I follow Yvette outside, cold air stinging my legs. The sound of sirens continuing to screech through the air. We run down the brick steps, past the admissions building with its two-story Roman columns, and turn at the brass statue of Robert Middleton, the wealthy banker who built the school nearly a century ago. The story is told at every Greenwich Lake School fundraiser to remind benefactors that unless they donate a building, their contribution could be more generous. Needless to say, Kurt and my ex have buildings named after them.

Yvette moves quickly, and we reach the parking lot as the sirens momentarily fade. "Want me to drive?" I ask as we stop at her black Range Rover.

"No."

"You should let me drive, Yvette," I say for both our sakes. But in typical Yvette fashion, she ignores me, believing she can handle anything the world throws at her, no matter what.

She lifts her bag against the door lock. Nothing like my classic convertible, which needs an actual key. I climb in and smell lavender as Yvette presses the Start button. The engine roars to life, and she hits the gas, barreling out of the lot and onto the pavement.

"If you won't let me drive, can you at least slow down?" I pull the seat belt tightly around my body. She eases up, but only because we reach the stone gatehouse, where a guard needs to wave us through.

She speeds back up and turns right onto Lake Drive, keeping her gaze straight ahead. I study her profile—chin set, jaw tightly drawn down, like she's willing herself to maintain control.

"Who was on the phone?"

Yvette tells me it was her neighbor and that he said police cars kept arriving at her house. "The signal was bad, and I couldn't hear everything . . ." She grips the steering wheel so tight the skin of her knuckles lightens.

"Let's see if your phone still works." I retrieve the scarf I wrapped the broken phone in and carefully open the bundle. The whole face is shattered, but her home screen pops up, a summer picture of Kurt and their daughter, Dylan, resting on matching wicker lounges under a lush canopy by their pool. Dylan's hand is shading her eyes from the sun, and she seems annoyed at being interrupted for a photo. Dylan has the same bright smile as her father. Although she's much slower to share a grin than her dad.

Where is Dylan? I know she was supposed to be at the gym with my kids, but I can't remember seeing her. It's possible I just didn't notice. Or that she was working in one of the art rooms where some volunteers were building papier-mâché creatures. I steal a glance at Yvette; do I ask her about Dylan? I decide against it. Dylan is always Yvette's first priority, so she either already knows her daughter's whereabouts or doesn't want to think about Dylan possibly being at the house.

"So far, so good," I report to Yvette and ask for her code. She gives me a complicated combination of numbers, which I type over and over without luck. "You're going to need to get this fixed," I tell her.

The sirens sound again. I leave Yvette to her thoughts and stare out the window. Daylight succumbs to night, despite the early hour. In what universe is it all right for nighttime to start before cocktail hour? Granted my body didn't grow up under these dreary conditions. My mom moved my brother and me across the country to Northern California when we were toddlers. When I came back east, I adjusted fine to the cold temperatures, just not the premature arrival of night.

Yvette turns right onto North Street, and I glimpse hints of extraordinary wealth. A tiled roof peeking between branches and a Palladian window shining from an upper floor. All hidden behind manicured hedges and high gates. Yvette proceeds under large oaks arching together to create an umbrella of intertwined leaves—shriveled and shrunken, ready to fall to the ground in a pile of autumn decay. Ugh, I'm feeling morbid. *Shake it off, Kate.* This could all be a false alarm.

Yvette eases up on the gas as her front gate comes into view. I hear myself gasp. No chance of a false alarm. This many police cars don't race through Greenwich for no reason. About a dozen cop cars line the circular driveway of Yvette and Kurt's estate. The red emergency lights revolve like disco balls, casting a grim glow against the limestone facade of the Robbinses' mansion, which is described in magazines as a fusion of an English castle and a French château. It boasts six chimneys and a tower with leaded windows and a finial plopped on top that reminds me of the tower Rapunzel might be locked inside.

Uniformed officers cluster like ants in distinct sections of the sprawling property. One group by the arched wooden front doors. Another on the right of the mansion's flat grass lawn, where a pathway leads to the backyard with the lounge chairs I just saw in Yvette's photo.

In the rearview mirror, a small army of gardeners—ignoring the police activity—employ surgical precision to place flowers in pots at the foot of a neighbor's cobblestone driveway despite the darkening sky. The juxtaposition of activities feels offensive. There's an emergency going on. Shouldn't they pause?

Yvette inches toward the traffic cop, who stands redirecting vehicles. A few reporters wander the perimeter of the iron gates. Any marquee basketball player draws reporters, but with Kurt it's bees to a honeypot. If he gets a splinter, there are six NBA analysts and a doctor discussing the implication at a television roundtable. What will the recovery time be? Will the splinter impact his shooting form? On and on.

It's only a matter of time before the national stations, like mine, arrive. Back on the road, the officer holds up his hand to stop the opposing traffic and waves our lane forward. Yvette honks, and the young officer shakes his head and motions for her to roll down her window.

"Lady, what's your problem? We have an emergency here."

"This is my house." Her voice catches on the last word as indignation melts to fear. "What's going on?"

The young officer peers into the car. "Mrs. Robbins? I'm terribly sorry. I didn't realize it was you. Let me radio the detective in charge of the scene."

"The *scene*?"

"I mean . . . in charge." He steps back before she can ask anything else, and I see him fumble with his portable radio.

Yvette turns to me for the first time since we got in the car. Her eyes pleading for reassurance.

"Don't assume the worst . . ." is about all I can muster. Like I said, I don't lie.

A news van inches past us and pulls onto the curb of a neighbor's home, with the rear sticking out into the road. The signature news-truck position—screw you, I can park anywhere I want.

The cop returns from the shadows and leans toward Yvette. "If you could pull behind the blue sedan. The one over there." He points toward an unmarked cop car parked in front of Yvette's home. "The detective will meet you there."

"Pull over? Can't you tell me what's going on?" Yvette's voice cracks. "I want to go inside."

The young officer looks at the ground and says nothing.

"Please." She chokes. "Is it my husband?"

A car behind honks. Someone yells for us to move. The cop raises his eyes and looks at Yvette. I see pity in his expression. "The detective will be out to speak with you in just a minute. I promise."

"Please. Is it Kurt?" she whispers.

"I'm so sorry. Really." He steps back to let her pass into the cordoned-off area.

"Yvette." I put my hand on her arm. "That cop's just a kid. He might not even know what's happening. Let's do what he says."

She eases her foot off the brake and pulls behind the blue sedan.

I sit back in the seat and take a deep breath, hoping the lavender smell of her car will calm my racing heart. Midbreath, a new burst of sirens jolts me from the task. Yvette's front lawn now looks as if a spacecraft landed on it with all the activity and lights.

"That's it." Yvette opens her door, violently throws her purse over her shoulder, and steps out. I jump out of the car and sprint to her side. The air smells of pine and reminds me of Christmas, though the holiday is months away—a jarring contrast to the worrisome activity around us.

"Do you see Gene's car?" she asks, referring to her brother-in-law. "He usually comes over on Sundays to watch football with Kurt."

I step into the street to get a better angle of her driveway. It's hard to see past the reporters lining up outside her gate. I walk closer to the edge of the activity and peek through a small spot not blocked by bodies. Amid the police cars parked in her vast circular driveway sits a blue Mercedes sandwiched between another Range Rover and an ambulance. I step back to where she waits and tell her Gene's car is parked in front of her house. I decide not to mention the ambulance.

"What about Mason?"

"Mason Burke?" I can't hide the surprise in my voice.

"I know you and he have had some . . . issues. He also comes over most Sundays. Sorry, but could you see if his car is there?"

Issues? The dude got me suspended and then lied about it. But given the dire circumstances, I let Yvette's portrayal of my interaction with Burke go and ask what type of car he drives. Again, I walk closer to the house and scan all the vehicles. I return to her side and tell her I didn't see any car resembling a gold Corvette. I put my hand on her shoulder and feel her shaking. Poor Yvette. Her life is about to be completely upended. She must sense it. But just how bad the news will be, we don't know yet.

In the distance, the young cop huddles with a taller, middle-aged man dressed in a tweed sports jacket and jeans. He's bent down, nodding as the young officer speaks. In the dark, he looks more like a professor than a police officer, with a narrow frame, John Lennon glasses, and a closely groomed goatee. He walks briskly in our direction, quickly closing the gap between us.

"Detective . . . ?" I step in front of Yvette and reach my hand out. He looks at me through the round frames.

"Bernard. Detective Bernard." He shakes my hand while keeping his gaze on Yvette.

"Mrs. Robbins." He pivots.

"Yes. What's happening? Why can't I go inside? Where's Kurt?" Yvette sputters.

"Could we go somewhere to talk?" Detective Bernard keeps his voice monotone.

"Inside my house," she says. "Yes. The young cop wouldn't let me . . ."

"I'm afraid that's impossible." He gives a thin smile, as if commiserating with her, and suggests they speak at the police station.

"The station?" she whispers.

"It will be warm. I can get you some coffee."

"Detective," I interrupt. "Can you please tell her what's going on? We saw ambulances."

"What?" Yvette turns to me. A car drives by and kicks up a pile of leaves; a fresh burst of pine reaches my nostrils. The detective clasps his thin fingers together and again suggests going somewhere private.

"Stop playing games with me, Detective," Yvette cries, "or I'm going to march inside my house right now." She takes a step toward her estate.

"Mrs. Robbins." He puts his hand lightly on Yvette's arm to stop her. She turns and looks at him.

"I'm listening."

"When was the last time you saw your husband?"

"Excuse me?" She reaches for my hand and crushes my fingers in her grip. She must be thinking the same thing as I am. That's a question you ask if someone is dead. At least the TV cops do.

He takes off his glasses and rubs his eyes. "Mrs. Robbins . . ." He puts the wire frames back on and looks directly into Yvette's eyes. "Please. When was the last time you saw your husband?"

"At breakfast."

"When was that?"

"I—I don't know. Nine thirty. Nine forty this morning. I was rushing to the school. To volunteer. And he had practice."

"In the city?"

"No. Gene's gym. The Greenwich gym that his brother runs . . ."

Detective Bernard folds his arms in front of his chest. "There is no easy way to say this. Your husband is dead." Bernard watches Yvette intently.

"Dead?"

Bernard locks eyes with Yvette. "He was shot."

"Shot?" I ask as Yvette screams, a gut-wrenching cry that reverberates through the air.

Detective Bernard clears his throat. "I'm truly sorry for your loss."

Yvette screams again and starts shaking, her body overtaken by tremors. She sways toward me and then away. Detective Bernard grabs one arm, and I grab the other. Between us, she hangs like an accordion.

"Who would do this?" she whimpers.

Before Bernard can answer, his radio crackles: *Bernard, you gotta see this* . . . He fumbles and quickly turns the volume down.

Yvette snaps up straight, her eyes blinking like butterfly wings. "Oh my God. Dylan. Dylan."

Bernard looks at me. I mouth, "Her daughter."

Yvette's voice cracks. "She can't hear this from someone else. We need to go." She grips both my arms. We step toward the Range Rover.

15

"Wait." Detective Bernard reaches for Yvette's arm and offers to take her. "It will be a lot quicker in a police car. You won't be able to get out of this traffic on your own." I'm thinking what a nice man, offering to take her to Dylan, when I realize he just wants to get her alone to question her. Isn't the spouse always the prime suspect?

"Yvette, I should drive you."

"Bring her car to the police station," Bernard orders, glaring at me. "I have some questions for her. We'll get her daughter and meet you there."

He keeps his tone casual, but I'm not buying the helpful bit anymore. He inserts his body between us by placing an arm on Yvette's back. "I'm afraid I have to insist." He narrows his eyes. This officer is nobody's friend. In a trance, Yvette goes with him. He's quick and opens the back seat door before I even move.

I run to them, push my body past the detective, and lean over the back seat. A forceful hand grips my arm and tries to jerk me back. I plant my feet, bend at the knees, and brace my body as a shield. He pushes against me, but I don't budge. I spent my career keeping top-level opponents away from a soccer ball, so I can certainly keep this police detective from Yvette. I wrap my arms around Yvette's neck and lean close. "Call an attorney."

"Move," Detective Bernard orders. "Or I'll arrest you for obstruction."

I ignore him and continue giving Yvette instructions. "Don't say anything until you get an attorney. I'll take your car and meet you at the station." I step back. He glares at me but doesn't say a word, just gets into the driver's seat and shuts his door.

I sprint to Yvette's car, press the engine button. I'm ready to race to the police station, but her Range Rover refuses to start. I try again. Nothing. Then it hits me. The key sits in Yvette's bag, which resides next to her in the police car. Damn.

I lean back in the seat and close my eyes. This is bad. Very bad. Someone shot Kurt Robbins. The police have whisked Yvette away. I'm stuck on a country road at the crime scene with no mode of transportation. *Someone shot Kurt Robbins.* My mind returns to those words. In the rush to help Yvette, I didn't digest that information. The weight hits me, and tears sting my eyes. Can Kurt really be dead? I mean, I know he is. The detective just told us. But I can't fathom that the larger-than-life, gregarious Comets superstar could be dead. Not just dead—murdered.

CHAPTER 3

I need to get to the police station. That's what she'd do for me. I take out my phone to order a Lyft. The icon shows a fifty-minute wait. Probably because of all the congestion. I get out of the Range Rover and survey the area. Maybe I can bum a ride.

Yvette must feel so alone. I need to reach her. Kurt was everything to her. Yvette often joked that it was her, Kurt, and Dylan against the world. But that wasn't really true. Kurt came from a loving home. His parents always sweet and supportive. And despite Yvette's reservations about Kurt's younger brother, Gene, he was around.

Yvette is a different story. Her mother suffers from dementia and lives in a nursing home in upstate New York. Her father died when she was young. She once mentioned a sister, but apparently, they had a huge falling-out and don't speak. I'm the closest person Yvette has to family. And, since moving to Greenwich, she's proven to be the one friend I can count on.

Yvette stayed with me during Jackson's recent episode, sleeping next to me in the hospital waiting room. Making me eat when I had no appetite. Letting me cry and cry. She was also there more than a decade ago when I finally decided to leave my egomaniac ex-husband.

I study my surroundings. Reporters buzz about at every corner. Artificial fluorescents shine bright, illuminating the street as if it's the middle of the day at a carnival. I move from the shadows toward the light. Like cogs along an assembly line, mini studios hug the fence of the Robbinses' estate. I recognize the equipment: LED lights, monitors, and cables. Snippets of their stories float toward me.

"Sources say Kurt Robbins's younger brother found the body in the kitchen . . ." CNN.

". . . a huge loss for the black community. Kurt and his wife had founded the Robbins Foundation, which provides mentorship and support for black athletes." CRE Sports.

"Fans will never see Kurt Robbins play again at Madison Square Garden . . ." David Lopez, from my station. My cheeks flush at the sound of his baritone voice. David and I almost hooked up recently at an after-work get-together. I was very drunk and upset about the whole bad-mom thing. To make matters worse, when I tried to kiss him, he rejected me. So humiliating. My cheeks heat up just thinking about it.

Until that night, I'd never even thought of David romantically. Yes, he's super handsome, with his olive skin, strong jaw, and expressive hazel eyes. I may have even described his eyes as kind before the whole nonkissing fiasco. And I really thought he was interested in me. He'd always make a point of talking to me at work. And I just sort of got that vibe. Clearly my romance radar remains deeply impaired.

I move farther into the chaos, traveling with the tide of bodies. The young traffic officer yells at reporters standing by the Robbinses' front gate. "Cars coming, cars coming—move back." Uniformed cops, with their backs to the media, push against the crowd to keep them from scurrying closer. It's like watching from inside a balloon as it's being blown up. Two CSI vans drive through. The vans proceed to the circular driveway and then bypass the parked cars by pulling onto the grass.

"Kate," a gravelly voice calls out. I turn to see TRP cameraman Bill Salvatore striding toward me, a cigarette dangling from his mouth. He bends his lanky body over and gives me a little hug. His leathery skin brushes my cheek. A musty smell wafts from his worn jeans and grungy army jacket. "You working?" He flicks the butt of the cigarette onto the ground.

"I'm not," I answer. "I came with Yvette."

"No shit. Where is she?" He looks around.

"Went to find her daughter."

Bill pulls out another cigarette, cups his hands against the wind, and lights it. "Hell of a thing." He takes a long drag and then exhales out of the corner of his mouth. He waves the smoke away from my face. It's nice to see Bill. He was the first cameraman I got assigned to work with at TRP. Bill helped me navigate the station politics, which required even more strategic thinking than playing professional soccer.

A light flashes, and I raise my hand to block the glare. A camera operator finishes setting up an LED fixture next to us. He quickly adjusts the light away as a reporter smiles and nods to the camera.

"One, two, three . . . one, two . . ." The reporter speaks into the microphone for a sound check.

Bill studies me. "They would have called you into the studio for this story . . . talk about the impact on athletes or something."

"Probably better this way."

Bill raises a brow. I know he feels partially to blame for my suspension. It was his camera that malfunctioned and missed recording the whole conversation. Whoever posted the video only provided the part that made me look bad.

"Is there any chance you can give me a ride into town?" I ask. He checks his watch and tells me he was planning a coffee run after David's next live shot and could drop me then.

"Bill—" David's voice sings out. "Kate." David flashes me a big smile. "What a surprise. Are you back working?"

"No. Still suspended."

"I'm sorry to hear that." David takes a step closer and squeezes my arm, then looks at Bill. "Don't mean to rush you, Billy boy, but we need to get moving—I'm about to go on."

Bill fishes keys from his pocket, tosses them to me, and tells me to wait in his van. I watch Bill and David walk over to one of the mini studios. David bends down to check his reflection in the camera lens. I return to the shadows, kicking at the gravel along the edge of the road.

Gas-powered generators moan as I pass the CNN and NBC trucks before spotting Bill's TRP van. A river of Burger King wrappers and Styrofoam cups cover the floor, making it impossible to rest my feet without losing sight of them. The strong smell of bacon and coffee fills the van, mixing with the faint aroma of curry—an olfactory reminder of recent meals ingested within the vehicle. Is it the smell making me queasy? Or the realization that a murderer is loose in my town?

I wonder if Kurt knew his killer. I know the estate maintains a kick-ass alarm system. At least the panel by the front door looks impressive. To drive through the front gate, you also need the code or someone to buzz you inside. But how generous are they with the code? Hell, I know it. I'd imagine Kurt's and Dylan's friends do. Also, maintenance and cleaning crews? That estate requires serious upkeep. My mind returns to Dylan. None of the reporters mentioned her. Could Dylan have been home during the attack? I know Detective Bernard claimed he'd take Yvette to find Dylan. Does he know her whereabouts? Could his whole cop-in-shining-armor thing be an even bigger ruse than I imagined?

My thoughts are interrupted by the trunk banging open. Bill secures the tripod with bungee cords, throws the rest of the gear into a milk crate, then comes around to the driver's side. He yanks open the door with one hand and flicks his cigarette to the ground with the other. I imagine Bill's in his late sixties now; but he's always looked old, so it's hard to know.

He turns on the engine. "Sorry. David wouldn't stop talking . . . even mentioned you got a raw deal."

"Right." I can't keep the irritation out of my voice.

"I always thought you two had chemistry," Bill says, and I feel myself grimace.

Bill flashes a nicotine-stained smile at me. Does he know I tried to kiss David? Did David tell people? Maybe have a good laugh about it? "Anyway—what are you, five miles from here? Fern Street, right?"

"Good memory. But could you drop me in town? There's something I need to do."

He puts the car in drive. "Sure. I'm heading there anyway."

"Need some caffeine to go with your nicotine?"

"Coming from the queen of caffeine?" He laughs. "That's rich."

"Touché."

Between Bill and me it's hard to determine who requires more coffee stops. We both lead the TRP pack for most caffeinated. For secret Santa, I always get some variation of a coffee gift, from mugs to beans to silly bumper stickers like CRANKY WITHOUT COFFEE. Bill starts backing out of the spot and slams on the brakes, inches from smashing into the side of a moving police car. The officer gives Bill a dirty look but doesn't stop.

"They got bigger fish to fry tonight." He snorts and screeches onto the street. The tripod in the trunk rattles as we bump along. Bill merges into a major traffic jam.

"I forgot what an adventure it is to drive with you."

"Ha ha." He lights another cigarette and cracks the window. "You think Yvette could have offed him?"

"Wow. Harsh."

He honks at the van in front even though there's nowhere the vehicle can go. "That's what the speculation is. They're saying all sorts of things, as you can imagine." The car in front moves forward, and Bill steps on the gas. "They're saying Yvette got jealous 'cause Kurt was getting serious with someone."

Kurt would never leave her. Yvette explained that years ago.

"For one thing," I say, "Yvette didn't have the time. What else are they saying?"

"There's been talk recently that Kurt's bromance with Burke had cooled."

That's interesting. Yvette asked me to check for Burke's car when we got there.

"Did you hear why they weren't getting along?"

"Nope," Bill says.

Maybe Kurt finally came to his senses. I never understood their friendship. Yvette said Burke took Kurt under his wing when he first got to the Comets. Kurt was just out of high school, and apparently, Burke looked after him. Like a big brother. But they are completely different. Kurt was friendly and . . . well, not an ass. And Burke is a malicious, sneering, condescending human being with zero redeeming qualities. Except that he used to be an extraordinary point guard. Now he's mediocre at best.

At the yellow light, Bill accelerates, shoots through the intersection as a minivan slams on its brakes. Bill swerves. "Have you talked to anyone at work?"

"No. But . . ."

I feel his eyes on me. He takes a long drag on his cigarette. "But . . . ?"

I think about the message I got a few days ago saying my boss wants a face-to-face meeting. Those types of meetings are never good.

"But I've been summoned to the station this week. For a *meeting*." I look out the window as Bill turns onto Greenwich Avenue, the commercial hub of town, and drives by the Prada and Jimmy Choo stores. Designer chains now occupy most storefronts, having pushed out high-end mom-and-pops. While the retailers changed, for the most part, the architecture still dates back over a century. A person will find the same stores on Greenwich Avenue as on Rodeo Drive, but they won't find the glitz. Greenwich likes to think of itself as understated.

"I feel terrible about the whole thing. If my battery hadn't died, we would have had Burke's comments on tape," Bill says more to himself than me.

"It's not your fault," I reply. "You didn't force me to lose my temper."

Bill pulls over and stops, igniting a small tornado in the trunk. "Keep your chin up—this whole thing will blow over."

"I'm not holding my breath."

Bill flicks his cigarette out the window and parks. "Everyone understands you were under stress. My God. It was right after your son's—you know, when Jackson—"

"I know. Hence the bad-mom thing and all that."

"Kate—I've known you for a long time. What's it been? At least ten years. You're not a bad mom. You are a great mom. And what happened with Jackson was not your fault."

"Thanks. But you're wrong." I reach over, hug him, and hop out of the van before he can say anything else. He drives down the hill and pulls over by Starbucks, the back of his van sticking into the road. Darkness hangs over the Avenue, which is a good thing, because I don't want anyone to see the tears welling up in my eyes. Even now, thinking about the whole Jackson scare makes my heart wrench. I push the feeling down and walk toward the Greenwich police station and Yvette, hoping I won't fail her the way I failed my son.

CHAPTER 4

I cross the street to the police station, which is shockingly grim considering Greenwich is one of the richest towns in the country. The building looks 1970s shabby with a flat roof, dirty windows, and tired granite. I walk through the narrow hallway to the front desk, where a female desk sergeant with unruly red curls, freckles, and deep wrinkles around her eyes sits reading a magazine.

"Yes?" she says from behind the glass, eyes fixed on her magazine.

"I'm here to see Yvette Robbins."

She turns the page of the glossy publication. "Who?"

"Yvette Robbins. Detective Bernard brought her in."

"You her lawyer?"

"I'm her friend."

"Well, then, friend. Take a seat. Only the lawyer gets in."

Behind her, giggles erupt. Must be pretty boring if rudeness gets such a reaction. I ignore them and head to the small waiting area, where I sit on a chipped green plastic chair across from a man wearing a stained Patriots jersey. A gray clock hangs above, precariously attached to the chipping white-painted wall. The clock reads 6:15 p.m., less than two hours since we learned Kurt died. It feels a lifetime ago. The hand of the clock ticks away seconds that feel like days.

A door opens from inside, and a familiar man appears in the door-frame, wearing gray sweats: Kurt's younger brother. I motion to Gene, and he lumbers over.

"I'm so sorry about Kurt."

"It doesn't seem real." He rubs his salt-and-pepper scruff. "What are you doing here?"

"Waiting for Yvette. I was with her when she heard."

He shakes his acorn-shaped head and tells me he'll wait too. Gene lowers his wide body into the seat next to me and stares at the man in the Patriots jersey. Gene resembles Kurt, but where Kurt's features were sharp and strong, Gene's hang fleshy and soft.

"You found him?" I ask. "That must have been awful."

He swallows; his Adam's apple juts out. "It was. At first, I thought maybe he had fallen. But there was—" Gene looks at his hands and cracks the thick knuckles of his fingers. "There was so much blood. He had no pulse. I tried CPR . . ."

"I'm sorry."

"I was covered in blood. The police gave me this to change into." He points to the sweat suit, and I wonder if he knows the police will also be testing his clothing for DNA, gunshot residue, and stuff like that. As if reading my mind, he adds, "Guess that's standard. They're probably testing the clothing too."

"Did they say what happened?" I try to ask as tactfully as possible.

"Shot." Gene keeps his head down. "The gun was right there in the kitchen by his body." Gene puts his hands over his face, and I can tell he's crying.

The front door opens, letting in a gush of cold air. A teenager in flannel pajama pants, an oversize sweatshirt, and purple sneakers walks in, nods at the desk sergeant, and proceeds over to the guy in the Patriots jersey. She folds her arms across her chest and kicks him in the shin.

"Damn," he grumbles. "Leave me alone."

She kicks him again, harder. "Get up, Dad!"

He mumbles and groans but stands and follows her outside.

Gene's phone rings. He doesn't seem to hear it at first but finally picks up. "Hello. Yes. It's true." He cups the phone between his shoulder and ear so he can return to cracking his knuckles. "I can't believe it . . . should we close tomorrow? You sure you don't mind handling everything? Yes, if you don't mind. Thank you."

He clicks off the phone and looks back at me. "We're lucky to have good staff." He pauses and looks up at the ceiling. "I'm lucky to have good staff."

The Robbins Brothers Gym was Kurt and Gene's project. Basically, Kurt's money and Gene's time. Yvette told me Kurt had bought the gym because he got tired of bankrolling all Gene's crazy money-making schemes. Gene hadn't always lived off the kindness of his brother. Out of college, he'd successfully built a start-up music app. Apparently, he was quite the tech wiz. But Gene had lived large, lost his money, and sunk the business.

Detective Bernard appears with Dylan and Yvette, both wearing the same gray sweats as Gene.

"Uncle Gene!" Dylan runs to her uncle and hugs him. He drapes his arms around her shoulders.

"Are you okay?" I walk over to Yvette.

She shakes her head and asks if she and Dylan can stay with me tonight. "We can't go home."

"Of course." I watch her try to smile, but her face crumples into tears.

Detective Bernard clears his throat and gives her a sympathetic smile. His manner seems kinder than before. "Mrs. Robbins." He puts his hand on her shoulder. "Again, I am sorry for your loss. I will see you tomorrow."

Yvette nods and starts toward the door.

Bernard turns to me. "Could I speak to you for one second?"

Detective Bernard takes off his glasses and rubs his eyes. Under the light, I get a better sense of him. He's a few inches taller than me, probably around five nine. Fit, with a long, thin nose that turns down, reminding me of an owl. "What a night . . . ," he says more to himself than me. "I left New York thinking I'd get away from these kinds of cases."

"You worked in the city?" I feel my body tense.

"Yeah. NYPD. Came here to escape the rat race." He shakes his head. "I worked with your dad."

I remain silent, unable to formulate any words.

"Isn't Liam Murphy your old man?"

If Detective Bernard wants to unnerve me, it's working. Liam Murphy may be my biological father, but my real father is my stepdad, who, along with my mom, raised me.

"Your dad is quite a guy. I can tell you some stories . . ." He pauses for a second, distracted by an officer at the desk trying to get his attention. "Anyway, I'm hoping you can come in to give a statement tomorrow."

I agree without asking questions, just so I can avoid hearing anything else about the father who abandoned my brother and me so long ago. Not much shakes me, but mention of Liam Murphy does.

CHAPTER 5

Yvette, Dylan, and I sit in my family room, which also serves as living room, den, and study. I'm what you'd categorize as Greenwich poor. Translation: I don't reside in a mansion, estate, or château. My house is one of the few remaining three-bedroom original Victorians near town. After leaving my ex, I wanted a simple, cozy home unlike the modern monstrosity we lived in. And I love that my street is walking distance from Greenwich Avenue. Actually, *street* is too generous a word; it is more of a stub with five modest, century-old homes crowded together. Back in the day, my cobblestone block represented the heart of a thriving working-class neighborhood. Faux mansions replaced the old homes that occupied the surrounding blocks, but somehow Fern Street remained relatively untouched. Now our homes stand riddled with historic-preservation plaques stamped on the narrow, two- and three-bedroom abodes.

Yvette has washed the streaks of mascara from her face, but her eyes remain red and swollen. I sit across from Yvette on one end of my Pottery Barn leather couch, and Dylan sits on the other end. Only the lamp by me is on, which creates a shadowy glow across the wood-paneled room. I banish all thoughts of Detective Bernard's surprising mention of my father, Liam Murphy, and focus my attention on Yvette and Dylan, both of whom look like they just returned from the front line of a war.

"Why don't you try and eat?" I point to the three plates of lasagna I reheated. I know how lame my effort must seem. Encouraging them to eat while their world spins out of control.

Dylan lifts the plate and takes a forkful, chews methodically, her long braids hanging over her cheeks, the bronze cuffs in her hair catching the light. The sound of the grandfather clock clicks from the hall, amplified against the deadly quiet of the room.

Dylan clears her throat as if trying to get Yvette's attention. But Yvette remains lost in thought.

"Mom." Yvette raises her head. Now that Dylan has Yvette's attention, she looks down at the rug as if she's reconsidered.

The doorbell rings, and I go to answer it. Zeke, Dylan's boyfriend, flashes an eager smile and asks to see her. He's one of those good-looking kids who knows it, dirty-blond curls, tan skin, and large diamond earrings shining from each lobe. He's wearing a red wool cap pulled over his bangs and a jean jacket. He and Jackson used to hang out all the time, but then Zeke seemed to just dump my son. I know it sounds very mama bear of me, but I get a bad vibe from the kid. And not just because he ghosted Jackson. At least, I don't *think* that's why. I tell Zeke to wait in the hall, and I return to the family room.

Dylan and Yvette sit on the couch huddled together. Yvette's arm over her daughter's shoulder, their foreheads touch in a conspiratorial fashion. As soon as Dylan hears Zeke's at the door, she bolts up and rushes past me.

"What did Dylan need to tell you?" I sit back down. "She seemed . . . nervous."

Yvette gets up and returns to the chair by my big picture window that faces the front yard. Under the glow of the antique streetlights, I see the low limbs of our majestic oak tree. Jackson and Nikki loved hiding in those branches when they were little.

"Dylan had another fight with Kurt last night." She meets my gaze. "She feels guilty that the final thing she said to him was in anger."

Last week Yvette mentioned to me that Dylan and Kurt had been fighting a lot. I chalked it up to teenage angst, but Yvette seemed worried there was more to it. I ask her if she knows what they were fighting about.

Yvette shrugs and turns back to the window. I repeat my question.

She keeps staring outside but tells me she has her suspicions. "They could have been fighting about Zeke. Kurt didn't like that he kept sneaking into our house after curfew . . ."

Yvette picks up her plate of lasagna and takes a bite, forcing the food down. She takes another, as if eating were preferable to talking.

"Or?" I ask.

Yvette puts her plate down on the coffee table. "Or . . . it was about Kurt's latest . . . indiscretion." Yvette sighs. "Maybe because the tabloids have been so cruel . . ."

Dylan shuffles back into the family room, her eyes bloodshot, and asks to go to bed. I bring her upstairs, get her settled. With the twins at their father's house tonight, I tell Dylan she can stay in either Jackson's or Nikki's rooms and borrow whatever she needs.

I come back to find Yvette curled up in the chair, her knees pulled against her chest with her arms wrapped around them. She looks so fragile, like a piece of glass. I can't imagine what's going through her mind right now or how much she's been able to process. I get out a bottle of cabernet, our favorite, pour two glasses, and hand her one.

She takes it and gives me a weary smile. "Can I ask you a favor?"

"Of course."

"It's going to sound awful . . . but will you come with me to the morgue tomorrow? I need to see him. I mean, I know he's dead. But, at the same time, I just can't believe it."

Of all the requests she might make, that was not something I expected. But I agree to go with her. "Thanks." Yvette sort of whimpers and starts crying to herself.

Feeling like a voyeur, I take our plates and walk down the narrow hallway to the kitchen. This is my favorite room in the house. It's bright and cheerful, with a large bay window that reminds me of the window in the kitchen from my childhood home in Berkeley, California. I cut another slice of lasagna, nuke it, and sit down at one of the stools at my butcher-block island. I gobble up the second slice before returning to the family room, where I find Yvette cupping her phone inside my scarf, holding the device near her ear.

"Yes. I understand . . . ," Yvette says. "See you tomorrow."

"You got it working." I sit across from her.

She turns to me and wraps my scarf back around the phone. "Oh, yes. I'm able to receive calls. Strange . . ." She puts the bundle back into her tote and picks up her wine. "That was the lawyer."

The grandfather clock in the hallway chimes a low, hollow gong-like sound, nine times. "Who did you get?"

She takes a long, slow sip and tells me she has a consult with an attorney who is also a mom at Greenwich Lake.

"I completely forgot about her," I say, impressed that Yvette thought to phone the town's top defense attorney.

I refill both our wineglasses, and we sit in silence. Eventually, Yvette goes up to bed. For a brief second, I consider trying to sleep myself. I am exhausted. But recently I've found myself suffering from insomnia. Dreading the idea of a fitful sleep, I top off my wine and turn on the flat-screen television above the brick fireplace and, out of habit, click on my station, TRP. The main anchor sits at his desk, flashing an easy smile, white teeth against pinkish skin. He's the ultimate guy's guy, the person you want to toss back a couple of beers with at a game. Right now, he's talking hockey, breaking down a Rangers power play, his eyes glistening with excitement. Or from the heat of the studio lights.

I imagine Kurt's murder took up most of the first block of the show. They will get back to it at the top of the hour. I sip my wine and wait for the grandfather clock to mark 10:00 p.m.

The anchor says good night as the grandfather clock chimes. TRP Sports TV's opening montage zips into focus, music blaring. *TRP Sports Television: No one covers the world of sports like we do.*

I remember the first time I appeared on the channel. I was fifteen and playing on the US Under-16 Women's Youth National Team in the semifinals against France. That was the year my age group was finally poised to win the tournament after a five-year slump.

I was the youngest player on the team, and the other girls didn't let me forget it. I may have been the fastest, but I lacked their maturity and strength. And their friendship.

Our team was down by one goal with five minutes left in the game, when the coach pulled our star winger and put me in. I could feel the resentment emanating from the other girls. I was so scared. It felt like I was running through pudding. The crowd was thunderous; the vibrations pounded in my head. A player passed me the ball right in front of the net. It should have been an easy goal. One I'd made a thousand times. But I struck the ball too low. I knew before I looked that I'd missed. To add to my teenage misery, not only did my teammates ice me out, TRP ran the clip of my failed shot over and over again in their feature on youth sports.

Back on screen, the anchor gives a somber smile and starts speaking. "Good evening. It's a sad day across the sports world. One of the NBA's greatest talents is dead. It was supposed to be just another Sunday—watching football, hanging out with family. Instead, the day turned tragic. We go live to the mansion where the Comets-franchise NBA forward lived"—the anchor takes a dramatic pause—"and died. Our own David Lopez has the latest."

The screen changes to two boxes, one with the anchor and the other with David, whose warm eyes glow on screen. Behind David, the Robbinses' mansion is awash in artificial light, giving the white limestone facade a bluish hue.

David nods his head and recaps the information I'm already familiar with. That Kurt was found by his younger brother in the afternoon
inside the kitchen. He talks about the crime scene investigators who
remain at the mansion and even mentions that Yvette and her daughter
are staying with friends, since the mansion is a crime scene. I peek outside to make sure no media followed them to my house. I hadn't even
processed the idea that reporters will be searching for a sound bite from
Yvette. So far, I don't see reporters through my window.

On screen, the anchor thanks David and turns to a guest in the
studio. "Joining me is a local *Greenwich Times* reporter." I tune out as
the young reporter's name is mentioned, distracted by how he shifts
uncomfortably in his chair, rapidly blinking his eyes as if his lids were
windshield wipers in a storm.

The anchor starts easy. "Tell us about Greenwich."

"Well, Greenwich is where a lot of really, really rich and famous
people live. Most people live in mega mansions. The average house is
probably five million dollars. You have actresses, Wall Street executives,
sports stars—um, obviously sports stars; you know that . . . people like
that." The young reporter flashes a quick smile, revealing braces.

"What makes Greenwich so appealing?" The anchor tilts his head.

"Oh, so many things. It's about a forty-minute train ride to
Manhattan. There are beautiful beaches on the Long Island Sound.
Lots of residents with yachts in Greenwich." He stops and scratches at
a pimple on his face. "But, you know, the thing I think makes it most
appealing for celebrities is that no one in Greenwich cares if you're
famous or rich, because pretty much everyone is. You don't find many
gawkers or stalkers there. And no one gets into your business. Most
neighbors don't even know each other."

"How do you think the Greenwich Police will handle this case?"
The anchor leans forward. "Do they handle many murders?"

"Well . . . this is the first high-profile murder since the 1970s,"
the young man starts. "Since the Martha Moxley case. You know, the

one where that fifteen-year-old girl was killed by Skakel. The Kennedy relative? But, well . . . there have been some drug and domestic violence murders over the past decade. And the local police handled those. Also, the detective assigned to this case, Detective Peter Bernard, comes from the NYPD homicide department. I also heard the NYPD is going to help with the Manhattan stuff—you know, interview the Comets staff at Madison Square Garden."

I click off the television, not wanting to hear more about the NYPD homicide department. I take out my phone and send my mom and stepdad an *I love you* text before heading up to bed. As if they can magically shield me from anything Liam related. But I have a bad feeling that my biological dad will make his presence known. And soon.

CHAPTER 6

I hear the whistle in the distance. The sound gets louder. It's the commuter train pulling into Greenwich station. Just last week, it was the train I took to work—coffee in hand, newspapers tucked under my arm. Now it marks an interruption of sleep. As the sound disappears, I float back into oblivion, riding a cloud toward unconsciousness. Quiet. Warm. Mindless in my cocoon of a bedroom. And then it hits me: This is not an ordinary Monday. Not even close. This is the day after Kurt Robbins was murdered.

The sudden recognition of the horror jars me alert. My eyes fly open. Yesterday, Kurt's death seemed surreal, like watching another person's dream. Or nightmare. But now the magnitude of the crime pulses through every nerve in my body. I push myself into a seated position and lean against my velvet headboard as the train whistles again.

The light from the sun shines through the room's lace curtains, highlighting the attic-like space. Usually my bedroom feels cozy, with its slanted low ceilings and white wicker furniture. Now it feels tight and hot and bright. I'm surprised by just how bright. I had planned to wake up early, but the sunshine suggests I slept through the alarm.

My phone rings: *Für Elise*, the Beethoven piece that Nikki programmed. "Hello?"

"Kate?" A raspy voice greets me. I haven't heard this voice in years, but I know exactly who it is. My whole body tenses.

"Kate? It's your father."

"I know . . ." I attempt to keep my voice steady, not wanting to give him the satisfaction of rattling me.

"I got a call last night from Detective Bernard." He pauses. "He . . . mentioned you spoke."

He waits for me to say something, but I don't. I can't. What should I say? *If I knew a murder would catch your attention, I might have hung out at crime scenes more often.*

"Kate?"

"Yes?"

"I will be in Greenwich today. I'd really like to see you."

A mix of emotions seeps through me. Deep down I've always hoped for a relationship with Liam. But, as my brother repeatedly points out, the father I concoct in my brain has no resemblance to the real one. That's why I continually find myself disappointed, while my brother remains unfazed.

"Why do you want to meet?" I hear weakness in my tone.

"Please indulge your old man?" He tries a laugh. It rings hollow. "I'm really just trying to help you. The Robbins case . . . I need to tell you something. Please. Ten minutes. Kate?"

"I don't know what to say," I answer, being completely honest.

"Think about it. I'll be at the Starbucks on Greenwich Avenue at one o'clock. Please meet me there."

I put my phone down and lean back on the pillows. I hate that Liam can unnerve me so easily. Should I just ignore his *invitation*? Does he really need to tell me something, or is it a ruse? I don't need to decide right now. What I should do is check on Yvette and Dylan. I saunter into the hallway clad in an oversize Velvet Underground tank top and fuzzy yellow socks. I listen for noise. Nothing. I walk to Jackson's room, where Dylan slept last night. The door sits slightly ajar.

"Hello?" Hearing no response, I push the door and peer inside. Dylan is nowhere in sight. But the room looks spotless, which is not its resting state. Did Dylan *clean*? Either that or the housekeeping fairy visited during the night. The pile of dirty clothing that usually lives on

Jackson's throw rug is nowhere in sight. The red-and-blue-patch comforter is pulled tight over the mattress, and the matching pillows fluffed
and set against the headboard. Jackson's glass-and-chrome desk, usually
invisible under a tornado of papers and books, is cleared, with a discreet
pile of stacked papers set on the upper right corner.

What I don't see is anything of Dylan's, no bags or backpack. I never
took Dylan as one of those people who cleans when she's upset. I can't
help wondering what this was really about. I step inside and walk over to
Jackson's bookshelf, where his science fiction novels are now neatly lined
up by size. The only space untouched seems to be the top of the bookcase,
where I recently put up some family photos. There's the one of Jackson at
his elementary school graduation, dressed in a polo shirt, his sun-bleached
sandy hair brushed back from his light-blue eyes. There is the picture of
him and Nikki bundled up in winter jackets, building a fort in the snow
when they were young. And my favorite, from two years ago, when he
and I went skating in Central Park. I pick up the picture of us standing in
front of Wollman Rink. He has at least four inches on me. His cheeks are
flushed, and his eyes sparkle. I miss that sparkle.

I put the picture down and move to Nikki's room, which is also empty.
Yvette made the bed, but no extra cleaning's been attempted. Downstairs
someone made coffee. Thank God for small favors. The full carafe sits on
the counter of my sky-blue kitchen, which radiates the morning sun. I fill
a yellow-flowered mug with coffee and take a gulp, savoring the strong,
bitter taste. I take another sip as a paper on the counter catches my eye.

> Dear Kate,
> I didn't want to wake you. We left early to meet
> with the attorney, but I made coffee. I think we might
> need to stay another night.
> Yvette
> P.S. Will you still come with me to the morgue?
> Let's plan to go in the afternoon.

So, she still wants to go. I've never seen a dead body, except at an open-casket funeral. I find the thought of the morgue super disturbing, and I sip some coffee to settle myself. *Für Elise* plays from the counter. *Please don't be Liam.*

"Ms. Green? It's Detective Bernard."

I don't know whether to feel relieved or more anxious. He continues. "You left so quickly last night; we didn't set a time for you to come in." *You didn't ask for a time,* I think to myself while agreeing to meet him at 2:00. I hang up and take a jar of peanut butter, an apple, and orange juice from the fridge and sit down on one of the light-blue stools at the butcher-block island. Too bad Dylan got tired of cleaning before she came down here; the kitchen could really use some tidying. From piles of mail to mismatched sneakers, everything gravitates to this room. A problem for another day. I take a few spoonfuls of peanut butter and then run upstairs to get ready.

What does one wear to give a statement to the police? I stand wrapped in a towel, staring into my overstuffed closet. Brown slacks? Black slacks? A skirt? Leather? Suede? Short? Long? Probably something conservative, but really, who cares? I grab black leather pants, a maroon turtleneck, and a pair of high platform boots for good measure. Just as I finish applying a second coat of mascara, the doorbell rings.

"Coming." I run down the stairs as the bell ding-dongs a second time and yank the door open to a familiar and unwelcome face. "What are you doing here?"

"Nice to see you too." My ex-husband, Tyler, pushes past me, knocking the coatrack, which ricochets against the wall. I can't believe I once found this three-piece suit attractive, with his resting scowl, narrow eyes, and military-style haircut. Not that to an outside observer Tyler Edison couldn't be considered handsome. His appearance just screams *uptight.*

"I brought Nikki her SAT book—she left it at my house."

"She probably left it because she doesn't need it."

He pushes the book into my hands. "Of course, she needs it." He moves past me toward the kitchen, his navy wool suit swooshing as he walks.

"What do you really want?" I follow him into the kitchen, where he helps himself to coffee.

"Want some?" He extends his arm in my direction, exposing a gold-and-red personalized cuff link with his initials.

I ignore him and pour my own. The pungent taste amps my adrenaline, which is already high, considering the call from Liam and the two cups I've already had. All the gray from Tyler's hair is gone. In fact, the shade appears lighter than when I saw him last.

"Milk?" Tyler opens my refrigerator and extends my container of milk toward me. I shoot him a look. "That's right, you don't put anything in your coffee." He says it as if there's something wrong with being a coffee purist. So I shun sugar, Sweet'N Low, and stevia-type things. And never, ever use milk, soy or otherwise. And yes, I might look down—just a tad—at people who order frilly lattes or cappuccinos with whipped cream and syrups and sprinkles.

"Did your therapy session go all right with Jackson?" I ask. Jackson's psychiatrist requested each of us accompany him this week. Tyler yesterday and me tomorrow.

Tyler shifts his body, blocking part of the window, which causes the sun to cast shadows across the ceramic tile floor. "Something came up."

"What could be more important?"

"It doesn't matter." He takes a sip of coffee and looks away. "I'll go with Jackson this week. It's just routine. Not a big deal."

"What then? You have my attention. Why are you *really* here? If it's not Jackson, are you separating from your third wife? Did Nikki get a C on a test and screw up her chances of getting into an Ivy League school?"

"Well, Nicole's grades are slipping a little. Legacy doesn't get you as far as it used to," he says, referring to his Dartmouth degree, which

40

he thinks is superior to mine from my alma mater, UCLA, especially because I was there to play soccer. He likes to skip over the part where I graduated summa cum laude.

"But that's not why I'm here," he says. "I'm concerned about the kids. And you. With Kurt's murder."

I always forget about Tyler's connection to Kurt, besides the obvious school dads. Yvette told me Kurt recently moved a chunk of money to Tyler's investment firm, the Edison Fund.

"You were with the kids last night, not me. How did they seem?"

He takes another sip. "Got any food? A protein bar? Some fruit?"

"How did the kids seem?"

Tyler walks back over to the refrigerator and pulls it open. He picks up my jar of peanut butter to search behind it and then puts it back, closing the door. "They seemed shaken. Have you heard anything?"

"What do you mean?"

He closes the refrigerator and walks around the butcher-block island, closing the gap between us. "I imagine Yvette is a suspect. And you spend a lot of time around her . . ."

"Are you suggesting that it's dangerous for the kids to be around Yvette?" I fold my arms across my chest. "What happened to innocent until proven guilty?" I can't help feeling that Tyler has an ulterior motive. Maybe spite? He always resented how close Yvette and I were.

"Easy," he says. "I'm just putting it out there. Are there others?"

"Other what?"

"Suspects." He puts his hand on the island and leans toward me. I smell his sickeningly sweet cologne. I inch backward as he continues to talk. "Because if there aren't, maybe we should stay clear of Yvette until the whole thing blows over."

The train whistles again. Probably a good thing, as I'm about to hurl some choice expletives his way.

He continues, "We should know more after the news conference."

I know he's playing me. And it's working.

"When is the news conference?" I ask.

"The radio said ten thirty. Guess that's something you would have been covering . . . if you hadn't lost your temper."

"I wasn't exactly myself. You of all people know that." I glance at my phone to check the time: 10:10 a.m. "Did you come over just to be an asshole?"

His frown deepens, and he shakes his head. "You always think the worst of me. I need to run." He starts toward the front. I follow. He opens the door, and I step outside behind him. I don't know why I'm surprised to find it's a beautiful fall morning. Maybe because the idea of sunshine the day after a murder seems wrong? The air smells crisp and clean; it must have warmed up at least ten degrees from yesterday.

"Are you walking me to my car?" Tyler's leather loafers barely make a sound against the brick walkway.

"No. I'm getting my newspapers." For effect, I reach down and scoop up the *New York Post*, *New York Times*, *Daily News*, and *Greenwich Times*. Tyler strides past me and opens the door to his car. I hesitate and then step toward him, thrusting my papers into his arms. "Wait here. I need you to drop me in town."

He frowns.

"I left my car at the school yesterday. Nikki is going to bring it home, but I need a ride."

"You're going to the press conference."

I run into the house, grab my bag, run back to Tyler's car, and open the door to a white Mercedes I don't recognize. He has dumped the newspapers onto my seat, totally disregarding the fact I'd be sitting there. I move the papers into my suede tote and settle in. The car has that new leather smell. "When did you get this car?"

"I have a few cars," he mumbles.

Looking out the window as we drive, I see workers in matching white-and-green jumpsuits sweeping leaves into giant rubber containers and then dumping them into a large truck. I look back at Tyler, his square jaw locked in that same perma-frown.

"Why are you staring?" he growls.

"I'm not." I avert my eyes and look down at my hands. How did I stay married to him for seven years? Granted we jumped into things.

Met at physical therapy right after a devastating knee injury that ended my professional career. He was funny and charming and got me out of my funk. He was there for a skiing injury, and we started scheduling our sessions together. That led to dinners, overnights, marriage, and the twins. It was all fine, even good sometimes, until I walked in on him with his secretary. Could it have been more cliché?

"We didn't finish discussing the kids. They shouldn't interact with Yvette until this is resolved," he says as he pulls along the curb, a half a block from Police Plaza. I can only imagine how he'd react if he knew Yvette and Dylan were sleeping at my home.

"I don't necessarily agree." The grass in front of the police station has been transformed into another media mecca. Like a traveling circus, the press moved its show here, complete with satellite trucks, bright lights, and high-tech cameras. One of the TV stations even set up a podium for the police, so no one would have to fight for mic position—making it all civil and such. In the meantime, it's just another day around the water cooler for my chums, who are shooting the shit while waiting for the press conference to happen. Or not happen.

"Let's talk more later. When we have better information," I suggest, hoping to de-escalate the situation.

"We can talk more, but it's not going to change my mind." He snorts. So much for a détente. I slam the door as he guns the gas and speeds away. God, how he irritates me. It's so easy to ignore Tyler because . . . well, I can't stand him. But could he have a point? Should I be worried about the kids being in close proximity to Yvette?

CHAPTER 7

I walk toward the action at the plaza and immediately spot familiar faces. Cal Callahan from SportWorld.net stands talking to a female reporter from CRE Sports, the other sports television station. Cal looks like one of those skateboarders who hangs out at Venice Beach, with shaggy blond hair, a pockmarked face, and a Grateful Dead T-shirt. The woman wears an understated cream suit and UGGs. Television-ready on top and comfy and warm on the bottom. A lot of us female reporters dress that way. It feels like ages since I've seen them. Through the years, we tended to get put on the same stories and often grabbed drinks after work.

When I first moved to television, I was surprised at how congenial everyone was with their competitors. As an athlete, we respected our opponents, but we'd never, ever, ever do anything to help them.

Obviously, in TV, if you are pursuing an exclusive story, you don't share. Logical. But most of the time, we waited around for the same interview and spent a lot of time guzzling coffee, swapping stories, and more often than not, covering each other's asses. So, when someone misses a sound bite because her camera operator's battery dies, we give her a copy. And when we get stuck behind a bus in the Bronx and miss Aaron Judge's presser, she shares the interview. It's nice. But it doesn't completely sit well with me.

My stepfather laughed when I told him, reminding me I not only needed to win everything as a kid but that I also needed to be the first to solve everything. I was a wiz at the Rubik's Cube, Othello, chess. Hell, I aced standardized tests because the patterns in the questions seemed so obvious to me. My brother once said I'd be a great detective, which made my mom shudder. I think she was glad when I stopped wanting to be Nancy Drew and started idolizing Mia Hamm.

I'm winding my way toward my colleagues when I notice David join their conversation. I feel my cheeks burn, turn in the other direction, and creep along the perimeter of the media village. I don't know why he's affecting me. That's not true. Of course, I do. I was drunk, made a move, and he rejected me. *Easy, Kate. You've had a lot to drink,* he'd said as he placed his hands on my shoulders and pushed me back. I don't think I've ever run out of a bar so fast. Or felt so humiliated.

I find an empty bench away from the action, sit, and pull out the *New York Post.* The three-inch front-page headline blares, LIGHTS OUT: NBA SUPERSTAR GUNNED DOWN IN OWN HOME AFTER SIGNALING HE WANTED A DIVORCE. Of course, the paper is already weaving a narrative that paints Yvette as the villain. I skip to Page Six to face whatever shade they might throw at me today. I should ignore the stupid column, but the masochist in me can't. I skim past a story on the Kardashians and find my name in the fourth paragraph. The viral video that toppled the career of Olympic soccer star turned sports reporter Kate Green climbs— reaching over 500,000 views. *Barstool Sports* puts it in the top five for the week. Hardly a record to be proud of. Then again, Green's record is, in fact, nothing to be proud of. As almost everyone knows by now, the blue-eyed girl next door was caught on camera screaming at Comets point guard Mason Burke, where she called him "a talentless fucking asshole." Burke told our Page Six that Green often yells at players and he's just glad someone finally captured it on video. To think, young girls everywhere once looked up to her as a role model.

I slam the paper shut. I don't know if I'm angrier about the fact that Burke keeps lying or that I might have let down young girls everywhere. I hadn't considered that. I knew better than to lose my temper. I wish I could just crawl into a hole. A deep, deep hole.

But I can't. I need to stay focused. For Yvette, my only friend in this town. I remember again how Yvette stayed with me at the hospital for forty-eight hours straight, waiting to see if Jackson would pull through when he overdosed. And Yvette who provided unyielding loyalty when Tyler and I divorced. She remained Team Kate while every other family suddenly forgot my name and lost my number.

"Fancy seeing you here." Bill's tall frame appears in my peripheral vision. He grins, leathery skin stretching over his stained teeth, and sits down next to me, his red-and-blue flannel shirt smelling of stale smoke.

"I'm not even sure why I came."

He takes a puff of a cigarette and tries to blow the smoke in the other direction, but the wind carries it into my face. "Isn't it obvious?" He nudges me with his elbow. "You can take the reporter out of the station, but you can't take the station—well, hell, you know what I mean."

"But I'm not even a real reporter . . ." *I'm an athlete.*

"You are now." He snorts and glances at his watch. "Ten forty . . . hurry up and wait."

"Always the same," I say. "You hear anything about this Detective Bernard? He used to be with the NYPD."

"I hear he likes his fifteen minutes of fame," Bill says. "Or as many minutes as he can wrangle."

Bill gets up and heads through the thicket of reporters to the TRP satellite truck at the back edge of the square. It's a truck I've spent thousands of hours in—editing stories, napping on the couch, even watching *The Price Is Right* with the engineers.

I see David walk out of the truck and take his position in front of the lens, wearing a perfectly tailored tan suit. TRP must have asked him to fill some time since the press conference is running late. I can't see

David's face, but I see him moving his arms in a very animated manner. Bill signals activity behind David, who steps out of the way while Bill pans to the right. I follow Bill's line of sight to see Detective Bernard at the podium. Bernard looks like he showered and shaved for the photo op, sporting a crisp blue button-down and a fitted sports jacket. A general hush travels over the crowd. Bernard waits in front of the bouquet of microphones for quiet.

"Ladies and gentlemen. My name is Detective Peter Bernard."

Bernard tries to keep his expression serious, but his eyes give him away—he's enjoying this.

"I'm the lead detective on this case. First, I want to assure you that we are doing everything we can to find the perpetrator of this *horrible* crime. To cover some basics: Greenwich Police received a nine one one call yesterday afternoon that someone had been shot at the Robbinses' estate on North Street. EMTs were unable to revive the victim, and Mr. Kurt Robbins was pronounced dead at the scene." Like a stage actor, Bernard pauses and looks to his left, center, and then right. "We will leave no stone unturned in our effort to catch the person or persons who murdered Mr. Kurt Robbins." He pauses again, takes off his glasses, and then puts them back on. "I will now take a few questions."

"Can you tell us how many times Kurt was shot?" an old silver-haired reporter yells from the back.

Bernard smiles. "No. I cannot."

So, Bernard isn't only a stage hog, he's a controlling jerk. No one in TV, radio, or digital publishing can do anything with *No. I cannot.* We need *I can't tell you how many shots were fired.* Full sentences. And someone this media savvy would know he's making our lives miserable.

"Did he die instantly?" another reporter yells.

"Out of respect for the family, I'm going to keep the details of the death private."

Bernard points to my colleague in the back. She stands. "Do you have any suspects? We heard you questioned his wife."

"It's standard procedure to talk to everyone associated with the victim. We're looking at all possible leads right now."

"But you did interview her for two more hours this morning?"

"I can't share whether we interviewed Mrs. Yvette Robbins for two hours or not," he says, making a point of speaking slowly and clearly.

This guy's good. And a first-rate jerk. He knows that quote will get top billing.

David raises his hand. "We heard the NYPD is assisting in the case," David's baritone voice carries across the plaza. "You don't get a lot of murders in Greenwich. Can your department handle it? Or will NYPD take the lead?"

"Greenwich Police will be leading this investigation," Bernard snaps.

"What will the NYPD's role be, then?" David follows up, undeterred.

"The NYPD is assisting with the interviews in the city." Bernard spits out the words as if they're poison. He looks out on the crowd. "Someone will try to update you further tomorrow. In the meantime, we have more leads to pursue and more vital witnesses to speak with."

Is it my imagination, or does Detective Bernard look in my direction as he says *vital witnesses*?

CHAPTER 8

I walk toward Starbucks with the thought that I don't have to go inside. But I'm disturbed by the way Detective Bernard highlighted the police interview of Yvette. He clearly wants Yvette's interrogation to be the focus of this media cycle. The question is why. Has Bernard already convinced himself that she's guilty? And if he has, on what evidence is he basing that conclusion? Or is something more sinister going on and a bad cop is looking to polish his image. I march up to the doors of Starbucks and pull them open.

My legs stop working, and I languish in the middle of the doorway, blocking everyone from entering and exiting. So much for bold actions. This is going to be harder than I imagined. Liam Murphy may be a celebrated NYPD homicide detective, but he's a miserable father. Worse, actually. He could have abandoned us and ripped off the Band-Aid. Then I would have mourned and healed. But Liam let the relationship fester, pouring alcohol on the wound with glimmers of new beginnings. A trip talked about for months that got canceled just as we arrived at the airport. A visit to the zoo that my stepdad ended up escorting us to when Liam proved a no-show. And then, just when I was ready to write him off, he'd make a grand gesture, like a forty-eight-hour whirlwind trip to Disney, and start the whole gut-wrenching cycle in motion again.

Deep breath, Kate. Go.

I march inside and immediately hear Neil Diamond mixing with the whir of steamers concocting whipped something or others. I look for Liam amid the crowd, but don't see him in the front of the store. The clock above the counter reads 1:05 p.m. I walk past shelves of pumpkin and black cat porcelain cups set under a sign advertising **FANG-TASTIC FRAPPUCCINOS**. The strong smells of cinnamon and pumpkin waft from the counter. Past that, I spot his six-two frame crammed onto a wooden bench. Dressed in a gray T-shirt and jeans, he gives a half smile, which is about as enthusiastic as I remember him ever getting with that expression. I walk over and sit across from him as he stands to give me an awkward kiss on my cheek, combined with a little pat on the back. My body stiffens at his attempt at fatherly affection.

"I got you a drink. No milk. I remembered that you hate milk." He pushes a cup of coffee forward, a proud look plastered across his face. The music changes to Norah Jones—something dark and soulful.

"Thanks." I take a sip and nearly spit it back. He remembered about the milk, but forgot I don't add sugar. Meanwhile, my tough as nails *father* sits sipping some sissy drink with froth that sticks to his upper lip. The froth doesn't soften his overall tough-guy demeanor. He's not someone you want to mess with. His face looks like Picasso had a whack at him, with a long scar on his right cheek and a nose clearly broken numerous times.

"I'm glad you came." Liam's raspy voice makes it sound like speaking is painful. Something with his vocal cords. If I closed my eyes, I could remember the times he read me Nancy Drew and how sinister the stories sounded with that voice. "I wasn't sure you would."

"I wasn't either."

He laughs. I don't.

He asks the obligatory questions: how I am, the kids, my brother. I respond with one-word answers, squirming the whole time. I am a grown-ass adult, yet sitting here I feel like a ten-year-old reliving hurt after hurt.

"How is your friend holding up? Yvette?"

Here we go. The reason he likely asked to meet. To pump me for information. And so, the chess match begins. "You probably know more than I do. Did the police really question her for two hours this morning? On top of last night?"

"She was his wife—there are a lot of things to discuss." He peers at me with the same powder-blue eyes I see in the mirror every day. He once told me our family's blue eyes are special—that, science be damned, our stock carries a *dominant* gene for the color.

I ask if he personally questioned Yvette. Liam makes a point of saying he didn't *question* her, which makes me think he might have listened to the interrogation. He confirms my hypothesis by adding that Yvette seemed nervous.

"Don't you think most people would be nervous speaking to the police? Especially if their husband was murdered?"

He changes the subject to her lawyer. "I heard she hired the infamous defense attorney who gets Mob bosses and murderous heiresses set free."

"And some innocent people, I imagine."

"What's Yvette like?"

I don't know whether I feel disappointed or vindicated. My prediction was that Liam had a self-serving reason to meet. And I'm right. I knew this would be the case—still I can't help feeling deeply let down. Screw him. Two can play at this game. "I'll answer your questions if you answer mine."

He folds his arms across his chest and gives a half smile. He's enjoying himself. He agrees to my terms, with the provision that he won't answer if it will jeopardize the investigation.

That's the best I can expect. Besides, I only have good things to say. "Yvette is the kindest, most loyal person I know. She's also very gentle."

He rubs the scar on his face and asks me just how well I know Yvette. I tell him we've been friends for nearly sixteen years.

"How does she handle all Kurt's infidelities?"

I share the stock answer that Yvette blames his indiscretions on fame. "I think some people turn a blind eye, and some don't," I say. "But she loved Kurt. And he loved her. When they were together, they were always laughing, holding hands. They shared a deep bond."

My mind goes back to my girls' trip with Yvette that we took years ago. Time away from the toddlers. We headed to the wineries in the North Fork of Long Island and spent the weekend drinking and eating. In one of my tipsier moments, I asked Yvette why she put up with Kurt's infidelities. She didn't answer at first. In fact, she waited so long that I figured she either hadn't heard me or wasn't going to respond. Then, in a low voice she told me they had an *arrangement*. She would look the other way, and he would make sure his *dalliances* would be just that—dalliances. And he'd never leave. *I don't know who I would be if I wasn't Mrs. Kurt Robbins,* she'd confessed. *My whole identity is tied to him and has been since middle school. I don't want to be just another ex-wife. Another cliché. He was thrilled with the deal. He gets his cake, and he doesn't become the bad guy who abandons his wife and child. Image matters to him, more than you'd think.*

Ironic that I became that cliché when I caught my husband cheating and divorced him. But I made a bargain too. I stayed in a town where I'm not welcome so my children could grow up with their father around.

"What are you thinking?" Liam asks, watching me.

"You don't want to know," I respond.

A woman knocks into me as she pulls the chair out from the table next to ours. She's wearing pastel-purple yoga pants and chirping into the phone. *"Sorry,"* she mouths before diving back into her call. "Yes . . . I know. It was a great class. He's *fan-tahs-tic.*" She sips a chai latte thing and sits down, turning so her back is to us. *"Bik-rahm* yoga is *soo* much better . . . I agree totally."

Liam gives his half smile. "Do you ever do yoga?"

"I run."

"Like your mother."

"She hasn't run in decades. She teaches yoga. Your son loves yoga too." I immediately regret mentioning my brother. He wants nothing to do with Liam, and sharing this information feels like a betrayal. My brother was three when my mom moved us to the West Coast, which made me six. I remember the night everything went to hell. My dad got shot, his partner died, and Mom gave him an ultimatum: us or the force. He chose the force, and that was that.

"It wasn't an easy decision . . . it was complicated," he says as if reading my mind. "You know I'm retiring in a few years."

"And you want a second chance at a family?"

"Would that be so bad? I'd love to get to know my grandkids, spend some time with you . . ."

"You don't get to do that. You played with our emotions our whole lives."

"I always wanted a relationship. Things just got . . . I wish you would understand . . ."

"I don't want to talk about this." I cut him off. "You get one more question, and then it's my turn."

He gives me that half smile again, emphasizing how much fun he's having. A fact that irritates me immensely. "Was Yvette acting strange when you saw her at the school?"

"You mean when we found out about the police showing up at her home?"

He nods his head yes, which means he's super plugged in if he knows that detail. I think back to yesterday. She arrived at the gym, already on the phone with her neighbor. That was at 2:30. I remember looking at the clock on the wall.

"She seemed shaken. But that makes sense. Her neighbor told her the police were at her house."

He drums busy fingers on the table. I forgot how fidgety he is. "One last question," he says. "Did you notice Dylan at the gym?"

The woman who had been chitchatting about yoga gets up and walks away. Two middle-aged women take her table. I can see them checking out Liam. He has those rugged good looks that always attract glances. I tell Liam that I don't remember seeing Dylan at the gym. That doesn't mean she wasn't there. With dozens of kids volunteering, I didn't notice everyone. In addition, some of the students were working in different rooms. Could he really think Dylan capable of murdering her father? She's a kid.

"My turn," I say. "Why is Detective Bernard so focused on Yvette?"

"She's the wife. The spouse is almost always . . ."

"Yeah, yeah. I know." I cut him off. "Who are the other potential suspects?"

"That's not a question I can answer." He practically laughs.

I fold my arms across my chest and glare at him, hoping I have the power to make him at least a little uncomfortable.

"All right. In very broad terms. We are speaking to all his family, friends, and teammates. There are one or two whose answers seemed to me to be . . . questionable." I make note of the fact that Liam said seemed to *me*. Not seemed to *us*.

"What about the woman Kurt was allegedly fooling around with? Have you spoken to her?"

"I'm speaking to her later today," he says, but refuses to reveal her name.

Good luck with that. Media vultures will suss that out soon enough. I check my phone; I have twenty minutes to get to the police station for my interview with Detective Bernard. I have two questions left. First, I ask him if there was any security footage.

"What makes you ask that?"

Because I'm not an idiot and this is Greenwich. "I thought I noticed cameras at her house," I say.

He tells me the cameras at the Robbinses' mansion weren't working, but police retrieved security footage from the neighbor. "The quality isn't great, but the tech department is working to enhance it."

"Last question," I say. "Why did Bernard leave the NYPD?"

A shadow passes over Liam's face. "He apparently had some *issues* at his precinct in Queens."

"*Issues*? Can you elaborate?"

"I don't want to spread gossip," he says with finality.

"Should I be worried about Bernard?"

Liam doesn't answer. He doesn't have to. His feelings are written across his face. And all of a sudden, the apprehension I felt about going to the Greenwich Police Department turns to a stomach-twisting dread.

CHAPTER 9

The visit to Starbucks was worth it, despite the fact that I feel like I've regressed from a forty-two-year-old mature woman to a child.

I step outside and head toward the police station while reviewing what I've learned. First, beware of Bernard. It's concerning that Liam—a cop's cop inside and out—has his doubts about Bernard. Second, there are other suspects. Third, Liam himself plans to speak to Kurt's mistress. Since Bernard said the NYPD was handling interviews in the city, the mistress must either live or work in Manhattan.

A high-pitched whistle jars me out of my thoughts, and I see one of the town's famous traffic officers standing in the middle of an intersection; his lips pucker as he blows mightily into a shiny silver whistle. Dressed in a bright-yellow vest and Secret Service sunglasses, he points to a man who had the audacity to step into the road midblock. A very serious no-no here. The man pulls back, spilling coffee on what looks like an expensive suit, and curses under his breath.

Always the Good Samaritan, I come up beside him to offer sage advice. "You probably want to walk to the corner. They take jaywalking pretty seriously here."

The man pulls out a handkerchief and blots his shirtsleeve, steam pouring from his ears. "You'd think I robbed someone." The man dumps the remains of his coffee on the sidewalk. Lucky the traffic cop doesn't see. "Shouldn't they be busy worrying about real crime?"

I shrug, step past him, and walk to the corner. I'm a Good Samaritan, up to a point. Besides, I'm in a rush. Two women stroll past me and turn into a juice bar that specializes in organic-kale-and-wheatgrass smoothies. When we moved to Northern California, my mom fed my brother and me so many green health drinks that the sight of kale makes me gag. One of the few good things Liam did was send candy for holidays. My brother and I would curse Liam while stuffing our faces with chocolates and caramels.

Only a few reporters remain outside the police station, no doubt in case any interesting witnesses come in or out. That's exactly what I don't want to become—an interesting witness. I need to figure out how to get into the police station while keeping my colleagues from thinking I'm part of the story. I skirt the border and edge my way toward the back of the building. But more crews sit camped out by the rear door.

My only option is to act like I belong. "Hey there." I walk up to them, hoping my friendly demeanor offsets their urge to lift cameras. "Anything going on back here?"

"Nah. Dead as a doornail," the female camera operator says. Next to her stands a photographer with a *NY Post* badge around his neck. The *Post* makes a sport out of humiliating me, but he seems engrossed with his phone. Now's my chance.

"I need to check on something . . ." I reach for the doorknob, trying to act casual. Like I said, I don't lie. But misdirection or obfuscation is allowed.

"No one is talking, but knock yourself out." The woman grabs hold of the door for me and yanks it open. I step inside when I hear a man yelling, "Sam. Sam! Shoot her. Get the pic . . ." Sam must be the name of the *Post* guy because I hear him grunt and move toward me. The shutter clicks as I step inside and try to body-slam the door closed. I can imagine the headline now: DISGRACED SOCCER PLAYER QUESTIONED IN ROBBINS MURDER TRIES TO BODY-SLAM DOOR IN CAMERAMAN'S FACE.

It just keeps getting worse.

I press the intercom and announce I'm here to see Detective Bernard.

A buzz and then the lock releases, granting access to the narrow hallway with the familiar dank linoleum flooring from yesterday. Reaching the front, I recognize the desk sergeant from last night. She looks much more pleasant today. Under her red curls, I notice her active eyes and rosy cheeks.

"There." She points to the door across from the waiting area. So much for appearances.

"Ms. Green." Bernard steps forward. "Thanks for coming in. Another detective is using my office, so I hope you don't mind if we go into the conference room. Please follow me." Bernard leads me to a narrow staircase with scuffed flooring. Unlike last night, he makes no attempt at small talk—not a *Thanks for coming* or *Did you find the station all right?* At least he doesn't bring up dear ole dad.

He leads me past a small kitchen, more desks with officers hunched over computers, and stops at a door with a metal nameplate that says INTERROGATION ROOM.

"I thought we were going into a conference room."

"At this station, it's one and the same," he says as if I'm complaining about getting a brownie instead of a chocolate chip cookie. "After you." He ushers me into a gray cinder block space that's about ten feet by ten feet. There's a distinct smell of smoke despite a large no-smoking sign tacked onto a cork bulletin board on the far wall. In the middle of the room is a bridge table and two metal folding chairs. He points at one and sits in the other across from me. Above, fluorescent strip lights give off a dull, unnatural glow. I push down the feeling of anxiety growing in my gut and focus.

"Pulling out all the stops." I pull my chair forward; it squeaks against the concrete floor. "I'm flattered."

Again, no smile. "Mind if I tape our talk?"

"You mean record the interrogation?" I fold my arms over my chest, signaling I'm taking this seriously. He may have won our tango challenge last night when he whisked Yvette away, but I'm not losing twice.

He clicks the record button.

"Let me start with the basics." He clasps his long fingers together in front of himself, and I notice a thin silver wedding band. "Can you tell me about your activities yesterday?"

"Well, I spent the morning at home. And then went to the school around . . ." I think back to yesterday. I left my house around 1:30, so I probably got to the school about fifteen minutes later. "I must have arrived around one forty-five."

"Arrived at Greenwich Lake School? Please be specific."

"Greenwich Lake School, where my kids, Jackson and Nicole—Nikki, as she prefers—attend the eleventh grade." If it's details he wants, it's details he'll get. "I was assigned to hang banners, spider webbing, and . . ."

He puts up his hands. "I don't need *that* many details—I'm sure you realize. Tell me what time Yvette arrived at school."

"I just missed Yvette. She ran out for coffee and supplies." The fluorescent above buzzes, making the light flutter.

"When did you see her?" There's exasperation in his voice, which confuses me. Doesn't he have her timeline from, like, *all* the volunteers? And the coffee shop? It's not like she was even gone more than an hour. The sound of a radiator kicks on, and I feel heat hitting my legs. Maybe leather pants were not the smartest attire to wear, because I'm starting to feel uncomfortably warm.

"Do you remember the time?"

"I do. It was two thirty. I remember hearing the sirens and glancing at the gym clock."

"All right," he says. "Was Dylan there the whole time?"

"I don't know. Most of the kids were working on their own. I didn't notice Dylan."

"I see," he says and writes something on his pad.

"Let's talk about Yvette and Kurt's *marriage*," he says, derision in his tone.

The radiator kicks off, and the heat slowly recedes from my legs. I remain still, knowing he's hoping I will fill the silence.

"How did Yvette handle all the humiliation? All his affairs. I imagine she had a lot of built-up anger." Energized by his narrative, Bernard speaks faster. "Now this new affair and all the talk that Mr. Robbins would leave. One could even surmise that after what Mr. Robbins put her through that he deserved what he got."

"You're making a lot of assumptions, Detective," I say.

"Mrs. Robbins might even be able to launch an abuse defense . . ."

"If she were that upset, she'd divorce him, not kill him." I hear my voice rise.

He leans back, as if he's caught me. "If that were true, why didn't she divorce him already?" He folds his arms over his chest, a smirk crossing his lips.

"Because it didn't bother her," I reply.

He scoffs. "How could it not?"

I realize he's baiting me to spill private details of their marriage. And I'm not going to fall for it.

"I'm sure she already answered that for you during your two-hour interrogation."

The radiator kicks back on, and again, I feel the warm air against my legs. Bernard glances back down at his pad. "How did you and Yvette learn about the shooting?"

"Yvette got a call from a neighbor. He said there were police and an ambulance at her house."

He looks up from his pad and locks his hard eyes on mine. "How do you know it was the neighbor?"

"What do you mean?"

"Did you hear the conversation? Or just see her talking on her cell phone?"

"I saw her talking on her phone . . . but that's a ridiculous question. She wouldn't lie about that."

"Would she lie about anything?"

"Absolutely not."

He closes his pad, leans over to click off the record button. "Mrs. Robbins may have you fooled. But I know she did it, and I will prove it."

"Let me ask you a question." My outrage is building. "Why did you leave the NYPD?"

"That's absolutely none of your business." Anger flashes across his eyes. My goal was to put him off balance. Instead, it appears I poked the bear.

CHAPTER 10

I don't even bother to hide from the *NY Post* photographer. At this point, he got his pic, so who cares if he shoots more? It's not like the paper will do a collage of Kate Green photos. And, if they didn't get a picture here, no doubt they'd pull something from their archive. I can already imagine the outrageous headline. KATE GREEN INTERROGATED ABOUT HER MURDER-SUSPECT BFF. The headline should read: POLICE WASTE TIME QUESTIONING KATE GREEN ABOUT DECORATING GREENWICH LAKE SCHOOL GYM FOR HALLOWEEN. But whatever. At this moment, I've got more important things on my mind.

I take a left and walk onto a side street, a few blocks from home, the cold air slapping against my face. It's clear Detective Bernard has it in for Yvette. Giving him the benefit of the doubt, just for a minute, would Yvette have even had enough time to commit a crime?

She left the school around 1:40 and arrived back at 2:30, which gave her less than an hour to get coffee and supplies. Her house is ten minutes from the school, about the same distance as the coffee shop. I know she got the coffee because she had the tray with her. I'll have to ask her where she went for supplies. Even if the supply store was close to the coffee shop, it just appears like the timeline is too tight for her to also have gone to her house. And theoretically shoot her husband.

It feels more like Bernard is trying to smash a square peg into a round hole. I'm troubled that he doesn't seem interested in other scenarios. At least, that's the impression I got from the press conference. And then Liam made a point of saying *he* believes there are multiple red flags. He didn't say *we* or the *police*. And I know Liam to be very precise with his words.

My phone rings, and Yvette starts talking a mile a minute. She's at the mansion, and police are making her check every room of her house. I hear voices in the background. She hangs up, but not before confirming I will still go with her to the morgue.

As soon as we say goodbye, the phone rings again, and the loud, booming voice of my agent blares from the phone. "How's my favorite client?" my agent greets me.

"Don't ask."

"I know Yvette is a good friend of yours. I'm sorry about her husband."

"Thanks."

He tells me he got a call from TRP. "They would like to move your meeting to Wednesday morning." He pauses and adds, "That's the day after tomorrow," in case it skipped my mind that today is Monday.

"What if that's a problem?" I say.

"I told them it wasn't."

A leaf blower turns on, drowning out his voice. I cross the street as he continues a diatribe on how I need to make things right. I only half listen because I've heard it all before. When he stops for a breath, I jump in and ask if we could have the meeting over Zoom.

"They want a face to face with you," he says. "Kate. This is serious. You need to show up. And . . ." He pauses. "You're probably going to have to issue another apology."

"I already apologized! Burke didn't even deserve the first one."

"It's not just about Burke." My agent sighs, exasperated. "Did you see Page Six today?"

"I did. Apparently, I've let down every young girl in the country." I take a deep breath because I feel that part is true. "Let me ask you something—if a male athlete said the same thing, would he get casti-gated the way I am?"

"I don't know," he says. "But hypotheticals won't get us anywhere. Just go and play nice. This is your future we're talking about."

He waits for an answer, but I don't feel like supplying one.

"Call me after the meeting." He hangs up.

Part of me just wants to tell TRP Sports to shove it. But I need a paycheck. And, if I'm honest with myself, I love the job. Really, really love it. Reporting saved me. When I tore my ACL and learned my professional soccer career was over, I went to a dark place. My whirl-wind marriage to Tyler and having the twins helped. For a little while. But everything I'd known revolved around soccer. Not just playing the game, but the camaraderie, the training, even the smell of the locker rooms. Getting a chance to cover sports brought me back into the orbit that felt most like home.

A school bell rings at the neighborhood elementary school; boys and girls pour out the doors, and I watch the kids run into the arms of parents and nannies.

I'm lucky my mom met my stepdad, a gym teacher at the local high school. He was always there for my brother and me. When I developed my love for soccer, my stepdad supported me all the way. We'd stay out-side practicing in the backyard long after sunset. *Left, Kate. Now right. Lower your shoulder. Hesitate and then go. Yes. Great!* Once I kicked the ball so hard, it broke his nose. Even after that, he insisted on playing goalie—although he started to wear a hockey mask and three layers of clothing as protection. In the grand scheme of things, we really ended up better off without Liam.

I turn onto my street and stare at the plastic ghost and goblin blow-ups in front of what the kids and I call the Puke House. Until a few years ago, the color palette of the five homes on our cul-de-sac matched well. We each painted our homes in blues and greens. We picked his-toric but subtle shades. Then a young eager family moved in. They went in a different direction. A brighter direction. Restoring their house to its original pinks and purples. The historical society responded with utter glee, featuring the pastel home on the front page of their magazine and tour brochures. The rest of us were kind of horrified.

I'm usually the first on the block to decorate for Halloween. But I'm behind schedule. I would pass this year, except if you don't embrace Halloween on my block, you get egged and toilet papered.

Personally, I love Halloween; always have. Growing up, we went all out for the holiday. My stepdad and mom even dressed up as vampires. Unfortunately, Jackson and Nikki claim to have outgrown the holiday and only participate with Grinch-like enthusiasm.

I find Nikki sitting in the kitchen eating a bowl of Cheerios.

"That looks good." I smile, grab a bowl, and pour some cereal and milk together.

"Mom, slow down."

"I'm so hungry," I say between mouthfuls. "I haven't eaten all day. Where's Jackson?"

"Upstairs."

She tells me about her day, most of it filled with talk about Kurt's murder and how everyone can't believe it. The school administrators even brought in grief counselors for students who wanted to discuss their feelings. Some reporters tried to sneak over the school fence to interview students. I let Nikki know that Dylan and Yvette will spend the night again, and she agrees to bunk with me and order dinner from our favorite local Mexican restaurant. She's about to head upstairs when I realize I haven't returned the book Tyler dropped off. "By the way, your father dropped off your SAT book. You left it at his house."

She furrows her brow, and I notice she's wearing bronzer. "I told him I have too much other work this week. I don't have time for SAT stuff."

"Then don't do it," I say. "The SATs aren't till the spring."

"Yeah." She grunts, stands, and brings her bowl to the sink, clearly troubled by her father's continued nagging. I need to tell Tyler to back off.

Yvette pulls up at precisely 4:00.

"Are you sure you still want to do this?" I say as I open the passenger door and climb into her car.

"I don't *want* to. I *need* to," Yvette says as I close the door.

"How are you holding up?" I study the prominent circles under Yvette's eyes, visible despite heavy makeup. The merry melody of a Mister Softee truck rings out. I can't see the truck; it must be on another block. But it's definitely on the way.

"I feel as if I'm walking around in someone else's body. More than anything, I'm numb." She presses her lips together.

I ask one last time if she's sure she wants to go to the morgue.

"I need to, Kate. I need to see him." She hits the brakes as the ice cream truck turns onto my block, and then she pulls out of the cul-de-sac. As she drives, she tells me her in-laws want to hold a service this week. They are talking to the priest about having it on Friday. I wonder if the police will even release the body by then but don't tell her my concerns. Instead, I ask how her second interview went with the police.

"Awful . . . ," she replies.

"What do you mean?"

Yvette meanders through the side streets and toward the highway. "They keep attacking me. I feel like they think I did it. They're going to try and railroad me—I can feel it. And the worst of it is Kurt's real killer will go free."

Yvette sniffs back tears.

"What does your lawyer say?"

"She's worried that the police are overly concerned about the optics and want a fast, public win. I don't think she likes Detective Bernard."

I wonder what the attorney knows. I definitely need to look into Bernard sooner rather than later.

Yvette tells me the gunshot residue test came back. "Obviously, there was nothing on my clothing. You'd think that would be the end of it. But my attorney says the cops will argue I might have changed. Can you imagine?"

I can. Unfortunately. So, on top of everything else Detective Bernard thinks Yvette accomplished within fifty minutes, he assumes she dumped her clothing covered in gunshot residue somewhere and changed outfits. I watch Yvette as she drives through town and turns onto Route 1, past the corner doughnut shop. Ah, the memories. It was my and Yvette's morning spot for years. The first day our kids started kindergarten, we dropped them off and then went to get coffee at Starbucks. The coffee was great, but the place was full of moms sizing us up. It wasn't that we just felt uncomfortable; one whispered so loudly that we heard, clearly, *Tyler Edison with her? Total rebound. I give it a year before he asks for a divorce.*

I thought soccer was tough, but these women were vicious. The next morning, we got our coffee and Yvette told me we were going somewhere else. She drove us to the doughnut shop, where we walked in holding our cups at our sides and hid in a corner table. We ordered a chocolate sprinkled doughnut to share and enjoyed relaxing without prying eyes. Except for two old men reading the paper and a few construction workers, the place was empty. It became our routine. I smile at the memory. Yvette merges onto the highway and toward Stamford, where the morgue is located. The downtown Stamford exit comes up quickly, and Yvette gets off, taking us by a modern chrome-and-glass apartment complex, a new shopping plaza, and trendy restaurants before she turns right and heads toward the outskirts of this small city. Yvette pulls into an old corporate park and drives up to a one-story structure with a flat roof and small windows. "This is it." Yvette turns off the car. "City morgue."

We walk into the lobby, which I expect to be as dismal as the exterior. But it's not. In fact, the interior appears almost cheerful, with pink—albeit plastic—chairs, yellow walls, and a framed photo of the staff bowling team, the Morguers, holding up a trophy.

"Can I help you?" a small woman with an easy smile and dimples asks. Yvette explains our situation, and the woman tells us to wait on the pink chairs.

A silver-haired lady with a flower-print dress walks over. "Hello. My name is Patricia Kalyn." She looks at Yvette with overly sympathetic eyes set in a grandmotherly face with soft, loose skin. Patricia explains that she's a grief counselor and that most family members prefer to just see photos of their loved ones. She suggests that option to Yvette. "Your brother-in-law already identified your husband," she says. "You don't need to see him. Viewing the actual body can be very upsetting."

"I understand," Yvette says. "But it's something I need to do."

"Are you sure?"

"Yes."

Patricia agrees to Yvette's request and disappears down a hallway.

Yvette turns to me, tears in her eyes. "I still can't believe this is real. I keep expecting to see Kurt walk into a room and say this is all a big, stupid joke."

Patricia reappears and tells us to follow her. We walk down a dimly lit hall and stop at a glass window that faces a small space about ten feet by twelve feet. It resembles the rooms in *Law & Order* episodes. "One minute. The lab assistant will bring his body out."

Bright light floods the room, highlighting white walls, a white floor, and Formica cabinets. The door opens, and a bald man in a lab coat wheels a metal gurney toward us. A white sheet covers the table. Pinpricks of sweat break out across my back. The grief counselor looks at Yvette. "Tell us when you're ready, dear." Yvette stares through the glass at the gurney and nods her head. Patricia signals the man, and he lifts the sheet from Kurt's head and stops at the chin.

I hear myself gasp. The body resembles Kurt, but looks more like a mannequin or statue—like someone carved a stone figure of Kurt.

"Oh my God . . . no." Yvette pounds her fists against the glass. "Wake up!" she cries, her body shaking. The grief counselor signals to the lab technician, who quickly draws the sheet over Kurt's head. Together the counselor and I pull Yvette away from the glass and lower her into a nearby chair. I sit beside her, rubbing her back as she sobs. Out of the corner of my eye, I see the counselor shaking her head, in an *I told you to just look at the photos* kind of way.

I don't know how long we sit. Ten minutes? Twenty? Yvette's sobs turn soft and then stop. "Let me take you to the powder room, dear," Patricia says. "You can splash some cold water onto your face." Yvette and the woman walk down the hallway and disappear through another corridor.

I get up and step over to the door to the room where we saw the body. I turn the knob—it clicks and opens. "Hello?" I enter the brightly lit room.

"You can't be in here." The bald man in the lab coat appears from behind a cordoned-off area.

"I'm sorry. I just wanted to ask—did he suffer?"

The man looks at the ground. "You're the wife's friend?"

"Yeah. I thought the information could comfort her. If he passed quickly . . ."

"I'm afraid there's nothing comforting about how he died. Bled out slowly . . . he might have even lived if someone found him sooner and got him to a hospital. It was a painful, slow way to go." He points to the door behind me. "You really can't be in here."

I step out just as Yvette and Patricia round the corner. If Patricia saw me, she doesn't say. But I can't help feeling like she's looking at me funny as she escorts us out of the building.

Yvette can't stop shaking. I put her in the passenger seat and drive. She curls herself into a fetal position and closes her eyes. All I can think about are the words of the man in the lab coat.

If Kurt had been found sooner, he might have lived.

CHAPTER 11

Inside my kitchen, the kids stand around the butcher-block island unpacking dinner from large shopping bags. My mouth waters from the smells.

"Perfect timing." Nikki smiles a bit too brightly. Jackson and Dylan don't even look up, locked in a quiet exchange. I recognize Jackson's defensive stance: arms folded across his chest, sneaker kicking at the floor. I try to get Jackson's attention with a hello, but he just grunts and keeps staring at the floor.

"What's going on with Jackson and Dylan?" I follow Nikki into the dining room as she carries a platter of tacos and enchiladas inside.

"Nothing." She places the dishes down on the flower tablecloth. I slide past a chair to get closer to her, banging my ankle on the leg of the table. This is the one room in the house I don't like. It's small. Dark. But five people won't fit at the kitchen counter, so we have no choice but to squeeze around the little wooden dining room table I found at a garage sale.

"Jackson seems upset."

She shrugs and tries to return to the kitchen, but I remain in her path.

"God, Mom." She shakes her thick blonde hair. "I think he's fine. Maybe he's stressed about your appointment tomorrow. Did you consider that?"

She slides by me. Jackson and I have our group therapy session in the morning. He must have mentioned it to Nikki. I look at him through the doorway, his skin still pale, his lips pulled tight in a frown. Dylan seems angry, with her hands clenched at the sides of her body. This is about more than our appointment tomorrow. Something is going on between these two.

"Coming through." Yvette strides past me, carrying a bowl of guacamole and another of salsa. She's pulled herself together since we returned from the coroner and even pasted a slight smile across her lips.

"Any idea what Jackson and Dylan are talking about?" I ask.

"You know those two. Always drama . . ." Yvette dips a chip into the guacamole and takes a bite.

Always drama is not how I'd categorize Jackson and Dylan's relationship; but it wouldn't be the first thing I've gotten wrong about Jackson.

We bring the rest of the food to the table, and I open a bottle of cabernet. Jackson picks up the plate of tacos, takes some before passing the serving dish around the table. Nikki and Dylan both choose the vegan option, while I put two large beef tacos on my plate with a heap of guacamole. I try to think of a way to fill the silence, but the only idea I come up with is to chew louder. Not an appealing option. I am so hungry, having only had Cheerios for lunch. The savory beef taco mixed with guacamole tastes divine, and I lose myself in the food.

Nikki can't stand quiet, and my chewing isn't enough for her. I see the wheels spinning in her mind while she weighs options to fill the void. "Dylan," Nikki says a bit too loudly. "Is there anything you need from school that I can get you?"

"I don't think so." Dylan shrugs. "But . . ."

We all turn to Dylan.

"Speak up, Dylan," Yvette prods. "But. What?"

"Well, I was wondering what kids at school are saying." She keeps her gaze planted in her taco.

"Dylan Robbins. You shouldn't care about idle gossip. We're better than that."

Dylan looks as if she wants to dive into the guacamole.

"Don't worry about that." Nikki rushes to the rescue. "People weren't talking about it."

Jackson gasps. Unlike me, it appears my daughter has no problem lying.

"We got loads of homework in chemistry. At least you don't have to do that," Jackson throws out there. Mourn a father, skip chemistry. Not the most tactful response. Lucky for Jackson, he's literally saved by the bell. The house phone rings. Nikki jumps up to answer it, even though only her dad and salespeople use that number. She returns to tell me that her father would like a word with me, and mouths, "Good luck."

"Yes?" I take the phone and step into the kitchen. Across the street, I see activity at the blue Victorian next to the Puke House. The retired elementary school teacher carries a black plastic cauldron onto her porch. On Halloween, she transforms her quaint porch into the most terrifying spot in town. Every Halloween, my prim and proper neighbor dresses as a witch with green face paint and a large hairy wart glued to her chin. She sits in wait—so still, kids believe she's a decoration. Then when they get close, she stands, reaches her arms around them, and lets out an ear-splitting cackle. It scared the crap out of me and the kids the first time we went trick-or-treating on our block.

I tune back in to Tyler, who is presently berating me for letting Yvette and Dylan into the house for dinner. He doesn't know they are also sleeping over. "I can't believe you allowed our children to have dinner with that woman. We agreed you wouldn't expose the kids to her."

"We didn't agree. You demanded," I hiss into the phone.

"You can't make this decision alone. I have rights . . ."

"I'd love to discuss this further, but I have guests I need to return to." I hang up on my maniacal micromanaging ex and return to the dining room.

Nikki and Jackson start clearing plates. Dylan informs us that Zeke is outside and runs off to see him.

I refill Yvette's wineglass and top mine off. She tells me that Kurt's parents want to look at coffins tomorrow. Outside, the crickets start *cree-crawing* through the window. I ask Yvette where her in-laws will stay, and she tells me she expects to be allowed back in the mansion tomorrow and that they will stay with her.

"That seems quick," I respond.

"With all the police there today, you'd think we could be back in now." She takes a big gulp of wine.

I remember she told me the police had her check every room of the house to see if anything was missing. I ask Yvette if she found anything that was stolen or out of place.

"Fifty thousand in cash was taken from the safe in our bedroom."

I nearly spit out my wine. Who has $50,000 sitting around in their house safe? But then I realize the answer is probably most of Greenwich.

"Was it definitely taken? Could Kurt have removed it?"

"That's what the detective asked. I guess it's possible, but they didn't find any cash on him. And, I'd have noticed if the safe was open before I left in the morning." She picks up her glass of wine and takes another big gulp. "The strange thing is that whoever took the money left my jewelry, which was worth a hell of a lot more than the cash."

Again, I let the obscene value of her jewelry pass and wonder why someone would take the money and not the gems. "Did the detective have a theory?"

"None he shared with me." She reaches across the table, picks up the bottle, and refills her glass. I'm debating telling her to slow down, but she's earned the right to drink.

"Something else was really strange." She looks toward the kitchen, where we can see Jackson and Nikki washing the dishes. Yvette lowers her voice. "The police didn't find Kurt's diamond studs or gold chain when they . . ." She closes her eyes and pauses. ". . . when they found his body. The only time he ever took them off was during games. He slept with them and everything."

"Do you think the killer took them off his body?"

"It's the only thing that makes sense."

I let that sink in. Someone came into the house, shot Kurt, ran upstairs to steal cash, and then took jewelry off Kurt's dead, or dying, body. "Couldn't Kurt have handed over the jewelry before he was . . . you know, at gunpoint?"

She doesn't answer. I'm not even sure she's listening. I've been anxious to ask Yvette about Dylan's whereabouts. Now seems as good a time as any. "Detective Bernard asked me if I saw Dylan at the gym Sunday. Where was she?"

"Dylan and Zeke made a run to Home Depot. The police were able to confirm that with Zeke."

"At least he's good for something," I say, and she laughs.

"The police asked me where you were. I knew you went to get the coffee, but I wasn't sure where you went for the supplies," I say.

Yvette puts her wineglass down and looks at me with her strong copper eyes. "First the police. Now you?"

"Don't get defensive." I put my hands up. "It's going to be at the center of their investigation."

"Sorry." She sighs. "I just feel like everyone is out to get me." She takes a sip of her wine. Then another. "After getting the coffee, I drove to Montgomery's Hardware store to get industrial glue. I got all the way there when Dylan called to say she was at Home Depot. So, I had her get it and I headed back to school." She looks down at her hands. "I should have gone into that damn store. I was right outside. That detective is saying I had *opportunity* because of those stupid twenty minutes."

"Maybe your car is on some traffic camera or something," I say, trying to offer hope. But we both know those twenty minutes will be a problem. Still, even with twenty minutes, that's awfully tight. She'd need to have driven back from the coffee place and then to the school, which would have left her about five minutes to allegedly commit the crime. And they didn't find any clothing of Yvette's with gunshot residue. I make a note to myself to find out what Yvette was wearing in the morning to see if she changed. Because if she hadn't, I can't see how the police explain away the lack of gunshot residue.

"Yvette, when they checked for gunshot residue, they checked your hands, right?"

"Yes," she says. "Obviously it came up negative."

After she heads to bed, I take out my computer and google Detective Peter Bernard. I find basic information: age forty-five, joined NYPD twenty years earlier. Was a homicide detective with the 104th precinct for ten years, before leaving two years ago. I google the 104th precinct to see if anything interesting pops up and gape at the result. If this is true, then my hunch about Bernard is right. And he is someone who will stop at nothing to make his case, whether he's right or wrong.

CHAPTER 12

At 8:00 a.m., Jackson and I sit in the office of psychiatrist Dr. Aaron Michelson. Jackson on one end of the faux-leather couch and me on the other. The morning sun shines through the windows of the psychiatrist's office.

"How are you feeling today, Jackson?" Dr. Michelson leans back in his chair and crosses his right leg over his left, as if to indicate he has all the time in the world. His tone sounds like forced warmth. Dr. Michelson reminds me of a small Thomas Jefferson. About five three, he wears a well-fitted three-piece suit, slightly wide tie, and has silver hair reaching down the back of his neck.

The office feels like it should belong to an art-history professor. There are African masks on one wall, a large watercolor painting of a Japanese koi pond on another, and in the corner, a modern swirling sculpture in blues and greens.

"'K." Jackson squirms in his navy school blazer.

"How about you, Ms. Green?"

"Well, it's been a tough couple of days, to be honest," I say. "We are friends with the Robbins family. And, with Kurt's death . . ."

Jackson fidgets, bouncing his ripped sneaker up and down on the rug.

"Do you feel the same, Jackson?"

Jackson looks at me with his light-blue eyes. They appear flat, like a still pond. "I think it's harder on Mom. She's closer to them."

"What about Dylan?" I turn toward Jackson.

He shrugs, and I'm reminded of Yvette's comment yesterday about how there's always drama between Jackson and Dylan. Dr. Michelson interlaces his fingers and puts them on his lap. "Jackson, do you want to talk about what happened to Kurt Robbins?"

Jackson shrugs again.

"Ms. Green." Dr. Michelson turns to me. "There's something Jackson has been working on. Not surprisingly, children sometimes have trouble expressing themselves to their parents. I encouraged Jackson to write you and Mr. Edison letters he can read here within this safe space."

"Oh." I look at my nails to hide my discomfort; the blue polish has chipped. Is Jackson about to tell me that his overdose was, in fact, a suicide attempt? And that I'm the one to blame?

"Is it okay if Jackson reads yours now?" Dr. Michelson asks.

If Jackson needs to get things off his chest, I should be encouraged about that. I should know what my son thinks. I brace myself and turn to Jackson. "Of course. Read me your letter."

Jackson doesn't meet my gaze. Instead, he stares into the glass bowl filled with Halloween candy that rests in front of us on the coffee table.

He picks up a chocolate pumpkin, unwraps it, and places it into his mouth. Jackson chews the candy, swallows, then fishes a piece of paper from his jeans pocket. He opens the yellow sheet, clears his throat, and starts. "Dear Mom."

"A little louder, Jackson," Dr. Michelson chimes in.

"Dear Mom." His voice still thin but louder. "I—I kind of feel like you—you don't trust me."

I open my mouth to speak, but Dr. Michelson puts up his hand. "Let him finish, Ms. Green. It's important not to react until he's done."

Jackson clears his throat again. "Every time you look at me, I—I feel like you think I'm—um . . . that you think I'm reckless or some-thing. Like you don't believe I can get healthy on my own."

Jackson stops. His hand is shaking. He inhales deeply, holds the air, and then lets it out.

Dr. Michelson keeps his eyes on Jackson. "You're doing great."

"'K," Jackson says. My son puts the paper on his lap and looks directly into my eyes. "I . . . can you—can you . . . please . . . back off and like . . . give me some space? I . . . know I scared you. But I'm okay. Really. And I *need* you to believe that. Otherwise, I don't see how I can fix myself."

The words hang over me. I've always seen myself as a laid-back, go-with-the-flow kind of person. But then, with the *overdose* . . . maybe I'd been *too* laid back? I knew Jackson smoked a little pot. And we spoke endlessly about how to be safe; never driving if you're drunk or stoned. But in my wildest dreams, I never suspected he'd get addicted to amphetamines. And I didn't notice the symptoms until he ended up overdosing and nearly dying in the hospital.

"Ms. Green, what are you thinking right now? It's important to have a conversation."

"I feel like I should have been watching *more* closely. I should have protected him. I hadn't even noticed he'd been taking Adderall."

Dr. Michelson puts up his hand, stopping me again. "Tell Jackson."

I turn to Jackson and notice for the first time that he shaved and brushed his hair. His skin, always pale, no longer looks sallow. But the darkness under his eyes remains. Then the image from the hospital flashes across my brain. He's in the emergency room, and his heart flat-lines. The doctors rush in with a crash cart. We stand there, not sure if he will return to us. I close my eyes against the burning of tears forming behind my lids. The water trickles down my cheeks.

"I feel like it's my fault. I should have been there. I failed you."

Dr. Michelson gets up and holds out a tissue box. I take a handful and dab my eyes.

"But, Mom. That's the point." Jackson's words come fast. "I need to take responsibility for my actions. My actions! I'm not a kid—I'm seventeen. You didn't take the drugs, I did. And with you blaming yourself and hovering and all . . . it makes it worse. I need to own my mistake."

We lock eyes, and I wonder if the emptiness I've thought I've seen in his gaze is really frustration. Or anger?

"We used to have fun," Jackson says. "Remember going skating in Wollman Rink? You never laugh around me anymore. Everything's so stressed."

I stand and walk to the sculpture. It's circular, like an abstract Ferris wheel with hundreds of shades of blues and greens—lime, light lime, dark lime, darker lime, sky blue, and on and on. So many different shades I could never even name them all. I turn and face Jackson. "I want us to laugh and have fun. Of course, I remember the day we went skating. It's just—I'm just so worried." I walk back to the couch and sit next to him. "But I will try. Really."

At 8:50, Dr. Michelson ends the session. "Jackson, do you mind if I speak to your mother alone for a minute?"

"Nah." Jackson leaves the office.

"Thank you for coming in. We made good progress this morning." He squirms in his chair, uncrossing his leg. It must be hard to sit all day like that. "I imagine you were also expecting an update?"

"Yes. I was."

"Without divulging anything personal, I can tell you that Jackson is making progress. He seems very committed to trying to lead a healthy life."

"I'm so happy to hear that." I stand up. "Thank you, Doctor."

Dr. Michelson stands too. "There is one thing."

A red light blinks by his chair. "My next patient," he says by way of explanation. "Like I said, there's one thing . . ."

"Yes?"

"Jackson also prepared a letter to read to Mr. Edison. He planned to read it to him on Sunday. I hope Mr. Edison comes to our next session."

"I'll tell him."

"I appreciate that." Dr. Michelson tilts his head. "It's important."

I assure Dr. Michelson that I will do everything I can to make sure Tyler shows up. I thank Dr. Michelson again and then head to the elevator. Tyler is helicopter-dad focused on Nikki, but God forbid he pay attention to his son. I don't know why he continues with this outrageous behavior. I hope Jackson's letter to Tyler is a whopper.

Deep breaths. I don't want Jackson to see how angry I am. I plaster a smile on my face, step out of the elevator into the cramped lobby, where Jackson is watching the small TV screen on the security guard's desk. My impulse is to ask Jackson what excuse Tyler gave for missing his appointment. But this moment isn't about my ex, so I summon every ounce of self-control and tap Jackson on his shoulder. "Want to get breakfast? I can give you a note for school. You're already late as it is."

"True." He looks in my direction, but doesn't make eye contact, focusing about three inches to the right of my nose.

"You worried I'm mad?"

He turns his blue eyes on me. "Kind of. Yeah."

The elevator opens, and an elderly man shuffles out on a walker. A woman with him. "Come on, Dad, this way." She leads him past us and out the front door.

"I'm not mad, Jackson. I'm proud of you for wanting to take control. And you're probably right that I've been hovering a bit."

"A bit." He gives me a half smile, and I notice, for the first time, how much he looks like Liam. It's more than just the blue eyes. It's the wry smile and strong jaw.

"Why are you staring?"

"Sorry. You just look so grown-up."

"God, Mom, stop." He wrinkles his nose.

We walk across the street to the 1950s-style Greenwich City Diner. The place is decorated with red vinyl booths and stools on top of a checkerboard-patterned floor. Movie posters featuring Gene Kelly and

Elvis Presley hang on hot-pink walls. A waitress sits us at a booth in the corner, and Jackson immediately starts flipping through the jukebox. He puts two quarters into the machine, and Elvis Presley's "Hound Dog" plays.

"Good choice." The plump waitress hands us large laminated menus and flashes an easy smile. She's wearing dangling pumpkin earrings and a goblin necklace over her white uniform.

"All righty. My name's Joanne, but everyone calls me Jo. Coffee?"

"Yes," we both say at the same time and laugh.

Jo returns, carrying a pot of coffee, and fills each of our cups. The coffee smells weak. I sip it anyway, craving the caffeine despite the muddy taste.

"Mom, you're staring, again." Jackson pulls his lips into a grimace.

"Sorry." I shift my gaze down to look at the red laminated tabletop between us.

"Just ask . . . obviously something is on your mind." He picks up his coffee. "You want to know about Dylan, right?"

I nod my head. But Dylan was not who I was thinking about. I want to know what excuse Tyler gave for missing the appointment on Sunday. "I thought you and Dylan were close."

"She just became dumb when she started dating Zeke. He's a jerk," Jackson says.

"I noticed the two of you arguing at dinner last night."

His mood changes in an instant, and he mumbles that he needs to use the bathroom. I didn't even bring the topic up; he did. I'm going to get some serious whiplash from this kid.

My gaze wanders to the television, where video from one of Kurt's games flashes across the screen.

"What an awful story. He was a regular here, you know." Jo reappears, topping off my coffee. I didn't realize that. But it makes sense. Gene's gym is only a block away. Jo looks sad. "He was such a charmer. He always greeted me by name. *How's it going, Jo? How are your grandkids?* It says something about that Kurt Robbins that he paid attention to me and the rest of the folks at the diner." She motions toward the line chef. "He even helped pay for our chef's cancer treatment last year. And didn't tell anyone either. That's the kind of man he was." She sniffs. "To be honest, I was a bit worried when I saw him Sunday."

"You saw him Sunday?" I say.

"Around lunchtime." She leans toward me. "He got into a huge fight with the guy he was with. The manager had to ask them to lower their voices."

"Really?" This is the first I've heard about a public fight between Kurt and someone on Sunday. "Did the police talk to you about this?"

"I tried to call that detective from the TV. I think his name is Bernard."

"It is. What did he say?"

"Nothing. No one called me back."

I'm flabbergasted. This is important information for their investigation. Kurt had a fight with someone hours before he died. If I ever needed proof that Detective Bernard was set to pin this on Yvette, here it is. He's willfully ignoring an important lead. I'm more convinced than ever that I need to help Yvette. She needs someone on her side investigating this case. And since no one else seems committed to being objective, that someone will have to be me.

I look back up at Jo. "Can you describe the person Kurt was fighting with?"

"Fit, around sixty, bald, with a baseball cap and a Comets sweatshirt."

I pull out my phone and google Coach Sebastian "Seb" Bradshaw. "This him?"

"That's him. Boy, Kurt was mad, I'll tell you that."

I take out a pen and write Liam's phone number on a napkin. "This is another detective working on the case. Contact him."

A man at the next table calls out for Jo. She takes the napkin and excuses herself.

Seb and Kurt got into a huge fight hours before the murder? They both have explosive personalities, and I've seen them engaged in serious disagreements during practices. But to fight in public at a restaurant? That strikes me as unusual. Something must have really set them off. And I'm determined to figure out what that was. Soon. But now I need to focus on my son.

Jackson returns, and we order blueberry pancakes and bacon. The song on the jukebox switches to another Elvis tune, "Jailhouse Rock."

"Here we go." Jo places giant plates of pancakes and bacon in front of us. I breathe in the sweet and savory smells. Maybe some sugar and grease can lighten the mood. I pick up the syrup dispenser and pour the sweet liquid all over my dish.

"Save some syrup for me." Jackson grabs the bottle from my hand. "That's kind of gross, Mom."

I pick up a piece of bacon, dip it in syrup, and take a bite.

"Yuck." He drizzles a little syrup on the top of his pancake stack and returns the dispenser to the table. Jackson polishes off his bacon and almost finishes his pancakes before I get through half a stack. By the time we leave, he's smiling, and I feel a glimmer of hope. Things could be moving in a good direction for us, if I can just navigate the minefield of topics that are off limits.

CHAPTER 13

I pull up to the entrance of Greenwich Lake School to drop Jackson off. "Jackson," I say as he's about to get out of the car. "Did Dad explain why he missed Dr. Michelson's appointment Sunday?"

He shrugs and tells me Tyler got a work call and needed to go back to the office. "Typical, right?" he says and gets out of the car. *Not really.* Tyler is never one to give up his weekends for the office.

On my drive home, Yvette phones to say the police officially left her house, but she's nervous to go inside. I turn the car around and head to North Street and her mansion. I stop at the wrought iron gate with its gold tips and stare at the mansion that I've spent so much time inside. The beauty of the place will forever be tainted by the violent murder. I steel myself for what's ahead, enter the code, and proceed down the long gravel drive, parking behind Yvette's Range Rover. She gets out to meet me. From afar she looks good, wearing a crisp maroon blouse and tailored trousers under her long cashmere coat. But up close I see the pain etched across her face. I take her hand, and we stare at the carved arched double oak doors of her stately limestone estate. I wonder what she's thinking. Is it about all the family memories the house holds or the gruesome murder that just took place?

"We don't have to do this." I feel like that's my new mantra. But I know Yvette. She likes to face things head-on. "You and Dylan can stay at my house as long as you need." A gust of wind kicks up some leaves near us, and we watch them scatter on the ground.

"It's been two days since Kurt . . . passed," she says. "I think the longer Dylan and I wait to return to the house, the worse it will be. Dylan has lived here her whole life. I want her to remember all the good times and feel surrounded by Kurt's love."

Yvette unlocks the door and flicks on a light. I blink the two-story grand hall into view, taking in the ivory marble tiles and sparkling crystal chandelier hanging from a gold linked chain. The entranceway is nearly the size of my whole downstairs; I believe they call this a rotunda.

Yvette grips the polished mahogany table to maintain her balance. "Kurt bought me this table last year for our anniversary. It's an antique from the English court. He said the strong wood represented our strong bond—one that could never be broken."

Yvette has lots of these types of presents. Lavish and thoughtful gifts accompanied by beautiful sentiment. Kurt oozed love and romance toward Yvette. He really could take your breath away.

Yvette folds her arms over her chest and tells me a cleaning service will be coming in a few hours, but she wants to scope things out first. She starts toward the kitchen. I hesitate, unnerved at the thought of entering the room where Kurt was shot. But if Yvette can face it, I certainly should be able to.

As we enter the kitchen, I half expect to see signs of a crime, but it's more *Architectural Digest* than police blotter. The only hint of disruption is a faint odor of Lysol or ammonia instead of the scent of vanilla I usually associate with this room. The kitchen mixes brilliant greens with a bold diamond-patterned backsplash, which I personally find a bit too busy for my taste. The centerpiece is a long concrete island with brushed-nickel chairs that are as uncomfortable as they look.

The dark wood floor appears dusty, and I wonder if that's from the forensic team. I half expect to see a chalk outline of a body, but that's probably only on television shows. There's no indication of where Kurt died, and I walk gingerly across the floor, wary of each step. Yvette moves to the cooking area and stands before the massive Sub-Zero refrigerator. "This is where the police said it happened." She bends down and puts her hand gently against the floor as if trying to cosmically connect with Kurt. I stare at the floor and notice a spot that appears a little darker. I shiver, wondering if the stain is from blood or general wear and tear.

"Gene told me Kurt was face up." She keeps her gaze on the ground. "Kurt probably saw who shot him. Don't you think?"

I remember what the lab tech said to me. That Kurt bled out slowly. So, Yvette's right that he probably did see who shot him . . . and had time to think about it as the life drained from his body. Were his last thoughts about his wife and daughter? I shut my eyes against the tears I feel forming.

I still can't get over the fact that he's gone. He was one of those people who embraced life in every moment. When I started covering the Comets, he would always play silly jokes on me. Kurt loved practical jokes. I'd interview him after a game, and then when I turned to face the camera, he'd make funny faces for the viewers. It was silly. And the producers loved it. The first time I looked at one of those tapes, I laughed so hard, I couldn't breathe.

"You get a false sense of safety in this town." Yvette shakes her head and tells me they never kept the alarm on during the day and that their security cameras have been broken for months. A fact I already knew from Liam.

She's right about the false feeling of safety. Until Sunday, I never used my house alarm either. Let alone locked the doors and windows. Foolish, really. She stands up and tells me the police confirmed the gun found next to Kurt was in fact registered to him.

"Where did he keep it?"

She says most of the time he locked it in the safe in his study. "But sometimes after going to the range, he'd just leave it out. Especially if he came back with teammates and wanted to show off." This isn't the first time Yvette has relayed how lackadaisical Kurt could be about the gun. It was something they'd argued about. I remember Liam kept a gun safe at our apartment when I was a kid. And he was diligent about putting his firearm away and locking the safe.

"Did Kurt have his phone on him?" I ask, wondering if he could have called for help. She tells me his phone was found on the other side of the room, on the kitchen table.

"And there's something else . . ." Yvette looks down at the ground. "They also found a burner phone on the table."

"Why did he have a burner phone?" I blurt before I can stop myself. For his affairs, obviously. Since I already put my foot in my mouth, I might as well continue. "The police asked me if Kurt was getting serious with a mistress," I say. "Did you know anything about that?"

She narrows her eyes before answering. "Are you really asking that?"

"I can't help you if I don't know the situation," I say as kindly as I can.

"I mean . . . he seemed to be out more than usual." She shrugs and opens the refrigerator, taking out a can of diet soda. "But that's happened through the years." She opens the soda and pours it into a glass. "I do want to prepare myself and Dylan for whatever information will drop on the woman."

She takes a sip of the drink. "Could you try and find out who Kurt's last affair was with?"

"I'll see what I can learn," I say. Maybe someone at the Comets knows about the affair, I think to myself. I'll stop by Madison Square Garden tomorrow after my meeting at TRP. See what I can learn. And, more importantly, dig into Kurt's fight with the coach.

"I heard that Kurt might have had an argument with Coach Seb the day of the murder," I say to Yvette. "Do you know why they would have been fighting?"

She looks at me, her copper eyes wide. "It couldn't have been serious. Seb was like a second father to him. Remember when Seb came to the hospital when I had my appendix out?"

I smile at the memory. It must have been seven or eight years ago. Kurt called me, frantic, hardly able to string two words together. He said an ambulance just took Yvette to the hospital and could I meet them. When I got to the hospital, Seb was already there trying to calm Kurt down. But he couldn't stop crying. It was only when the doctor came out and told him the surgery went well that he calmed down. But not before he embraced the doctor in a hug and swung him around. We teased Kurt for years—if this was his reaction to an appendectomy, what would he do if something serious happened?

Yvette's phone beeps and I see she's replaced the old one. She reads a text and then tells me that the cleaning crew should be here soon. She seems jittery and asks if I would mind if she spent a little time alone.

I give her a hug and let myself out. About a mile down North Street, a gold Corvette speeds past me. Yvette told me Mason Burke drives a gold Corvette. Did she rush me out of her house because Burke was coming to visit?

I have a lot to mull over, and I'm not about to do it on an empty stomach. I pick up a sandwich and bring it home. After polishing off the turkey sub and iced coffee, I decide to start by looking further into Detective Bernard. I open my computer and pull up an article on the precinct he worked at in Queens.

The article reports that a man living in Maspeth, Queens, was recently freed from prison after being wrongfully convicted. It shows a blurry picture of the young man hugging his family at a welcome home party in a small living room. The article only hints at police wrongdoing, focusing on the family reunion instead.

I search for articles on the case, typing in the name of the man in the picture. A story from the same publication, *Maspeth Weekly*, pops up from an earlier date. It says that the NYPD reached an out of court settlement with the man for an undisclosed amount. It detailed the initial case, saying the twenty-seven-year-old was recently ordered to be freed after DNA proved he hadn't bludgeoned his girlfriend to death ten years ago. The story says the man, then only seventeen, always maintained his innocence. And even described an attacker. But the police detectives never looked beyond the teen and willfully ignored crucial evidence. I try to find more information, but nothing comes up. I'm sure the police made the man sign a nondisclosure agreement, so it will be hard to uncover the identity of the detectives. I find the email address for the reporter from the *Maspeth Weekly* and send her a message.

About to close the computer, I hesitantly type my name into the search bar. The first item that pops up is Page Six of the *New York Post*. Before even reading the copy, I know it will be bad because I'm staring at the most unflattering photo of myself. My hand's up, trying to block the shot, and I'm scowling in a way that suggests I'm seconds from assaulting the cameraman.

The copy matches the image. It says the Greenwich Police brought me into the station to be "interrogated" by the police regarding Yvette Robbins. Many people don't realize that soccer superstar turned disgraced reporter, Kate Green, is also BFFs with the prime suspect in the Robbins murder. Detectives spent hours grilling Green. Add bad judgment in friends to Green's already growing list of problems. How ridiculous can they get? If it weren't so hurtful, I'd laugh. I scan the rest of the column in case there's a mention of my meeting tomorrow at TRP. They don't mention the meeting, but they do end the article promising tomorrow's column will have more on Green's "meteoric fall."

I've had lows before, but I could usually dig out of them with hard work: more drills, weight training, fitness. But this is starting to feel insurmountable.

I need to clear my head. I change into running gear and go for a long jog, desperate to rid my brain of all things *New York Post*. By the time I return, the sky is gray and the weather dreary. The kids are with

Tyler tonight, so I shower, eat some cereal for dinner, and get ready for bed. As I'm settling in for the night, I get a text from my agent. Don't even think of skipping the meeting tomorrow. I silence the phone. I'll decide in the morning whether or not to go into the city and meet with TRP. My agent's warning be damned.

CHAPTER 14

From the depths of sleep, I hear an angry buzz. I try to ignore the noise, but it's relentless. I blink myself awake and turn off my blaring alarm. I feel so tired, I consider returning to sleep. Then I remember it's Wednesday and I have a meeting at TRP. With great reluctance, I force myself out of bed, into the shower, and to the train station. I guess I never really planned to blow off the meeting no matter how much I *thought* about it.

Coffee in hand, wearing a black wool dress and my new zebra-patterned heels Yvette insisted we buy.

We'll get matching pairs, she said on our last girls' trip. *Kick-ass heels so we can kick some ass.* She had laughed because she rarely used words like *ass*.

I stare out the window, ignoring the *Post* on my lap. I'm just not caffeinated enough to face the vitriol that awaits me. I sip my coffee and stare outside at the slideshow of roofs and power lines as we speed toward Manhattan. The floor rumbles under my feet; coughs and conversations surround. The power lines give way to clumps of green yards as the train whizzes through the suburbs of Westchester.

Coffee finished and approaching Manhattan, I can no longer avoid the task at hand. I unfold the paper and stare at the headline: MURDERESS IN HEELS? Below the words sits a full-page picture of Yvette rushing from the police station. Her head tilts down and shoulders slump, making her appear like she's hiding something. A picture perpetuating another false narrative. Whatever pose she took would become twisted. Head high and staring forward would translate into arrogant. Crying would become widow's crocodile tears. If the media has it in for you, consider yourself toast.

The media never sees the Yvette I know. The one who I've shared my deepest secrets and laughed over the silliest jokes with. The one who shares my love for cabernet and Billy Joel and my dislike for sushi. The one who also never had sex until college.

The conductor announces five minutes until Grand Central Terminal. I push my feelings down and turn to Page Six. Like one of those moviegoers watching a horror scene through open fingers, I begrudgingly scan the column. It appears I escaped unbruised. Then my eyes focus on the last paragraph. My heart sinks.

> Disgraced soccer star turned reporter Kate Green heads into a meeting today with TRP brass. A little birdie told Page Six she's expected to be canned.

Tears sprout at the corner of my eyes. Even though it's Page Six and I know they make shit up, I feel deflated.

I text my agent and ask if he's aware he's sending me into a firing squad. Pun intended. And apropos. He replies with don't believe what you read in the Post. Easy for him to say. I'm about to catch the next train home when I get another text from him; clearly my agent is clairvoyant. Or spying. He warns me not to even consider skipping the meeting. You've faced a hell of a lot worse. Don't be a coward. God, I hate when he's right. I leave the train, hail a taxi, and steel myself for what's ahead.

On Sixth Avenue, I stare at the sleek silver-and-glass skyscraper that is not just home to TRP Sports but all the global enterprises of NetWorld Media Corporation, including the company's newspapers, magazines, and news and entertainment channels. The smell of coffee and doughnuts overtakes bus fumes and smoke. Normally, I find the cacophony of honking and hollering energizing, but today the noise strikes an uneasy chord. Slowly, I walk to the building, questions ping-ponging around my brain. Will I come out of this meeting with no career? Will I need to reinvent myself yet again? I'm not sure I have that kind of energy. I was stupid to yell at Burke. No matter how he acted. I am better than that. At this moment, I truly hate myself.

Taking advantage of the unusually warm day, a crowd of tourists pushes against the two-story glass windows at the north corner of the building to peer into one of TRP's studios, where the anchor smiles at a teleprompter. The large black-and-red digital ticker above spews updates—NEW ENGLAND PATRIOTS LOSE IN FINAL MINUTES TO BALTIMORE RAVENS, 17–14. I stand up straight, plaster a smile on my face, and walk past the crowd and into the charcoal marble lobby, my heels click-clacking against the dark stone. Most people head toward the banks of elevators, but I veer left to the escalator at the far end of the lobby.

"Morning," the security guard says, nodding and unlatching the red velvet rope. Is that pity in his eyes? Did he read Page Six this morning too?

"Thank you, Mike." I step onto the escalator and descend into a wide, windowless vestibule.

A second guard, also Mike, stands by the glass doors to the newsroom. "Morning, Ms. Green." He opens the door, and I step into the caffeine-ingesting, adrenaline-driven newsroom. Shouts assault, televisions blare, and murmurs sweep across me. Like a Vegas casino, there are no windows and therefore never a sense of day or night—just constant commotion. The stadium-size space is packed with hundreds of desks arranged in clusters, divided by the shows.

"Kate." I turn to see a young producer logging an interview with LeBron James. "What's up?"

"Meeting with the boss."

"Good luck," he says in a way that makes it clear he read Page Six. I want to disappear into the walls. Once again, I consider bolting. But my agent's warning sticks with me. I'm already a screwup. I won't add coward to the list.

I hear my name again—this time from the front, where a commanding woman waves energetic arms at me. It's Chi Huang, the head assignment editor, perched on a raised platform about three feet off the ground—the queen bee running the station's day-to-day operations. Above her a digital clock reads 9:28 a.m., making me about a half an hour early for my meeting.

"Kate!" she yells again, shaking her short black hair. "Kate!" I give a weak wave and maneuver past rows and rows of reporters, producers, and writers toward Chi, who wears a jean jacket over a fitted T-shirt. Chi's all smiles right now, but I can't help wondering if part of her might feel happy about my impending demise. It's not like we don't get along. It's just she thrives on drama.

"What's going on?" She wraps her arms around me. "What are you doing here—not that I'm not happy to see your ugly mug."

"Summoned by the boss." I stare at her. "Surely you read the papers."

"Who believes anything Page Six says? Come on. It's fiction. Truly, I didn't even know you were coming in today." I can't tell if she's *truly* out of the loop or giving an Emmy-worthy performance.

"Hey," a young man sporting a scraggly beard, Yankees T-shirt, and gym shorts yells from below. "Why didn't the crew leave yet for the Comets practice?"

"They're leaving in twenty. Hell, we're only ten minutes from the Garden and the Comets aren't showing up to practice till noon," Chi yells back.

"It's gonna be packed! And Lopez found out who Kurt was messing around with. He's got an interview with her!"

That gets my attention. David discovered the identity of the mistress, and she's at the Garden. "These kids think they know everything," Chi mumbles as her screen beeps, and she hits a key with one of her fingers. "Gotta deal with this," she says without looking up.

I'm aware she's done with me, but I need more information. "The Comets are holding an open practice?" I try to sound nonchalant.

"I think they're so buried in media requests, they want to give everyone access and then be done with us. Plus, they do have to train." The phone rings, and she picks up. "Gotta take this. Good seeing you. Don't worry about what the paper said. It *should* be fine."

Her tone reminds me of a nurse promising you won't feel the needle as he jabs it into your arm. I descend back into the maze of desks, feeling eyes on me. Needing fortification, I wind my way to the break room and the Keurig machine. I pop a Peet's Major Dickason into the machine and listen to the hiss of liquid spurting into a Styrofoam cup. The coffee makes me feel momentarily better, but I'm still on the receiving end of side-glances and whispers. It's as if I'm wearing a scarlet letter. Desperate for a place to hide, I head toward the edit bays.

I would sometimes seek refuge in the edit bays, savoring moments away from fluorescents and high frequency noises. Now I just want to escape the glare of all the people waiting for the *Firing Kate Show*. I'm like the impending car accident everyone rubbernecks to observe. I open one of the mint-colored soundproof doors. Inside the small dark room, a man and woman sit facing computer screens and speakers.

"Go to Kyler Murray's first touchdown pass," one of our new female producers orders, pointing to the computer. The editor, a bald man who seems to be missing a neck, hits a button on the keyboard that sends the video backward.

"Lose the first five frames."

"This what ya want?" the man asks in a flat bored tone.

"Yes—that's it. Put it in." The producer turns around and narrows her eyes. "We have the room for another hour."

"Sorry. I wasn't trying to kick you out." At least she seems just regular hostile, not *I read the Post* hostile. I shut the door and move to the next room, a replica of the first one. A low buzz emanates from the machines, though they stand unused. I sit in the swivel chair, spinning in circles, grateful to get away from prying eyes. My brain goes back to the preseason matchup between the Comets and Wizards. The game that sent my career into a tailspin.

I never should have returned to work—just a week after Jackson's overdose. But he had been moved to an inpatient recovery facility, and we weren't allowed to visit. My boss called and suggested it would *take my mind off things*. I welcomed an opportunity to stop agonizing over the fact that I hadn't known my son took drugs.

Jackson had been purchasing nonprescribed Adderall as a pick-me-up for over a year. And he never thought mixing it with alcohol would cause his heart to stop and land him in the hospital. The familiar pit in my stomach surfaces. The bad-mom feeling. I obviously wasn't paying enough attention. The door opens, light pours into the room, bringing me back to the present. The kid in the Yankees T-shirt steps in. "Hey—I'm scheduled for this room."

"Sorry." I shoot up, squeezing past him and into the hot newsroom. It's time to head to my meeting anyway, and I wind my way back through the desks. I look through the glass wall of the small office belonging to my boss, Charlie, with its desk and two folding chairs. At any Manhattan law firm or financial institution, his office would be where they put the first-year employees. But on the main floor of TRP Sports, this tiny spot represents prime real estate—the only private office on the whole floor. Charlie sits at the desk, bobbing his head up and down. His face reminds me a bit of a goat's head—long and thin. Everything about him is thin, from his lips to his narrow eyes to his receding hair. Even his red-and-white-striped tie is thin.

"Hello, Kate." Charlie's assistant forces a smile. "Take a seat." She's a pleasant older woman who has worked for Charlie since the station began. And she knows all the secrets, including, I'm sure, the exact tactic Charlie will employ to fire me.

Waiting to find out my fate brings me back to my days playing for the US Women's National Team and all the times I sat outside different coaches' offices waiting to hear whether or not I was being cut. *You're just not physical enough. You're not gelling with your teammates.* Except for a few superstars, most of us ping-ponged back and forth through our early years. It was brutal. And, despite what people say about growing a thick skin, no skin is thick enough to withstand the rejection of no longer being part of something you want with every fiber of your being.

The assistant tells me I can go in. I get up slowly and take a deep breath to center myself. I hold my head high and open the office door.

"One minute." Charlie motions for me to sit without even glancing away from his screen. "Sit." Piles of paper cover the two chairs in front of his desk, so I lean against the edge of a narrow table. Behind Charlie hangs last year's Associated Press plaque for outstanding sports coverage, framed in dark wood, with gold-etched lettering. We won it for our reporting on the Super Bowl, which I was part of.

He looks up, eyelids fluttering. "Move the papers . . . so you can sit."

I would just as soon stand, but I lift a pile of papers from one of the chairs.

"Floor is fine," he says.

I drop the pile as neatly as possible on the floor and sit.

Charlie reaches for a big red mug with the letters *TRP*. He sips it and spits the liquid back. "Old," he says by way of explanation. He reaches for a blue mug, looks inside, and this time takes a slow sip. And a second. His screen beeps. He types again and thanks me for coming in.

I cross my right leg over my left. "I read in the paper that you are about to fire me."

"Since when do you believe Page Six?"

"So you're not?" I call his bluff.

"Here's how I see it . . ." Charlie puts his palms on his desk, jittering his right hand up and down. "We have to placate the brass. But I want you back."

I take a minute to absorb his words. "So, you're not firing me? But you want another apology?"

He presses his thin lips together, making them almost disappear into his face. "I'm afraid that won't be enough. You're going to—"

Someone opens the door. I turn and see David.

"Sorry to barge in." David swings his suit jacket over his shoulder, eyes moving from Charlie to me. "Kate." His cheeks redden. "Glad to see you in our neck of the woods." David smiles extra wide and asks Charlie if they could speak in private. "No offense, Kate."

"None taken."

Charlie clicks his keyboard and offers him a time slot in the afternoon.

"I mean before I head out." David gives a sidelong glance toward me. "It's about my story . . ."

Charlie mumbles to himself but gets up, strides across the office, and leads David out the glass door. Through the glass, I watch Charlie lean his long body down as David speaks. The two confer for about a minute. David seems ready to leave when Charlie says something, and they both turn and look at me. My skin prickles. What the hell is going on?

"Sorry about that." Charlie walks back into the office and returns to his seat.

"What was that about?" I can't help asking.

"Just a story. Nothing for you to worry about." He squirms in his chair. "Where were we?"

"You were saying that another apology isn't enough . . ."

"That's right." Charlie folds his arms over his chest. "I have a great idea about how to make this all go away. I'd like to have someone here interview you about the incident. So you can explain why you were . . . rattled that day?"

It takes me a minute to process his meaning. As his suggestion settles in, I feel my body fill with rage. "You want me to tell the world that my son overdosed, so I wasn't myself when Mason Burke taunted me about being a bad mother?"

Charlie puts his hands up. "Calm down. And yes. If you think about it, you'll see it's the right thing to do. For everyone."

"Everyone but my son."

"There's nothing wrong with discussing mental health issues in public." He seems prepped with that response. "The question is: Do you want to return to work? Because, as I see it, this is the only path forward." Charlie keeps his voice even.

"You know how crazy this is? There are male anchors here who have thrown computers at producers. And they haven't had to throw themselves on their sword."

"This isn't a sexism thing. It's a *you got caught and millions of people saw your tantrum* thing."

I am aware that my whole body is shaking. Is he out of his mind? I would never do what he's asking me to. Fuck this job.

Undeterred, he reiterates the fact that my only path back to work is to do an interview.

"My answer is a big NO." It's one thing if a person decides to discuss their mental health issues. But I'm not forcing that discussion on my son. I bolt up and accidentally knock over one of the stacks of paper. If someone was watching, they might think I'm having another tantrum. *Stay calm, Kate. Stay calm.* "If you want me to apologize again, I will. But I'm not going on television and throwing my child under the bus. And shame on you for even asking."

He shakes his head. "I'm surprised. It would be an important discussion to have in the public arena. But, if you won't agree to these terms, then we're at an impasse."

I never realized just how manipulative he could be. "Fine. I will collect my things."

He looks back at his computer screen. "I'm going to give you a few days to reconsider."

"There's no way in hell I'll change my mind."

"Then, next week, I will terminate your contract. You can pick up your stuff then. Now I'd just like you to leave." He stares at me with hard eyes. "Don't forget, if we terminate for cause, you don't get any money. And there's a two-year noncompete clause."

"Screw your money. And your clause." I storm out of the office and don't look up until I'm outside.

I step onto Sixth Avenue and fight the urge to scream. How could Charlie even suggest I tell the world about Jackson's overdose? Doesn't he understand the damage that could cause Jackson? Who sacrifices their child for a career? Well, we know one person who did. Liam Murphy. But even he might not go this far. I force myself to calm down. I can't do anything about TRP Sports, but I can try to help Yvette by tracking down Kurt's mistress. And it sounds like she's at Madison Square Garden.

CHAPTER 15

I hail a cab and settle into the back seat as my phone rings. It's my infuriating agent. I ignore it. But he keeps ringing, the stubborn bugger. Well, so am I.

"Did you know what he wanted?" I yell into the phone.

"Another apology?" his voice booms.

"You really didn't know?" I huff. "Charlie wants me to go on television and talk about Jackson's overdose."

A car honks, and my cabbie gives him the finger.

He takes a second to respond. "I can understand his reasoning."

"So, you did know?"

I hear him sigh like he's talking to an exasperating child. "That's not what I said. I did not know. But it makes some sense. From their point of view. And it's not the worst thing in the world to discuss this in a public forum."

"Only if it's something a person wanted to discuss. My God. I'm obviously not sacrificing my child's well-being for a stupid job." The driver turns around and stares. I lower my voice. "We should talk to other stations."

"It's not that easy. You have a noncompete clause. It's pretty iron-clad. But I will reexamine it. My guess is they can keep you from going to a competitor. And they can stop *paying* you. Maybe I could find you something if you moved . . ."

"That's bullshit," I respond, thinking about my last bank statement. I have a little money stashed away. We'll be fine for a few months if we're very careful. "How about endorsements?"

"No one is touching you with a ten-foot pole right now. Take a few days and consider Charlie's suggestion," he says.

"If you mention it again, I'm not only leaving TRP—I'm firing you."

"Stop being so dramatic. We'll talk in a few days." He hangs up before I can respond.

Stop being so dramatic? Seriously? He has kids. Would he throw them under the bus for his job? Actually, he might.

The taxi stops on Eighth Avenue, and I walk to the white awning near the loading dock for Madison Square Garden. If you don't know where the media entrance is, you won't find it. There are no signs. I yank open the heavy door and step into the damp, drab hallway with square, speckled linoleum floor tiles. A young security guard sits on a high stool, one eye on me and the other on a black-and-white screen mounted in the corner.

"Thought you were fired." He rubs his nose.

"Not as of today." Still suspended. So, technically not a lie.

"Credentials?"

"You kidding?"

"No."

I reach inside my bag and pull out my press pass, which Charlie probably should have confiscated. "Here."

He puts out his hand, and I place the rectangular laminated Comets press card in it.

His cell rings. "Hey, babe—yes. Aha ha." He returns my pass and motions me in.

I put the credential around my neck and step into the narrow hallway. The "world's most famous arena" is dreary here, with turquoise paint peeling off the walls, bare wires exposed on the ceiling, and fluorescent bulbs blinking at half strength. I get into the creaky, silver-scratched elevator and descend two flights.

The elevator opens on an empty corridor with bars locked over concession counters. The concessions may be closed, but the empty hallway still smells of hot dogs and beer. Boy, I wouldn't mind a beer right now. Or ten. To the right of an ice cream cart, I pull open the doors to the arena and stare down at the court. I've entered about two-thirds of the way below the nosebleed section; the moderate-to-high-priced seats are above, and the outrageously expensive seating below.

I walk down concrete steps to rickety aluminum ones that take me to floor level, where Bill kneels with his camera resting against his army jacket. "Hey, Bill."

"Kate?" Bill keeps his eye on the viewfinder. "What are you doing here? Did your meeting go well with Charlie?"

"I wouldn't categorize it that way."

"You here to work?"

"I'm here to find some answers." I scan the empty folding chairs set up at games for superfans like Spike Lee. Coach Seb sits in one at mid-court. I leave Bill and make my way toward the Comets' colorful coach.

"Coach." I plop down next to him.

"No comment." He lifts his Comets cap off his balding head.

"I haven't asked a question. What if it's something you *want* to comment on?"

"I never want to comment." He clasps his fingers together, flexing his muscular arms. Even after retiring as a professional basketball player decades ago, Coach Seb remains super fit.

"What if I tell you I'm not here as a reporter."

"Just a stalker?" He raises a brow.

"Very funny." I lean back. Seb and I have a reasonable relationship. I think because I know what it's like to be on the other side of the microphone. He respects my athletic achievements, and I appreciate the pressure he's under in a way other reporters simply can't. And we both understand the sacrifices we each made to succeed: studying film, training, missing family celebrations.

"I'm here for Yvette," I say.

"What does that mean?" he asks.

"I heard you and Kurt had an interesting lunch Sunday . . . at the Greenwich Diner."

Seb chuckles. "You want to know where I was three days ago? You playing detective, Kate Green?"

"I'm worried about Yvette," I say.

"I already told the NYPD everything this morning." He shakes his head. "A real son of a bitch too . . . Detective Murray or Murphy . . ."

At the mention of my father's name, I stiffen.

Of all the arenas in all the cities . . .

"That detective's got a real stick up his ass," Seb continues. Don't I know it. But he's diligent. I'll give Liam that—happy to learn he followed up with the waitress from the diner.

"Let me ask you something." Seb turns to me. "What makes you so sure Yvette is innocent?"

"Come on. You know her," I respond and then ask him what he and Kurt were fighting about.

"Care to wager a guess?" He raises a brow.

"Burke?"

"Burke."

Seb tells me that Kurt tried to convince him not to trade his friend. "But the decision was made, and nothing was going to change that. Kurt was pissed. But ultimately, it was what it was. Burke isn't the player he used to be. He hasn't been for years. Not to mention, he's a prickly motherfucker."

"If it were me," I say, "I'd have traded him ten years ago."

Seb laughs. "You know what's ironic?"

"What?"

"With the salary relief we'll get because of Kurt's death, we'll probably hold on to Burke for another season." He stands up. "Strange how things turn out."

Seb says goodbye and walks to the court, calling for the players to gather around. How badly did Burke want to stay on the team? Enough to kill his friend? I spot Burke on the court, the green body of his snake tattoo wrapped menacingly around his bicep and creeping up the right side of his pale neck. He flashes me a nasty grin, his fierce eyes mocking me. He takes the ball in his hand and smashes it hard against the floor, where it bounces before rolling out of bounds. Is that some kind of masked threat? Like I'm the metaphoric space under the ball?

"Well, look who's here!" My friend from SportWorld.net, Cal Callahan, taps me on the shoulder. "Kate Green. Welcome back." He smiles, his shaggy bleached blond hair falling over bright eyes.

"Cal! How are you?"

"How are *you*?" He leans against the back of a chair, wearing one of his many Grateful Dead T-shirts with ripped jeans and sandals. There is no business casual among our breed; you either dress to the hilt or, like Cal, about as grungy as grunge gets.

"You're back?" Cal asks.

"TRP and I are *talking*," I reply.

"It's bullshit what they did. Everyone knows what an ass Burke is—he probably egged you on, right?" Cal raises a brow.

"Nothing gets by you, huh?"

"I pride myself on that." Cal laughs. "Wonder if they're still going to trade him now that Kurt's gone." I look back at Burke, who grabs a Gatorade and, as if sensing me, turns and smirks. I feel visceral disgust inside my gut but refuse to give him the satisfaction of a visual response. He saunters over to his teammates, chest puffed.

The Dead's "Sugar Magnolia" plays from Callahan's phone, and he excuses himself to take the call.

Across the court, I spot David making his way toward the tunnel that leads to the locker rooms and some Comets offices and press rooms. I'd bet David's on his way to meet up with Kurt's mystery girlfriend. I motion to Cal that I need to go and speed walk around the sidelines to the tunnel entrance and security guard.

"You going to set up for the press conference?"

I hold up the credential around my neck.

"Go ahead," he says. "It's the large conference room—one twelve. Down the hall and to the left."

I step into the cavernous tunnel with cinder block walls, wide hallways, and exposed piping. At the end of the tunnel, a few camera crews head left toward an open door—likely room 112. To the right, a shadowy figure disappears around another bend. I recognize David's confident step. Hugging the perimeter, I follow, pressing my hand against the wall, the cinder blocks cool to the touch. The thumping of basketballs grows faint as I move deeper and deeper into the maze of tunnels. I turn left and immediately pull back, hiding my body at the edge of the wall. About ten feet in front of me, David stands outside one of the small Comets offices, speaking with a tall, slender woman with shoulder-length icy-blonde hair. I can't make out the rest of her features, but her clothing suggests she jumped out of *Teen Vogue*—a skimpy embroidered tank, jeggings, and leather boots.

They seem to be arguing. David flaps his arms around while she shakes her head.

"You can't be serious." David's voice echoes through the tunnel.

She shakes her head again, blonde hair falling across her face. "That's the deal. Take it or leave it." The rest of the words are muffled. She shuts the door on David while he's midsentence. He places his hand on the knob, but the door doesn't budge.

"Hey," he yells. "Let's talk. Come on. We had an agreement." He knocks against the door. Then tries the handle again. "Damn," he grumbles and turns in my direction. I react too slowly.

"Kate?" He starts toward me.

My brain short-circuits, and I feel completely embarrassed. *Run,* I tell myself. What will I say if he catches me? *Not only did I try to kiss you, but now I'm stalking you. Run,* I tell my body, as sweat breaks out across my back. My legs begin to work, slowly at first and then at full speed.

"Hey. Kate? Is that you?" David's voice draws closer as he continues to yell above the sound of his shoes slapping against the floor. This is the second time in a half hour that I wish I could become invisible. My heels clomp conspicuously against the concrete.

My blood pounds in my chest. Up ahead, Comets dancers enter the tunnel dressed in sparkling silver bathing suit tops and tight-fringed shorts. Rap music pounds through the tunnel. Guess everyone is practicing today. I hunch down and try to lose myself among the metallic fabric and fringe. Over my shoulder, I see David pushing through the mob.

I dart around the corner toward room 112, flash my press credential, step inside, and slow my pace. I walk down the aisle and sit in the back row of the auditorium, contemplating what I should say to David if he confronts me. Maybe I can just deny it was me? The room feels hot, stuffed with reporters facing a small stage with a long table and, at the moment, empty leather chairs. I don't see any signs of David and start to breathe a little easier.

Callahan enters, looks around, sees me, and waves before taking the only spot left in the front row. Coach Seb and a handful of players, including Burke, walk into the room and take seats on the dais. I see Liam slide in behind them and stand by the door. I push my body lower in my chair, hoping he won't notice me. He looks like he's going to bust out of the sports jacket hugging his arms. He's a big strong guy who appears intimidating in everything he wears. His square jaw is set in a tight grimace.

"Why did you follow me?" David drops into the seat next to me. His thoughtful brown eyes look confused, like a puppy dog's. "What's going on?"

I feel my cheeks flush.

"Sh" is all I muster.

"Excuse me." A heavyset ESPN radio reporter leans over David, who moves his body sideways to let the man pass. The reprieve only lasts a second.

David's hot breath hits my neck, and I smell citrus aftershave. "Why did you follow me? That was you. I saw you."

I turn my back to him and focus on the podium, where Coach Seb leans forward and starts talking. "There aren't words that can express the depths to which this tragedy has rocked all of us at the Comets organization. Kurt Robbins symbolized everything good about our team. He was hardworking, and he elevated everyone around him. He was a born leader. Personally, I believe he was the best forward I've had the privilege to coach." Seb looks down at his hands. "Kurt came to the Comets from high school . . . such natural talent. I had the privilege of watching him flourish and, well, it's . . . it's gut-wrenching to . . . just hard to wrap our heads around."

Seb puts his long fingers flat against the table, like he's trying to maintain his balance. "We will retire Kurt's number at our next game." Seb stops, his lips trembling. "Sorry. This is hard. All right. We'll take a few questions."

A young woman from one of the local stations yells out, "Had anyone threatened Kurt?"

"I can't comment on that, except to say that we have shared every single thing we know with the NYPD." At the mention of the police, he looks over at Liam. Between Liam and David, I just want to melt through the floor like the Wicked Witch from *The Wizard of Oz. Anyone have some water to throw on me?*

Meanwhile, Cal Callahan is drilling Seb about trades. "So, you might not make the trades you previously planned?" Cal repeats. "Maybe keep Burke this season?"

"We are going to reassess, Cal. That's all I've got for you," Seb says and then shoots a dirty look my way, apparently under the false impression I shared our conversation with Callahan.

Another reporter jumps in. "Burke, you must be relieved to hear that."

Burke leans into the microphone, the snake tattoo peeking out from his collar. He narrows his angry eyes. "Relieved? My best friend died. Relief is not the emotion I'm feeling."

"Ask Burke why he wasn't watching football with Kurt on the Sunday he was killed," I whisper to David, remembering that Yvette said Burke, Gene, and Kurt usually spent Sundays together.

"What?" David raises his brow.

"Ask him. Please."

David calls out, "Burke, why weren't you watching football with Kurt on Sunday?"

Burke looks shaken. "I—we—yeah. I should have been there. I ended up having to cancel. I wish I had gone. I should have been there. I usually was."

Callahan's bleached blond head pops up again. "Burke, did you skip the football game because of talk that you might get traded?"

"You are so off base it's almost funny." Burke rubs his neck. "This doesn't have anything to do with basketball, dude." Burke leans back in his chair and folds his arms over his chest, signaling he's done.

This doesn't have anything to do with basketball. If that's true—and clearly, with Burke, that's a very big *if*—then why did Burke skip football on Sunday?

The ESPN reporter next to me stands. "Seb, a police source told us there were hostile emails sent to Kurt from a fan. Some serious threats. Any word on that?"

The question ignites whispers; I catch Callahan's eye, and he shrugs. Something got by him. That's unusual. I wonder if that's another avenue that Bernard is ignoring. I make a mental note to ask Liam about the threats.

"I can't say anything except that the police are looking into it." Again, Seb glances at Liam.

"I'd like to comment." Burke leans forward, ignoring a glare from Coach Seb. "Kurt showed me a few of those emails. They were intense. And detailed. And I hope the organization took them seriously when they were first sent."

Seb ignores Burke and ends the press conference. Seb and the other players make a quick exit, but Burke remains in his seat. Reporters rush forward to ask him more about the emails. Out of the corner of my eye, I see Liam spot me. He nods for me to come outside, a barely perceptible tilt of his neck, but I know the cue. I break eye contact and debate my next move, having completely forgotten David for the moment.

"Be straight with me." David forces eye contact. "Are you trying to steal my story?"

I'm startled by his question. It hadn't crossed my mind that this would be his concern, which was kind of dumb of me. But it was so much better than him thinking I was stalking him. "No, I'm not. I promise."

"Then why did you follow me?" There's a rumble in front as two custodians wheel in a dolly. "Kate, why were you following me? And don't tell me it wasn't you; I know it was."

"Fine. I followed you because I wanted to know who Kurt was sleeping with. As you've probably heard, I'm friends with Kurt's wife."

"I didn't know that." His expression softens, and I see flecks of gold in his brown eyes.

"Really? I thought everyone knew." I can't help smiling at him; he looks so cute right now.

"So, it wasn't for the story?" He relaxes.

"No. Truly it wasn't." *Nor was it to stalk you.*

"Why were you meeting with Charlie?" He leans forward and puts his hand on my arm. "Are you returning to us? That would be great." He flashes a big smile.

"I hope," I reply, wishing even a little more now that David seems to want me to return. "I was there to negotiate whether I can come back. Which, at the moment, I can't. Or rather, won't." Up front, the custodians lift the table off the dais. David asks what I mean by that, but I tell him it's too long a story to get into. "They want me to do something I'm not comfortable with," I say.

"David." Bill walks up to him, holding his tripod and camera. "Live shot in eight minutes. Everything's set up outside."

"I'll be right there." David keeps his attention on me.

I ask him why the girl with the icy-blonde hair slammed the door in his face. He tells me she wanted to go public about her relationship with Kurt. But when he showed up, she insisted she'd only do the interview if she could approve the final story.

"Good for you, saying no," I tell him.

David lets out a quick breath. "You sound surprised I have ethics."

"That's not what I meant." I feel my face flush.

"I've got to get to my live shot." David rushes off, clearly offended. I feel bad I upset him. I can't get anything right when it comes to him. The only upside is that maybe our conversation lasted long enough for Liam to lose interest in waiting around. I step into the tunnel and look to my right. No one. I turn to my left and feel my whole body tense. Liam stands there, staring down at me, arms folded across his chest.

CHAPTER 16

"I'm getting the feeling you're trying to avoid me." Liam closes the distance between us, a large figure looming over me.

Because I am.

"We shouldn't be talking here," I whisper, feeling very uncomfortable.

He takes a deep breath and leans toward me, his blue eyes softening. "I'd like to know how it went with Bernard. And there's something I need to tell you about Yvette."

He certainly knows how to get my attention. Am I being manipulated? I'm aware of other reporters in the tunnel. Do they think I'm trying to pump the NYPD cop for information? Or do they notice the family resemblance?

Cal sidles up next to me and asks if everything's okay. Either he wants in on the action or he senses my distress. I tell him everything's fine, and he reluctantly walks away. I'm feeling incredibly self-conscious, but I know Liam won't let up. I didn't just get my blue eyes from him. I also got his obstinance. I suggest we meet in an hour across the street at L. M. Burgers and walk away from him as fast as I can. I hear his footsteps behind me, heading in the other direction, heavy and deliberate.

It's time to learn more about the icy-blonde woman. A light goes off, casting shadows across the tunnel just as I approach her office door. Now that I'm standing here, I wonder what I will say. *You were sleeping with my best friend's husband. Did you also shoot him?* I lift my hand to knock and stop. Maybe I should turn around. I mean, really, what in the hell do I hope to learn? But something keeps my feet from moving. I want to look in her eyes. For Yvette.

I knock and wait. Nothing. I try again and put my ear close to the metal door. A low hum sounds, like white noise. But I don't hear any movement. I grip the doorknob and turn. It gives way and squeaks as I push the door open and look inside.

"Hello?" I push the door farther and peer into the darkness. My heart beats faster as I step into the quiet square space and pat the wall to find the light switch and click it on. I blink my surroundings into focus, surveying the cramped, windowless room painted in Comets royal blue. The only furniture is a metal desk and one of those ergonomic chairs. On the metal desk, I discover the cause of the white noise: an egg-shaped diffuser circulating a liquid that smells like pineapple. A stack of business cards sits next to the diffuser, and I pick one up. Printed in the same Comets blue as the walls is a name: MIA MARS, ASSISTANT DIRECTOR OF SOCIAL MEDIA, COMETS ORG.

Mia Mars. I don't recognize her from the press department. She must focus on socials like Instagram, Twitter, and YouTube. I walk around her desk, sit in her chair, and study a photo in a simple wooden frame next to the computer screen. It's a woman with two toddlers, dressed in shorts and tank tops and holding ice cream cones.

A rumbling echoes through the office. It gets louder. Sounds like a laundry bin or cart being wheeled down the hall. I freeze as the noise stops just outside the office, worried someone will open the door. I scan the room for a place to hide, but there are no spaces big enough. I squat behind the desk and hold my breath. A carpenter ant creeps along one of the cracks on the concrete floor and scurries past my ankle. I focus on the doorknob, willing it not to turn. Out of the corner of my eye, I watch the ant take another lap near my foot. Good thing I'm not squeamish about insects. The rumbling starts again and grows softer. I let out a breath and stretch my legs as the ant scurries back to the corner. That was too close. I need to hurry.

I pull open the top desk drawer and find makeup, tampons, a few water bottles. The next drawer proves just as exciting with paper clips, rubber bands, a stapler. I'm about to move on to the last drawer when I notice a clipboard shoved in the back. I pull it out and flip through some papers and discover a Polaroid of Kurt and the woman I now know as Mia Mars. The first thing I notice is her eyes. I don't know if it's a photographic distortion, but one eye appears brilliant green and the other more of a hazel-green mix. Fine lines around the eyes and mouth suggest she's in her late twenties or early thirties, older than I first thought. Her lips are full, and she has an almost ethereal quality to her expression.

The image throws me. Kurt has his muscular arm wrapped around her thin body. He's looking down at Mia with a wide grin across his face. There's something disturbingly familiar about the photo, but I can't quite grasp it. I slowly scan the small picture to try and figure out what's bugging me. Is it Mia? Have I met her? Maybe at a game? But she's so striking it's hard to imagine I wouldn't immediately recognize her.

It's not Mia. I realize what's bothering me. It's so obvious. I recognize the painting behind them. It's a Picasso lithograph that Yvette hung in her study. The realization makes me sick. Not only has Kurt been cheating, he's brought his mistress to their home.

Footsteps sound in the tunnel. I take a final look at the picture, wondering if it's a selfie or if someone else was in the room. The steps get closer, and I shove the picture back onto the clipboard and the clipboard into the back of the drawer.

"Did you hear something?" A woman's voice travels from the hallway.

"Hear something?"

I crouch down again and knock the trash bin by accident. It clanks against the wall and starts to fall. I wedge my back against the rim of the bin to keep it pinned.

"From my office." The knob to the door turns.

"Coach Seb was hoping to talk to you. He said it's extremely important."

"I also don't remember leaving my light on," Mia says.

The light! How could I be so stupid? Panic creeps through my veins, adding to the tension.

"He just needs a minute." The male voice sounds irritated. There's some mumbling that I can't quite make out. I pull myself into a smaller ball. What will I say? *No one was inside, so I thought I'd let myself in. You don't know me, but you know my friend Yvette. You've been to her house . . .*

"Fine." The doorknob snaps shut. I start to relax just as the door reopens. "Let me just shut off the light." I don't dare look up, praying she doesn't glance in my direction. The room goes dark, but the door remains open. *Please leave. Please leave,* I think to myself.

"Come on," the male voice orders.

"Fine. Coming . . ." The door clicks, but I remain curled in the corner. Is someone watching me? Did she shut the door but remain inside? Is it a big ruse because she immediately noticed my body? Footsteps fade, but I'm not sure if I hear one set or two. My calves cramp so badly that I need to move. But I think I hear breathing. Mine? I'm not sure. I lift my head and squint into the dark. No lurking shadows to speak of. I reach my hand around and grip the edge of the trash bin but lose my footing. I fall, and the bin bangs against the concrete. *So loud.* I scan the office. No one by the door or on the other side of the desk. I got lucky. I reach down and pick up the trash bin, noticing a thick piece of folded paper that fell out.

If this were a movie, the paper would provide an important clue. *Silly, really.* I pick up the paper and reach my arm to toss it back in the bin. And stop. I recognize the shape and feel of the glossy, white square paper with the black-and-gray image. I can't believe what I've found.

I stuff the paper into my bag, open the door, peek to the left and to the right. The tunnel looks empty. I slide out, pull the door shut behind me, and speed walk past the closed locker room and out into the arena. I'm heading toward the aluminum stairs when someone touches my shoulder.

Callahan knits his blond bushy brows together. "Why are you so jumpy? Doing something you shouldn't?" He laughs, but I'm not sure he means it as a joke.

"Was just catching up with some people." I try for casual.

"I didn't realize anyone was still back there." He keeps his tone light.

"One or two." I look down at the ground and tell him I'm late for something.

"Don't let me stop you." He gives me a formal bow, which looks ridiculous coming from a guy in ripped jeans and a Grateful Dead T-shirt. He's trying for funny, but when he stands up, his eyes flash with something that looks very much like distrust.

CHAPTER 17

I find Liam waiting in a booth in the back of the dimly lit restaurant drinking a beer. "Hey." He gets up to try and give me a hug/kiss, but I quickly slide in across from him. He sits back down, squeezing his large frame into the vinyl bench.

"What were you doing at the Garden?" he asks. His tone rings more interrogation than conversation.

"I wanted to follow up on a few things," I respond. "What about you?"

He doesn't answer, but signals for the waitress and asks me what I'd like. I order a gin martini with extra olives, a burger, and fries. I don't want to prolong our meeting, but I'm famished. *Lesser of two evils,* I tell myself. *Liam versus starvation.* He orders the same meal, then asks if I was at the Garden to cover a story. I assure him that I'm still very much suspended, moving toward laid off.

"I'm sorry to hear that," he says. "I enjoy watching you on television."

I don't know how to respond, so I change the subject and tell him I heard he interviewed Coach Seb. "He said you were a 'real son of a bitch.'"

Liam actually laughs; the hard lines of his face momentarily soften. "I could say the same about him."

"Is Seb a suspect?"

He puts his beer down and tells me Seb's alibi checks out. "But I appreciate that you sent the waitress my way."

"What I don't understand is why Bernard didn't return the waitress's call. She left him a message."

"I know." Liam shakes his head. "She told me."

I tell Liam that I found a newspaper article about a case in Maspeth where DNA proved the man behind bars was innocent. "Was that Bernard's case?"

"Look at you, Ms. Nancy Drew." He smiles.

"That's not an answer."

"All right." He picks up his beer. "Bernard was one of the detectives on the case. But, as you probably read, the NYPD settled. No one is talking about it."

I give him my best skeptical look.

He puts up his hands in mock surrender. "I'll tell you what," he says. "Let me try to find out more. Okay?"

"Yes," I say.

He turns serious. "How did your talk with Bernard go?"

"It was more of an interrogation than a talk." I rehash the details.

Liam doesn't say anything, just orders another beer.

"My turn," I say. "Have you spoken to Burke yet? He usually watched football with Kurt and Gene on Sundays."

"I interviewed him myself," Liam informs me. "What a piece of work."

"Don't I know it." The waitress sets down my drink. As I nibble on the olives, Liam tells me that Burke claimed he had a stomach bug and stayed in his apartment that day. "We are interviewing the doorman and reviewing security footage from the building."

"Good. Because I wouldn't put anything past him." I finish off my last olive and take a sip of my drink.

Liam asks me if I believe Burke would murder someone to avoid getting traded. "It feels like a weak motive."

"I don't necessarily disagree," I admit. "But something he said at the press conference stood out. Burke said his reason for not going to watch football on Sunday at Kurt's had nothing to do with basketball. If it was just a stomach bug, why wouldn't he say that instead of being so circumspect?"

"Some people don't like to admit they got sick. Makes them feel weak."

"I don't buy that. Something is stranger than usual with him."

"And you're not just saying that because of . . ."

I glare at Liam. It hurts that Liam would imply that I'd consider Burke a murder suspect just because Burke instigated the viral video that upended my career. I'm bitter, but not vengeful.

The waitress sets down our burgers and fries. As someone raised on health food, I feel giddy just smelling the greasy food. I dump ketchup on the burger and take a huge bite as I wait for Liam to answer.

He's also enjoying his food and takes his time. I'm aware of the square paper in my bag that I took from Mia's garbage can. It feels like a brick weight. A baby ultrasound with Mia Mars printed on the image.

I ask him what he knows about Mia Mars.

He picks up his beer. "Why do you ask about her?"

"I know she was Kurt's mistress."

He keeps his eyes on me as he takes a sip. I think about the photograph I just saw in Mia's office—the one with the Picasso lithograph. "I know they spent time in Yvette's house . . ." *And she's pregnant.*

He says nothing, just keeps drinking. Behind us, the maître d' seats two businesswomen. I lock eyes with Liam and lean across the table. "I know she's pregnant," I finally say.

He puts his drink down quickly, the liquid splashing onto the table. "What?"

Unless he's an Oscar-worthy actor, he wasn't aware of the pregnancy. Score one for the good guy. I remove the crumpled ultrasound from my bag and open it in the middle of the table. "This belongs to Mia."

"How the hell did you get that?"

"It doesn't matter."

"Jesus. This is serious information." Liam rubs his scar. "This is something for the police to investigate."

"It is. But I don't trust the Greenwich Police to do it."

The women seated behind us turn to check Liam out, probably wondering if he's my father or robbing the cradle. But philandering wasn't his Achilles' heel. I glare at one of them, and she quickly looks away.

He reaches for the ultrasound, but I keep my hand firmly on it. "I'll only give it to you on the condition you tell me if the baby is Kurt's."

He grimaces. "Let the police handle it."

"I am letting *you* handle it. You just have to agree to my terms."

"Fine." He takes the paper and puts it in the front pocket of his button-down. "You know, if it is Kurt's baby, it gives Yvette a stronger motive for murder."

I pick up my drink. "Or it gives Mia a motive. Maybe Kurt wouldn't leave Yvette, so Mia got angry. Maybe Kurt didn't want another child. He wasn't a bad father to Dylan. But he also wasn't around much."

Liam opens his mouth to speak and then closes it. He seems to be struggling with his thoughts. "Do you believe people can change?"

"Like Kurt? Developing a new interest in children?"

"Yes. Maybe he was reevaluating his priorities."

There's weight behind his words. "Are you talking about Kurt, or you?" I ask.

He puts his hand on his scar and rubs it. "Maybe both. You know, it was the toughest decision of my life."

"You still made it." I feel the tension creep up my back. "And don't tell me the trips to Disneyland or SeaWorld made up for all the things you missed." I want to add, *like watching me in the Olympics*, but it would hurt too much.

"You were so far away."

"We were in California, not Antarctica."

He starts to say something, then stops. I don't have the energy to rehash this and remind him he had information about Yvette he wanted to share. His eyes cloud over, and he seems to struggle with what to say next. I notice the chatter in the restaurant is louder and most of the tables are now full.

Liam finally drops the other line of conversation.

His expression turns grave. He leans forward, speaking in his raspy voice. "A neighbor saw a black Range Rover pull up at the mansion just before the murder. Doesn't Yvette drive that type of SUV?"

"Yes—along with hundreds of other people in town," I say. "Any progress with the security footage?"

"Tech is still working on it," he says, looking at his watch. "I need to run."

"One last question," I say. "What's the story with the threatening emails?"

"We're looking into it." He puts down cash and stands. "I really need to go."

Liam reaches down in another effort at a hug/pat. "Be careful. This isn't a game," he says. "There's a murderer roaming the streets. I know I won't be able to tell you to stop looking into it. But be careful."

CHAPTER 18

I wake up early Thursday morning. It's been four days since Kurt's murder. It seems like both a minute and a year ago. My mind tries to piece together everything I learned yesterday.

First, Mason Burke. With Kurt gone, Burke will likely stay another year on the team. But so what? Is that enough of a motive for murder? I still don't think so. I feel like there's something I'm missing, but I can't put my finger on it.

Next, Mia Mars. She was obviously involved enough with Kurt to be in his house and in front of Yvette's favorite painting. Was it a one-time thing? Or did she frequent the mansion? The thought of her in their house makes me sick to my stomach. And not just out of sympathy for Yvette. It brings back memories from the end of my marriage. And the day I came home from work early to discover Tyler and his secretary in our bed.

I push my thoughts back to Mia Mars. What do I know about her? Not that much. She works in the social media department, which is a division of public relations. She must be low on the ladder if she's in a small office in the tunnels versus the bustling suites upstairs. Maybe she's a recent hire? Or she pissed off one of the directors of public relations? They are a prickly crew.

I also know she's pregnant. Or was pregnant as of this recent ultrasound. The big question remains whether it's Kurt's baby. And, if it is, what are the implications? Did she want Kurt to leave Yvette? He refused, and then she killed him in a fit of rage? Of course, the other scenario would be that Yvette found out and got jealous. But I don't buy that.

I take out my phone and dial Yvette's number. The call goes straight to voice mail, and I hang up, thinking better of leaving a message. Yvette asked me to figure out who Kurt was sleeping with. But I don't think I should tell her about the pregnancy until I'm certain it's Kurt's child.

I try texting Yvette, asking if I can come by this morning. She replies that I can come at 10:00.

It's only 8:00, which gives me a couple of quiet hours to do some digging. I set up my computer in the kitchen, pushing aside the breakfast dishes Jackson and Nikki left on the counter.

I start by checking the staff page of the Comets website and find about twenty employees listed in the public relations department. I discover Mia Mars toward the bottom. The picture shows her staring at the camera with two shades of green eyes—one brilliant and one with hints of gray. Her gaze feels distant, and her full lips turn up in more of a dare than a smile. Her hair looks darker than yesterday, which leads me to the conclusion that the icy-blonde shade comes from a bottle. Score one for Nancy Drew.

There's a very short bio under her picture, where I learn she's responsible for the Comets blog, that prior to the Comets she worked for the Brooklyn Nets, and that she's a New York native and graduate of Sarah Lawrence College in Westchester.

I google *Mia Mars / Sarah Lawrence*. An article from the *Westchester Guardian* appears. TRAGEDY STRIKES LOCAL SARAH LAWRENCE SISTERS with a caption mentioning Mia Mars and a sister. I click on the article, which leads me to a link that requires me to subscribe to the *Guardian*. I try a few other Google searches to see if I can get the information from another source, without needing to pay for a subscription. No luck.

Outside, the sun casts shadows in the kitchen. A red Toyota pulls out of the Puke House driveway, presumably on the way to work. I'm about to subscribe to the *Guardian* when my phone rings. It's Nikki, asking me to bring her tennis bag to school because she forgot to take it and has practice today. I grab the bag, close my computer, and head to Greenwich Lake School. The *Guardian* will need to wait until later.

I drop Nikki's bag in the front office and say hello to the office manager, who's been at the school forever. She hardly looks up, staring over her spectacles into the glass window of the principal's office.

"Everything all right?" I ask.

"A bit of drama this morning." She doesn't look at me. "That Christie still wants to hold the Halloween dance on Saturday night even though the kids are reeling from the death of poor Mr. Robbins." She shakes her gray curls.

I hadn't even thought about the dance. I guess I just assumed it would be canceled. I remember my mom once telling me that when her father passed away, she felt like the whole world paused and was shocked to see everyone continuing with their daily routines. I recall she told me how surprised she felt that the subways were still running. Even though, logically, of course they were.

The manager continues her tirade. "Who is Christie Orlow to make such a fuss anyway? She's just a *stepmom*." She turns to me. "It's just disgraceful."

"Stepparents can be great," I say, thinking about my own stepdad. "As for the dance, I hadn't even thought about it," I answer truthfully and excuse myself, heading for the lobby. As I'm walking to my car, I hear a familiar voice call my name. Part of me wants to run. But it wouldn't do any good. She'd sprint after me, so I stop and wait as Christie catches up. She's nearly panting as she reaches me. Her face is flushed, but every blonde hair remains in place. She asks me if I've heard about the *dance drama*.

"Just a little."

"Well, I think it's outrageous that the school might cancel. For one thing, the kids worked so hard to plan it. For another, if they don't attend the dance, which will be *supervised*, who knows what trouble they'll get into. Because you know they won't be sitting at home."

"I hadn't thought of it that way," I answer, wondering if it would be better for all the kids to be together and watched versus off on their own doing God knows what. On the other hand, I worry it will seem disrespectful to hold a dance the day after a classmate's father will be buried. The dance drama is so above my pay grade.

"Listen, I'm really late," I say and offer to call her this afternoon just so I can get away.

"Okay. But don't forget," she yells as I zip toward my car and drive away.

I stop in front of Yvette's mansion and look for the security camera that Liam had mentioned. I find it attached to a tree on the neighbor's property, posted near the border of Yvette's lawn on the right side, when facing her mansion. Besides covering the neighbor's home, the camera seems to point to the Robbinses' circular driveway. I wonder if the lens would cover the far edge of the Robbinses' lawn on the left side. It depends on the type of lens. But it would need to be a high-quality wide-angle to accomplish that. I make a mental note to check with Liam.

I roll down my window and enter the code into the keypad; the electric gate slides open. As I do, I'm reminded again of how many other people probably also have the code and could easily go in and out of the Robbins estate. I need to tell Liam to cross-reference the threatening emails sent to Kurt and the Comets with a list of people who can enter their home. Although, I'd imagine dear old dad already considered that.

Light floods the windows of the mansion as if Yvette is preparing for a party—bright, yellow, and bold. I even see smoke coming from one of the six chimneys. I step onto the pavers as the wind whips a pile of autumn leaves off the ground, whirling them in a little dance and then cavalierly discarding them. I step up to the double-arched wooden doors and reach for the bell.

Before I can even ring, the door opens.

"Kate." Gene steps forward, his button-down half tucked into ripped jeans. His soft features look bloated.

"Hi. Yvette asked me to come by."

"I see." He rubs the growth on his chin and explains he's spending the day at the house. "How'd you get through the electric gate?"

"I know the code. Can I come in?"

He tells me I should come back later because now isn't a great time. I'm about to argue when I hear steps inside and an elderly woman's melodic voice. "Who is at the door?"

Yvette's mother-in-law, Betty Robbins, appears behind her son, her eyes sunken, face drawn. "Hi, dear. Nice of you to come." She pulls me inside and gives me a hug. In my arms, I feel her bones protruding through skin.

"I'm so terribly sorry for your loss," I say.

"It's the worst news any parent could receive." She sniffs and wipes her eyes with a handkerchief. "We're in shock. Gene, go get Yvette, please."

He hesitates, then disappears up the stairs, gripping the polished wood banister that rests on intricately carved spindles.

Betty tells me to wait in the hallway for Yvette. "I'm going back to Gregory. My poor husband—his heart is so weak." Betty takes my hand and squeezes it. "You are a good friend. Yvette is lucky to have you." I watch her walk away, her slippers creating a soft swishing sound against the polished marble.

"Kate." Yvette appears at the top of the stairs, wearing leggings and an oversize cashmere sweater. From afar, she looks put together; she's applied makeup and wears the same extensions as Sunday. But as she gets closer, I see her mascara is clumped and baby hairs have escaped her efforts to slick them down.

There's movement on the landing. I catch a glimpse of Gene as I look past the lavish chandelier. Yvette suggests we sit in the family room and starts down the hallway. My mind screams for her to pick a different spot, but I follow her to the cloistered sky-blue room where Kurt and Mia posed for their picture. I still can't figure out whether the picture was a selfie or if someone else took it. It felt farther than I could reach a camera, but Kurt had long arms. I feel guilty just stepping into the beautifully appointed space—like I'm part of a cover-up. I dread telling Yvette about Kurt's affair even though she asked me to find the information. My eyes find the Picasso lithograph with the cubed face and mismatched eyes, one at the top and one at the bottom.

"It's my favorite piece of art," Yvette says. "Kurt bought it for my birthday this summer."

"It's beautiful." I wince at my words. Yvette lowers herself into the overstuffed plush, striped couch and immediately gets swallowed up by the cushions.

"I'm glad you called." Yvette looks at me with sad eyes. "There's something that's been on my mind."

"Me too," I say, staring down at the swirls of the Persian rug.

She sets her cracked lips in a tight line. "Can I go first? I feel like if I don't tell you now, I might not have the courage."

I nod as she taps her chipped plum-polished nails together.

"It's kind of hard." She makes eye contact, and I see fear creep into her expression.

"You can tell me anything," I say.

She forces a sad smile. "Thanks. I don't know what I'd do without you. You're really the only true friend I have."

"I feel the same way."

"It's about the afternoon Kurt died," Yvette continues.

She looks at the fireplace, just behind me, with its elegant gray stone mantel. "The last few days have been such a blur." Her voice is a whisper. "And we haven't had a lot of time alone." She tells me that she'd never keep information from me. "I owe you an explanation. It's been weighing on my mind."

She takes a deep breath and meets my gaze, and I see something new in her eyes. Defiance?

"Kurt and I had a fight Sunday morning," she says. In the distance I hear the whir of a leaf blower or lawn mower. "It actually started Saturday night." She bites her lip.

"What was the fight about?"

She ignores my question and proceeds to tell me she came back to the house before picking up the coffee. "I needed to smooth things over. You know how much I hate when we're fighting."

I process what she just said. Yvette came back to the house just before Kurt was found shot to death. "Kate, don't look at me like that." She sounds hurt. "We talked. And then I left just before Gene was supposed to arrive to watch the football game. But it doesn't look good. My lawyer is concerned."

I stand up and walk to the fireplace. The second hand of the sunburst antique clock beats a steady rhythm above me, click, click. I stare at the second hand as it rounds the roman numerals of the old clock and ask her what they fought about.

"It was awful." She starts to cry.

"Did he want a divorce?" I think again about the ultrasound. Maybe Liam was right and Kurt wanted a family do-over.

"Of course not." Yvette says something else, but I can't understand.

"This is too much for me, Yvette." I hear the tremor in my voice. "The one thing you owed me was the truth. Here I am trying to help you. But you lied to me. How do I know you aren't lying about the murder?!"

"Kate," she wails, a sound that comes out like a wounded animal. "How could you even . . . consider . . . that I'm capable of hurting someone?"

"Because you lied," I spit back.

"I didn't lie. I just didn't have time to tell you everything." Her eyes beseeching. "Kate, please."

I walk past her as she grabs at my arm; her hand knocks a vase on the side table. She swats at it, but it smashes against the hardwood floor. Shards scatter across the rug. I step over the broken pieces and rush out of the room. Yvette came back to the house on Sunday right before Kurt died.

Yelling in the hallway interrupts my thoughts.

"Evie. Evie." Betty's voice floods the room along with a breeze coming from the open front door.

I hear Detective Bernard before I see him. "Call Mrs. Robbins immediately," he demands. "And Gene Robbins. I assume he's here?"

Sirens sound from the driveway, and the blue disco-like light casts shadows across the entrance.

Bernard's eyes find mine, and he sneers. I stop in my tracks. Yvette passes by me and rushes to hold her mother-in-law. Gene walks down the stairs, stopping at the landing.

"What do you want?" Yvette's voice cracks as she grips her mother-in-law's hand. I study Bernard and note again that he's camera ready; hair gelled, crisp button-down, and the dead giveaway, powder on his face to keep away the shine. Disgusting. I move my eyes toward Yvette, who's doing her best to hold herself together.

"What are you doing here?" Bernard barks at me.

"I don't have to explain myself," I bark back, crossing my arms.

Detective Bernard adjusts his round glasses.

"Why are *you* here?" Betty demands of Bernard, puffing her body up as best she can. She may appear frail, but she's not a woman anyone should mess with.

"Mrs. Robbins." Bernard holds Betty's gaze. "I sincerely apologize." He puts his chin up in an imperious gesture. A door slams outside, and two uniformed officers emerge from a marked police car and settle just by the front entrance.

"The police," Dylan cries out, and we all turn to see her standing in flannel pajama bottoms and a tight T-shirt. She rushes down the stairs, nearly falling on the last step. But Yvette moves quickly and catches Dylan, keeping her from smashing against the marble floor.

Detective Bernard seems thrown by her presence, like Dylan's taken the fun out of his moment. He looks at Dylan and tells her that she has his deepest sympathy and then takes his handcuffs from his pocket.

CHAPTER 19

A hush falls over the group. Yvette locks eyes with me. Detective Bernard's second of contrition is gone, and he's back to enjoying his big-man-in-the-rotunda moment, like a TV host about to announce who gets kicked off the island. He waits for the tension to heighten. *And the loser is . . .*

We watch Detective Bernard make eye contact with Dylan, Betty, Yvette, and then Gene. He walks past Yvette and stops in front of Gene. Everyone seems surprised, except for Gene. "Mr. Robbins, you are under arrest for larceny and obstruction of justice."

"Uncle Gene?" Dylan's voice cracks.

Gene lifts his gaze to Yvette and tells her it's not what she thinks. "Trust me, Yvette. They are making a mistake. I swear."

Yvette looks at him like he has three heads.

Betty yells at the detective. "You can't take my son. He'd never hurt his brother . . ." Yvette wraps her arm around Betty as the police officers walk Gene out of the house and put him into the marked police vehicle. We watch through the windows as it disappears onto North Street and from sight.

"Get the car, Yvette." Betty pushes against her daughter-in-law to reach the door. Yvette keeps Betty's frail body in a hug.

Dylan runs upstairs, her long lanky legs carrying her two steps at a time. A moment later a door slams shut.

Betty yells again, "Hurry! Hurry!"

"Mama, sh," Yvette says. "You can't go to the police station. Dad—"

Betty pulls out of the hug and starts flailing her arms like a bird caught in a storm.

"Why don't I go to the station?" I offer.

Betty turns to me, surprised, as if she forgot that I was even here.

"What's all this?" Yvette's father-in-law, Gregory Robbins, appears in the hallway—a thin, tall man with curly silver hair and wide, liquid eyes.

Betty scampers to him and winds her arms around his lower back, which is about as high as she can reach. "Nothing, nothing. Everyone's emotional. You need your rest for tomorrow. Please, the doctor says you must rest. Your heart."

"I heard a door. And yelling. Where's Gene?" His voice shakes.

"Gene's upstairs," Yvette says. "He's sleeping. A neighbor stopped by and dropped off food. That's all the commotion was about."

Gregory stands there a minute, studying the scene. He looks confused, like he's having trouble processing information. Betty pulls on him again. "Come on. Back to bed." This time he listens. Betty turns her head and looks at me. "Thanks for your offer. It would be so helpful."

"What offer?" Mr. Robbins asks.

"Don't worry, dear. You need to lie down."

They disappear down the hallway, two fragile figures leaning into each other for support.

"You don't have to go to the station," Yvette says, averting her eyes.

"This doesn't mean I'm not still really angry at you," I say. "But I want to help. And Betty's been through enough."

"Kate, I'm so sorry." She grabs my arm. "It sounded so . . . unbelievable." She's crying so hard her body's heaving. "If I didn't know it was the truth, I would probably doubt myself too."

"I would have believed you," I say. "I do believe you. But you should have told me sooner."

"I know. I'm so sorry." She pulls my hand to her face; the wet from her tears moistens my palms. "I'm so sorry. I promise, only the truth, from now on."

I say goodbye and walk to my car, a tornado of thoughts swirling through my brain. I can't catch one long enough to consider it. I drive to the station in a trance and park outside the building. A few media vehicles are parked outside. I wonder if they got a tip about Gene's arrest. No one bothers me when I open the front door and walk inside. The same sergeant sits at her desk behind the glass window. From my angle, I can see she's browsing an online shopping website. She looks up, her ruby cheeks flushed. "You're back? Again?"

"Yup."

"Why?" She sounds cranky.

"Care to guess?"

"Robbins?"

I nod my head.

"For heaven's sake, sit."

I find an empty seat in a row by two parents huddled with a teenage boy and a professional-looking woman, likely an attorney. The station feels busier than Sunday. Besides the family next to me, a group of teenagers sits in the far corner. And the same guy as last time, wearing the same Patriots jersey, sleeps in the same chair. I wrap my scarf around my nose to block out the pungent odor of Lysol. The wall clock shows 12:30. And to confirm the time, my stomach growls its desire for lunch.

There's a lot I need to wrap my brain around. The biggest question is whether the police think Gene murdered his brother, because Bernard only charged him with larceny and obstruction.

A young officer steps into the waiting room and approaches the teenage boy, his parents, and the attorney. The officer puts out his arm, indicating that they should follow him through the interior door. I wonder if they will be brought to the so-called conference room too.

As I contemplate different Gene scenarios, a woman dressed in a suit strides up to the desk. I see my friend the sergeant point to the side door. As the woman waits to get buzzed inside, the sergeant gives me an almost indecipherable nod.

"Excuse me," I say to the woman. Her hair has natural waves that frame her brown eyes and long lashes. "I'm Kate Green, a friend of the Robbins family."

She doesn't take my hand.

I drop my arm. "I was there when they took Gene away," I say. "You must be his attorney. His mom asked me to come to the station—"

"You're a television reporter." She leans close, nearly spitting in my face. "Shame on you for misrepresenting yourself. I'm not going to fall for that."

"I'm actually—"

The attorney pushes past me and disappears behind the door.

"Ask Gene!" I yell, but I'm not sure if she hears.

The desk sergeant shrugs. "Tough luck. You should just go home."

She's probably right, but I sit back down. I notice a rhythm to the station. The Patriot jersey's daughter appears wearing pajama bottoms and a sweatshirt. She kicks her dad and orders him to get up. He grumbles and growls but follows. A short time later, the parents, teenager, and attorney emerge from behind the door and quickly scurry out. I unwrap my scarf—either the Lysol smell faded or, more likely, I'm now used to it.

The inside door opens, and I stand, hoping it's Gene's attorney. But it's not her. It's Liam. My body tenses, and I start to look away when I realize he could help explain what's going on. I take a step toward him. He shoots me a cold stare, which stops me dead in my tracks. I know that look. It's the look I got when I broke a family vase as a child. Liam Murphy's *don't fuck with me* stare. And just like that, I'm a little girl again. I slump back in the chair as Detective Bernard appears from the interior door and walks over to Liam, who dwarfs Detective Bernard both in width and height. They huddle close together. Detective Bernard's eyes focus on the floor, like he's hearing something he'd rather not. As the conversation seems to end, Liam pats Bernard on the arm and strides toward the door. I get up and rush outside behind him. I'm not a six-year-old. He can't shut me down with a look.

"Liam," I call, the cold air turning my words into fog.

He responds by accelerating his stride.

"Liam Murphy. Stop." I break into a jog. "Dad!"

At the word *Dad*, he pauses and turns around. Instead of looking happy, his eyes flicker with irritation.

"What's with the cold shoulder?" I catch up to him, rubbing my hands together for warmth.

"I'm in a rush."

Is this the same person who was so solicitous of me just a day ago? Typical Liam Murphy, making my head spin with mood changes. God, I hate him. I'm tempted to stomp off, but this isn't about me. It's about Yvette. "I want to know about Gene's arrest." I rehash the scene at Yvette's, emphasizing that Bernard only charged him with larceny and obstruction of justice. "Are they building up a case for murder?"

"I can't say." He looks at his watch. "I need to go."

"Don't you think you owe me some information?" I blurt out, hearing my voice get high and whiny. And needy. God, I hate myself in this moment.

"I owe you information?" he scoffs.

"What about the ultrasound? I shared that. Quid pro quo, right?" I put my hands on my hips and force the tenor of my voice an octave lower. *You are a grown-ass woman, Kate. Remember that.*

His phone rings, and he picks up. "I'm on my way . . . jumping in the car now." He looks at me, exasperated. "Kate, for God's sake, stop acting like a wannabe detective and be responsible for once in your life. Leave the investigation to the experts."

I feel like he physically slapped me. How dare he. For once in my life? He hasn't been in my life enough to earn the right to utter words like that.

"What the hell?" I begin, but he's already turned his back and walked away. Tears sting my eyes, and I despise myself for letting him upset me. Again. *God, when will I fucking learn?*

I look back at the police station and see Gene's attorney watching me. Did she hear our fight? I want to slink away, but she's walking toward me. She apologizes for being rude earlier and says she will try to get Gene arraigned in time for the funeral. She doesn't wait for a response. And I don't pursue more questions, still licking my wounds from Liam's tongue-lashing.

As I head home, I force Liam from my brain because Yvette never told me why she and Kurt fought Saturday night and, again, Sunday morning. If she wants my help, she owes me the full story.

CHAPTER 20

I sit at my kitchen counter, still smarting from Liam Murphy whiplash. I can hear my brother's voice in my brain. *Fool me once . . .*

Yvette calls to say she found a garbage bag in Gene's gym bag filled with what look like financial papers but that she can't make sense of them. I jump at the opportunity to pick them up so I can ask Yvette in person about her and Kurt's fights. I pull my jacket on and walk into the cold afternoon air. All around me Halloween decorations bob and bounce, chiding me for my delinquency. I avert my eyes from the giant Casper blow-up in my neighbor's yard. I swear the *friendly* ghost is throwing shade my way.

Yvette meets me at the door and lets me into the foyer. "Do you want coffee?"

"No, but I do want to ask you a question."

She sits down on the bottom stair and rests her chin on her hands. I face her, leaning against the door, the chandelier casting shadows across Yvette's face.

"You never told me what you and Kurt were fighting about," I say.

"Dylan," she says in a low voice, glancing upstairs. "The fight was about Dylan."

"What about her?" I ask.

"Kurt didn't like Zeke. He thought he was 'bad news.'" She puts the words in air quotes. "Kurt got very protective of Dylan. The night before he died, Kurt told Dylan she couldn't date Zeke anymore."

"That must have upset her." I imagine what would happen if I told Nikki or Jackson something like that.

"She was infuriated with him. She ran off hysterically crying. I tried to reason with Kurt, but he wasn't hearing any of it. Then he just stormed off to his study." She shakes her head. "I tried talking to him again Sunday morning. But our fight was even worse than the night before. I called him controlling and told him he would drive Dylan away if he was so strict. You know how I hate when Kurt and I fight . . . so I came back to smooth things out."

"Did it work?"

She shrugs and looks up at the glistening chandelier as if the crystals held some secret answers. "Kurt was calmer. He just said he knew guys like Zeke, and they shouldn't be trusted. Then I reminded him that the more you use the word *no* with a teenager, the more they will do the opposite of what you want. He laughed at that." Yvette smiles at the memory.

Betty walks into the foyer and asks about Gene. I give her my update. She wrings her hands together, head bowed down. "I can't take much more," she mutters more to herself than us. She then notices the garbage bag at my feet. "I can take that from you, dear." She extends her hand.

"That's okay." I stand up, lifting the bag. "I've got it."

Yvette tells her mother-in-law she's just going to walk me to my car and be right back.

"Kate," Yvette says as we approach my car. "I can't make sense of the charges against Gene. Larceny and obstruction of justice?"

"It's strange. They didn't charge him with murder," I answer, explaining they could be building toward that. "Could Gene have stolen from Kurt?" I ask, thinking about the money missing from the safe.

"I wouldn't have thought so . . ." Her voice trails off.

"But he had money problems?" I probe. "You once told me Kurt opened the gym with Gene to help his brother."

"He did." Yvette wraps her arms around her chest, shivering in the cold. "Kurt figured if they co-owned a business, he could keep an eye on Gene."

"Did Gene know where the safe was?"

She shrugs her shoulders. "It just doesn't make sense. Last year Kurt paid off the mortgage on the gym. I can't imagine Gene has money issues. He has no debt."

"But? Something is clearly troubling you," I say.

"It is." Yvette's lips quiver. "I can't stop wondering if he took the *other* stuff." She widens her eyes as she says *other*.

It immediately clicks what she's inferring. Yvette believes someone removed Kurt's jewelry from his corpse. Now she's wondering if Gene did it. "You knew someone took Kurt's diamond studs and chain because you saw him just before he died."

She nods her head as the information comes together in my brain.

CHAPTER 21

As I drive home, my thoughts wander back to Liam and the reason for his rudeness. Was he playing at something at the police station? He certainly didn't seem like a man on a mission to win back his daughter. The most likely reason remains that he doesn't care. But what if his motive was more duplicitous? Is he trying to manipulate me? He knows I'm not going to stop investigating. Maybe he hopes to push me in one direction or another?

My mind spins. If he's trying to manipulate me, which direction does he hope I go? More importantly, what does he want me to ignore? Because that's what I need to focus on. Maybe I'm losing my mind with this circuitous thinking.

As a competitive athlete, I learned to banish outside noise from my brain. That's exactly what I must do now. Don't play defense against what Liam may or may not be doing. Go on the offense. I park in my driveway and rush up the brick walkway, avoiding glances from Casper's judging eyes.

I grab a pen and paper and create a list of topics to investigate:

> Gene's arrest
> Mia
> Dylan and Zeke
> Detective Bernard & Maspeth incident

Gene's finances
I examine my list and add a final topic for good measure:
Burke and Yvette?

I open my computer and google Gene Robbins. A few reporters were outside the police station when I arrived. Maybe they dug up more information on the charges. I discover a photo of Gene, in handcuffs, being escorted into the police station by Detective Bernard. The story doesn't clarify anything. The text states that Gene was arrested in *connection* to Kurt's murder, which could mean all sorts of things.

I move on to Mia Mars. I pay the forty dollars to subscribe to the *Westchester Guardian* and return to the article with the headline TRAGEDY STRIKES LOCAL SARAH LAWRENCE SISTERS. This time, the full story appears.

> Two Sarah Lawrence students (sisters) lost their mother in a tragic accident yesterday. Ms. Sandra Mars spent Parents Day with her daughters, Mia Mars (senior) and Heather Mars (freshman), before heading home after the traditional parent-student dinner. Sandra Mars's car veered off the highway, crashing into the guardrails, according to local police. Doctors say she died during the night. No other vehicles were involved in the accident. The death remains under investigation.

What a horrible tragedy. I find myself feeling sorry for Mia and her sister.

I try searching *Sandra Mars*, but no additional articles appear. I check the date on the *Westchester Guardian*: October 28, 2000. A friend of mine went to Sarah Lawrence and would have been a freshman that year. I know it's a long shot, but maybe she remembers something. I send a text asking her to call me when she's free.

Next on my list is Dylan. I will have to think about how to dig up more information there, so I move on to Detective Bernard. I haven't received an email back from the reporter at the Maspeth paper, so I google the general phone number and call. I'm connected right to her.

"Hi, this is Kate Green, sorry to bother—"

"Hi," she says, cutting me off. "I've been meaning to get back to you. It's just crazy here. Only me and one other reporter covering everything . . ."

She's talking a mile a minute. Between that and a thick Queens accent, I'm having a little trouble following her.

I explain that I'm trying to determine if a certain detective was involved in the murder case that was overturned and . . .

"That guy now in Greenwich?" She interrupts again.

"Yes. Peter Bernard."

"He was the arresting officer. A piece of work. But NYPD settled. Brushed the whole enchilada under the rug, and now there's an NDA. So, nothing's going to get done. Gotta run . . . good luck."

She hangs up before I can thank her. My instincts about Bernard were right. He's the type who doesn't let facts or evidence get in his way.

A car backfires. I look through my window and see the red car pull into the driveway of the Puke House. A velvet dusk blankets the street despite the early hour—4:30. Dark, but not dark enough to mask the witches and skeletons jeering at me. No matter what else I do, tonight I must decorate.

I pour myself a glass of chardonnay and take Gene's garbage bag full of papers into the family room to tackle the next item on my list— Gene's finances. The kids are out at the nighttime SAT prep class that Tyler insisted on. The house feels quiet as I curl up in the corner of the couch and cover myself with a wool blanket. Time to see what Gene stashed away.

I dump the contents of the bag on the couch, by my feet. Papers upon papers cascade across the cushions. What a mess—different sizes, some crumpled, others folded. A lot of unopened mail. It looks like the remnants of a discarded junk drawer. I take a long sip of my wine and let the oaky flavor sit in my mouth as I inspect the mess. I can't make sense of the documents like this. I need to organize the material. I slide onto the rug, back against the couch, and start creating piles on the coffee table. An hour in, I've only sorted about a third of the material.

I stand and stretch; my body feels tight. I need a break. I change into warm jogging clothes and head outside for a run in the neighborhood park down by the water. It's a favorite spot for dog walkers during the day, but at night, the trail is relatively quiet. I like coming here at night to be alone with my thoughts. I jog past an old stone house that was a school in the 1700s and now is a small museum for elementary school trips.

I turn at the fork and start toward the water. Most of the boats are winterized, but a few sailboats remain tied to the cleats along the main dock. Two teen boys with blond hair and baseball caps skateboard toward me; one wears a Greenwich Lake School jacket. "Hey! Aren't you Nikki and Jackson's mom?" one of them yells.

"Yup." I slow down a little. "Are you in class with them?"

"They should make you give back your Olympic medal, Kate Green," the other boy says as they break out laughing.

I feel my cheeks flush with shame. It's one thing to live with my mistakes, but the last thing I want is for my issues to be foisted onto my kids. I increase my pace and veer right, opting for the longer, more isolated loop.

The darkness feels comforting, like a cool blanket enveloping me. I take in a deep breath full of pine-scented air and feel my heart slow to a steady pace. The cool air makes my face tingle, helping me shed the stress of the last few days. My jaw loosens as my muscles relax. I feel one with the earth—a symbiotic relationship I only achieve through exercise. The world slows, my mind clears, and it's just me and the physical movement of my limbs. My breath.

There's a rustling up ahead. A figure by the bench. I'm surprised anyone else chose this path at this time of night. I speed up, wanting to remain alone. As I pass, I see the silhouette of a man, buff, wearing a fancy running outfit. He looks a little like Tyler, only taller. His pace is slow, and it should be easy to put distance between us. I surge ahead, once again reaching that mind-body euphoria. I turn by the lake, glancing back, and see the man about twenty feet behind me. The person must be in good shape to keep up. I increase my speed again as I begin circling the lake. Suddenly it feels like he's following me.

I banish the paranoia from my brain, but push my body to run faster. My feet pound against the dirt path. One, two, one, two. My breath comes fast and heavy. I see the person increase his speed. I'm too fast, though, and I put a few more yards between us. And then a few more. I look over my shoulder and see the figure stooped over, hands on knees, as if trying to catch his breath.

I have half a mind to turn around and find out why the fuck he was trying to give me a scare.

"Hey," he calls out. Fear overtakes my nerve, and I start running again, my legs propelling me forward. I hear him behind me. Calling. This time I don't look back. My calves burn. My ears fill with the sound of my blood pumping through my body. By the time I reach the park exit, I'm panting. As my lungs fill with air, I wonder if my fear was just paranoia. But why did he speed up when I passed? And why did he call out?

I feel safer outside the park. The streets are empty, but the lights from the houses lining the sidewalks provide a sense of security. By the time I turn onto my block, my pulse has returned to normal. By now, the kids must be home, and I'm relieved to know I'll have some company in the house.

I open the front door and call out a greeting.

"What happened in the family room?" Nikki asks as I enter the kitchen.

"What?" I ask.

"There are millions of papers scattered all over."

Gene's financials. I promise to clean up soon. Talk about a role reversal.

"We brought you some pizza . . . if you want." Jackson points to a box on the counter.

"Bless you." I give him an unwanted kiss on his cheek and open the box with two slices of gooey cheese pizza. The kids sit down at the counter as I scarf down the first slice.

"Is Dylan a suspect?" Jackson asks.

"Why do you ask?" I say.

Jackson tells me that the police came to school today and interrogated all the students who had helped set up for the dance this past Sunday.

"That detective from TV interviewed me," Nikki says. "Bernard, I think?" I don't know whether to be relieved or angry it wasn't Liam.

"Bernard interviewed me too," Jackson says. "But a lot of our friends got interviewed by some nasty guy from the city with a big scar on his face."

As I suspected, Liam was at the school. He's going to force my hand and make me tell the kids about him. As far as Nikki and Jackson are concerned, their biological grandfather dropped off the face of the earth and never resurfaced. Which was true. Until recently.

"What did the police want to know?"

"The officer kept asking about Dylan. *Was she helping to set up? Did I see her leave? Did I see her return?*" Nikki says.

"Same," Jackson adds.

I guess Zeke isn't turning out to be such a strong alibi. By now, the police must have reviewed all the Home Depot security cameras. Something must be off with the timeline. I make a note to dig into that.

"What did you say?" I ask.

Nikki goes to the faucet and fills up a glass of water and then adds some protein powder to the drink. "Dylan and Zeke were making runs to the store to get supplies. I saw her drop stuff and then head out again."

"Me too," Jackson adds.

"We kept running out of construction paper, glue—"

"We even ran out of hay for the maze," Jackson chimes in.

Jackson changes the subject to the funeral tomorrow and tells me that the principal is excusing any absences for people attending. "She's being unusually reasonable."

Nikki finishes her drink, rinses her glass, and the two of them head upstairs to finish their homework.

I carefully move my piles of Gene's papers upstairs and spread the piles onto the floor of my bedroom and return the unsorted documents to the garbage bag. I'll finish tomorrow.

My phone rings. It's my friend from Sarah Lawrence. After we catch up a little, I tell her I'm looking for some information on a car crash that killed the mother of two students, Mia and Heather Mars. She has a vague recollection of the accident, but tells me her roommate worked on the school newspaper and probably knows a lot more. She promises to reach out to the roommate and get back to me.

"I also have a favor to ask," she says. "My niece is a big fan of yours. Could you send her an autographed poster or something?"

I tell her I'd be thrilled to and hang up, feeling good about the fact I didn't let down *all* young girls everywhere.

I hear the grandfather clock downstairs mark 10:00 p.m. I'm exhausted. My muscles ache from the run and the fight-or-flight adrenaline that's now receded, leaving me limp and stressed. But there's one more thing I must do. No excuses.

I retrieve the boxes of Halloween decorations from the basement and drag them to the front door. I pull on a down coat, scarf, and gloves and stomp outside, dragging the boxes with me. Each year, just after

Halloween, I buy one new item to add to our collection. Last year it was a box of two-foot-tall shimmering ghosts with a cool metallic finish. I pull one out and study the iridescent face. Dark cutouts represent the eyes, and a long oval hole stands in for a mouth. The ghosts appear caught in a scream like the Dementors from Harry Potter. These will look good tied to the branches of the oak tree in the middle of our front lawn. I grab a step stool and place it under the limbs, then reach my arms straight. I just manage to tie the string around the lower branch. Repeating this action, I get all six ghosts tied around the tree. Next, I wrap orange twinkle lights around the trunk to draw attention to our centerpiece attraction.

Then I pull out the thick plastic spider webbing and drape the white gauze around the rails of our front porch. By the time I'm done, the electric black cats glow from the front windows, plastic jack-o'-lanterns line the walkway, and a giant scarecrow flaps from a stake in the yard.

A good tired comes over me. The kind of tired I'd feel after a satisfying training. One that works out my body and rests my mind. I sit down on the porch and bask in the orange glow of the twinkle lights. Fern Street is now respectably scary. I glance over to the Casper blow-up as if to say, *See? I did it.*

His eyes appear less judgy. I start to turn away when I notice a shadow behind the blow-up ghost. I have the strangest feeling that a person is standing behind the plastic figure. But that surely is crazy. Still, my body freezes in fear. Am I losing my mind? Or did the person from the park follow me to the house? I don't wait around to find out, but rush inside, locking the door behind me and setting the alarm.

CHAPTER 22

Friday morning I'm up and dressed early. In the light of day, I'm more convinced than ever that the so-called person I saw last night was just a figment of my imagination. Casper playing tricks on me. I can't believe I thought someone was really hiding behind a blow-up plastic ghost. *Kate—meet reality.* With all the stuff going on with the murder investigation and the fact that today is Kurt's funeral, it's no wonder my imagination is going wild.

I can't believe we bury Kurt today, five days since his murder.

Yvette wanted a small private ceremony. Kurt's parents desired a public service to mark their son's remarkable life. They reached a compromise, agreeing to a public ceremony at the historic Greenwich Cathedral, which holds over four hundred guests. After that, they will gather for a small private burial. The biggest sticking point became media coverage—Kurt's parents insisted the service be televised for all his fans.

The biggest unknown is whether Gene will get out of jail in time to attend his brother's funeral. Over a second cup of coffee, I scan the newspapers for updates; I only find a rehash of what I already know, mixed with lots of innuendo. Arrested in connection with murder? Charged with larceny and obstruction. . . more to come?

Jackson comes into the kitchen wearing a navy suit, his sandy-blond hair combed to the side.

"You look handsome." I smile as he walks into the room.

He scoffs. "Mom, I just realized . . . you are always dressed like you're heading to a funeral." He raises a pale brow at my outfit of black wool pants, black turtleneck, and black blazer.

"What can I say—I'm not one for cheery colors."

"That's an understatement."

"Okay, smart-ass. Eat." I place pancakes in front of him, along with maple syrup. I top off my coffee as Nikki shuffles in, still wearing sweats. She wipes her eyes and tells us she didn't sleep well. I hand her a green shake and ask if she's *sure* she doesn't want any coffee instead.

"I'm sure." She wrinkles her nose at the thought of polluting her body with caffeine.

At 10:45, we pile into my BMW convertible, top up. A crack of thunder booms across the sky. Dark clouds hang low on the horizon.

"It's a creepy day to have a funeral," Nikki says from the back seat, wearing the only dark outfit she owns: a navy sweater dress. "The day before Halloween."

"Better than on Halloween," Jackson replies as I turn out of our cul-de-sac and drive toward the church.

"Why is the weather always bad at funerals?" Nikki continues. I look at her in the rearview mirror and see Nikki bundled up inside her jacket, arms gripped around her chest. Jackson asks what other funerals she's attended.

"Just Grandma's." She twists a finger through a blonde strand of hair that's fallen free. She's referring to Tyler's mom. Jackson reminds her it was sunny that day.

"Yeah," Nikki says. "I guess I was thinking about funerals on television." A comment like that would usually trigger a sarcastic snipe or eye roll from Jackson, but he remains quiet as another clap of thunder blasts from the sky.

I turn onto Greenwich Avenue and stop at the high-pitched whistle of the traffic cop, who's clad in fluorescent-yellow rain gear. He holds up his right arm, signaling me to stop. I hit the brakes and notice my check-engine light flash on. *Tomorrow. I will deal with that tomorrow.* I love my classic black convertible, with its sleek lines and high-speed engine, but I don't love the trips to the service department, which are happening more and more frequently.

The traffic cop points to the cars across the way, motioning them to proceed. Nikki asks if she can skip the cemetery. I turn my head to Jackson. "Would you also prefer not to go to the cemetery?"

"Yeah," Jackson says.

The officer blows his whistle and rotates his arm in spastic circles that begin at his shoulder, like a Ferris wheel. I ease off the brakes and proceed forward. "What about Dylan?" I say, before remembering the kids said police were questioning them at school about Dylan. If she's a suspect, maybe Jackson and Nikki should keep their distance. The rain intensifies, pounding against the soft roof and echoing through the car, which I wouldn't have thought possible, and I grip the steering wheel tighter, my knuckles hurting from the pressure.

"We're not really close anymore," Nikki says, trying too hard to sound nonchalant.

"Is there anything I should know about Dylan?"

Neither Jackson nor Nikki speaks. I sense tension. They are hiding something. I feel it in my bones. "Do either of you know why she cleaned your room, Jackson? That seemed so strange to me."

Dead silence.

"Please. Someone tell me what's going on."

Nikki speaks. "If we tell you, you can't say anything to Yvette."

"Or Dad," Jackson adds.

My first instinct is to refuse. But I can tell something serious is going on. And after Tyler skipped the appointment with Dr. Michelson, I certainly don't owe him anything. "All right. I promise."

Jackson speaks. "Dylan's—"

Nikki finishes. "She's the one who supplied Jackson with all the Adderall," she says. "Even when it was clear he was already drunk."

"Nikki!" Jackson yells.

"Well, it's true." Her voice sounds contrite.

"Why did she have the drugs?" Blood rushes to my cheeks.

"I don't know," Jackson says.

"We have a theory," Nikki says. "She probably got them from Zeke."

"Why didn't you tell me?"

"We didn't want to get her into trouble," Jackson says, squirming in his seat.

The rain rages against the window, and I try not to get distracted by this information.

I turn onto Putnam Avenue and squint to see the church's tall spire through the rain and clouds. A gust of wind sends a torrent of water diagonally against the windshield. I grip the steering wheel tighter, and Jackson turns on the defroster.

I force my voice under control. "Does this have anything to do with Dylan 'cleaning' your room? Was she looking for drugs?"

"Probably," Jackson says. "She asked me to hold her stash. But I had flushed everything down the toilet the day I got home from the hospital."

I whisper so I don't shout. "There was more? At our house?"

Nikki leans forward so her head is by the console, and I smell bubble gum lip gloss. "We got rid of all of it, Mom. We swear. But she didn't believe we really dumped it. She thought we were going to try and sell it on our own and pocket the money. As if!"

I follow a traffic officer, who points toward a field that they transformed into an extra parking area for the large crowd. The tires sink a little in the grass. "Does Yvette know?"

"I doubt it," Jackson says. "Dylan begged us not to tell her."

"Or you," Nikki adds. "We got the feeling Dylan's dad might have known something about drugs."

"Yeah," Jackson says. "I think he caught her stealing Oxy. He had a lot around."

"Yeah," Nikki says. "Dylan said her dad had a sixth sense for when she did something wrong but didn't give a sh—um, crap—about anything she did right."

I pull my car behind a green Mercedes and cut the engine. If Kurt caught Dylan stealing drugs, did he also know she was selling? And, if he did, what did he do about it? Because, knowing Kurt, he would have acted.

"Mom?" Nikki says.

I snap back to the present.

"Say something," Jackson adds.

"I need time to sit with this." I open the door and do the only thing that makes sense: grab my umbrella and get out of the car. They follow.

Inside the church, we shake the water off our umbrellas, hang up our wet coats, and proceed into the sanctuary. I haven't been inside this church since Dylan's first communion, nearly a decade ago. I remember how proud Kurt and Yvette were. Kurt had a childlike exuberance. He literally beamed. He kept going up to everyone, wrapping them in bear hugs, lifting them off their feet. *Who could have thought I'd have such a beautiful child and beautiful wife. I'm the luckiest man alive.*

I look around the church. In contrast to the Gothic stone exterior, the inside boasts modern decor, with bleached wooden pews, abstract stained glass windows, and a glossy wooden cross suspended over the dais. The air feels heavy and sticky; too many people mixed with too much humidity.

"That cute reporter is trying to get your attention." Nikki nudges me, pointing to the press section on our left. I glance at the media area, which makes up the last five rows of the sanctuary. Two security guards stand by burgundy velvet ropes that hang on brass bases. The section overflows with reporters sandwiched next to one another. I scan the group, recognizing many faces, but not seeing anyone particularly *cute*.

"Over there." She points to David in the last row. "Are you blushing?" Nikki opens her eyes wide.

He waves us over. Before I can decline, Nikki starts in his direction. She's worse than any dating app, and Jackson and I find ourselves forced to follow.

David's brown eyes glimmer, and a smile flashes across his face. "Hi there." He reaches out his hand and holds mine an extra second. I pull back and tuck my hair behind my ears, feeling fidgety.

He keeps his eyes trained on mine. "Are these your kids?"

"Yes. This is my daughter, Nikki, and my son, Jackson."

"Nice to meet you." He steps closer to shake their hands. "David Lopez. Your mom and I worked together." His use of the past tense *worked* stings. The momentary spell is broken. Even though what he said is technically accurate.

"Be right back." Nikki leads Jackson down the aisle to join some school friends. I hope David can't tell how manipulative she's acting. Daughters!

David steps closer, and I smell lemon aftershave. "I'm sorry for our misunderstanding. Sometimes the job can make a person crazy."

"Don't I know it." I feel my cheeks redden.

He touches my arm. "I was thinking maybe we could grab some coffee sometime. I know things got a little weird that night at the bar . . ."

Oh no. He just called my attempt to kiss him weird, and now wants to get coffee to further discuss one of the most embarrassing moments in my adult life?

Without making eye contact, I quickly excuse myself and squeeze past groups of people searching for seats. *Coffee, for coffee's sake—fine. But why mention the bar? Does he feel the need to define the friend zone for me? Maybe he thinks I'll jump him if we're ever alone again? Will the humiliation never end?*

I hardly notice the dignitaries I walk past in the VIP section—the governor and mayor seated next to other local officials. I will my mind free of David. Today is about Yvette. By the time I reach the middle of the church, I feel most of the humiliation has drained from my body.

"Kate." Christie steps from her seat and makes her way toward me. She wears a navy suit, silk blouse, and pearl necklace. She's sitting with a large group of parents and staff from Greenwich Lake. The cynic in me can't help wondering if they are here for support or spectacle. She's put on a little blush and lipstick and curled her blonde hair. She places her hand on my arm. "How is our Yvette?"

"About how you'd expect."

"It's devastating. And to think just five days ago she was doing errands while her husband was murdered." Her words feel laced with innuendo. "Just a tragedy," Christie says, not looking concerned at all.

A man in a wheelchair rolls past us, a young aide by his side.

"You didn't call me yesterday like you promised." Christie reaches for the diamond-studded flower on her ear and twists at it.

The encounter with Christie at Greenwich Lake School feels like decades ago. "I'm sorry. The day got away from me."

She sniffs. "Well, no matter. The dance is on. It's best for the kids. You will be there tomorrow night? I have you down for a shift."

"I . . ."

She air-kisses me goodbye before I can get a word out and returns to her husband, who must be twenty years her elder. He's bald, with a potbelly and yellowish teeth. Before Christie married him, she worked for him, running the rental division of his mega–real estate company. Now she's pretty much running the whole company. No one buys or rents a house without Christie's knowledge.

"Hey." Nikki pulls on my arm. "Everyone is going to Starbucks after the service. Is it all right if Jackson and I go too?"

"Sure," I say as we continue to make our way down the aisle. I still don't see Yvette or her family, but I know she saved us seats in front. As we get closer, the casket comes into view. A magnificent red-and-peach rose wreath rests next to a large ebony coffin. The finish on it shines so bright it appears to sparkle, kind of like Kurt himself. Next to the coffin, a poster-size picture of Kurt rests on an easel. Kurt wears a lavender button-down shirt and stares into the camera with his deep-brown eyes. A shadow crosses his skin, emphasizing the sharp angles of his nose and jaw. But his wide smile softens the sharpness and lights up his face.

"Nikki. Jackson." Tyler's voice draws my attention, and I turn to see him walking toward us, his third wife, Gloria, several feet behind him.

"Hey." Nikki stiffens.

Tyler gives Nikki a closed smile and a quick hug. "Hi there." He releases her and looks toward his son. "Jackson."

"Father." Jackson remains by my side. No one talks. The rain overtakes our silence as it batters the roof. The air feels heavy and tight. Gloria joins our circle, and the kids scurry off. I'd scold them for their rudeness, but they've watched so many women enter and exit their father's life, I can't really blame them.

"Hi," Gloria says in a soft voice. She used to be Tyler's accountant. She's about thirty, with wavy platinum-colored hair. She's very friendly and sweet, and I feel nothing but sorry for her having to be married to him.

"Hi," I say. "Sorry about the kids. Don't take it personally."

"I get it," Gloria says with a sad smile.

A hush settles over the room. The priest accompanies Yvette and her family to the front. Yvette scans the church, her eyes finding me from under the spotted lace veil that covers most of her face. She points to the empty seats behind her. Jackson, Nikki, and I make our way to the second row and sit. Dylan turns to us, her eyelids puffy and swollen.

"Have you heard from my uncle?" she whispers, her lower lip quivering. Dylan's dressed like her mom today, in a black silk suit and gold cross necklace. Her braids are wrapped into a bun and pinned at the back of her head.

"No."

She nods, and I can't tell if she's happy or sad about his absence. Add that to all the questions I have for her. Why did Dylan give drugs to Jackson? Is she supplying drugs to other kids? Did Kurt know? Is Zeke involved? In fact, where is Zeke? I scan the church for him and spot Zeke with some boys with blond, wavy hair. Something about them looks familiar, but I don't think I know them from school. Are those the boys I saw in the park?

I ask Nikki who they are. "Trouble," she says and rolls her eyes. I study Zeke, who, despite being in church, has his wool hat pulled over his hair. The boys with him are laughing and smirking, rude on any occasion let alone a funeral.

The organ begins. The rich, somber tones ring through the sanctuary. The choir sings a lilting hymn. I lean back against the pew and close my eyes. We rarely attended religious events growing up; my mom and stepdad were born Jewish but embraced more of a Buddhist mindset. More Zen than amen.

A door clanks at the back of the church, and I open my eyes to see Kurt's teammates enter. Mason Burke stands in front, wearing a black suit and turtleneck. Gold aviator glasses cover his eyes, and he keeps his bald head tilted downward. The men move quickly down the aisle.

Most file into the seats behind us, but Mason comes over to Yvette and bends down, kissing her on the cheek. "Sorry we are late, Evie." He extends his pasty-white hand and takes hers. "I'm here for you. We will get through this."

Watching them, I'm more convinced than ever something is up. Burke releases Yvette's hand and stands straight. He walks past me, inches from me, and winks. Rage courses through my veins. Wow, he really thinks he's beaten me. *Just wait, Mason Burke.* Nikki must see my reaction because she leans over and tells me not to let him get to me.

From the podium, the priest raises his large hands. "Ladies and gentlemen." His strong voice resonates through the church. "Thank you for coming to offer comfort to Kurt Robbins's family and to remember a special man taken away too early from this earth."

My gaze returns to the coffin and settles on why we are here. The husband of my best friend is dead. Murdered. What a horrific loss for her and all of us. Such a vital force. Snuffed out in his prime.

"Here." Nikki nudges me, offering a tissue. I blot my eyes.

The words of the priest wash over me—somber words about the Lord, his mysterious ways, and the fragility of mortal life. There's a hypnotic lull of music, and I feel a little collective comfort. The intense rain gives way to light tapping. The choir sings a mournful tune that sounds both sorrowful and heartening.

Nikki elbows me. "That detective keeps looking at us. The one with the scar from school yesterday."

Liam Murphy had all day yesterday and this morning to call or text. He ignored me, and now he's drawing attention to himself and sparking curiosity in his granddaughter. I don't want to acknowledge him, but something pulls my eyes upward, and we make eye contact. He starts to give me his customary half smile, but I look down before the greeting forms.

"Have we met him before?" Nikki asks. "There's something familiar about him."

I shrug so I don't have to lie.

She loses interest, staring straight ahead. I turn back again. Liam's powerful figure bulges against a tan sports jacket and corduroy pants. He leans against the wall under the stained glass window with geometric shapes of yellow, blue, and red. I imagine it symbolizes some religious scene, but it's too abstract for my eye. He's not the only law enforcement present. Detective Bernard and a female detective both stand nearby.

"Before we conclude," the priest says, "Mrs. Robbins would like to say a few words."

Yvette rises, gripping a lined paper in her gloved hand. She walks deliberately, her pointed satin heels clicking against the wooden stairs. The congregation goes silent.

Yvette pushes her veil over her hat, exposing dull copper eyes. She opens the paper too close to the microphone, sending a crackle through the speakers. She pulls the paper lower on the pulpit and presses her hands over the sheet to straighten it.

"Thank you all for coming today." Her voice cracks. She clears her throat and tries again. "Thank you for coming today. Kurt would have appreciated having all of you here." She stops, coughs, clears her throat. "I'm sorry. This is even harder than I thought." She lifts a handkerchief to her eyes. "I . . . first met Kurt at a church. It wasn't like this one. It was in upstate New York. Small. Simple. Kurt was an altar boy, believe it or not." She giggles. But it's an uncomfortable laugh, and no one joins in. "I hardly remember life without him. We didn't have much back then, but we were happy. Kurt used to wait for me after school, every day, and carry my books home." She smiles, lost in the memory. Tears sting the corner of her eyes.

"Mom . . ." Nikki elbows me again.

I'm aware of whispers around me, like a jolt of electricity coursing through the sanctuary. Did something happen?

I put my finger to my lips in a *sh*. She shoves her phone into my hands, where I see a photo of Kurt kissing Mia outside Madison Square Garden. I'm confused. Why does Nikki have this? Then I see it's part of an article that just dropped on the internet. And the headline is even worse than the picture.

CHAPTER 23

A collective gasp rumbles through the congregation. I WAS HIS ONE TRUE LOVE—the first line. HE DESPISED HIS WIFE—second line. The article also prominently features the photo of Kurt and Mia taken at Yvette's home. I grab the phone from Nikki and scan the hurtful words.

> Mia Mars, a junior staff member of the Comets public relations department, says she and Kurt fell in love while working on a community service program for underprivileged children. "I never wanted to get involved with a married man. But he was so unhappy in his marriage. He said Yvette tormented him. He said the marriage was over in every way but the paperwork."

"This is outrageous," I whisper.

"*I know,*" Nikki mouths.

I think back to my conversation with David at Madison Square Garden—he refused to interview Mia when she insisted on story approval. What unethical chump agreed to her conditions? I scroll to the top. Disappointment seeps into my stomach: the byline reads Cal Callahan. I knew he was relentless. But I hadn't thought he was also unethical and slimy.

On the altar, Yvette keeps speaking, voice shaking. "Kurt and I had so many dreams." Giggles rise from the sanctuary. Turning, I catch Zeke's friends among the most disrespectful. Yvette grips the sides of the podium. "It's true: Things got tough when Kurt entered the NBA. He only planned to stay for a while, but, well, I guess it's hard not to want to be a star." Her lips tremble. "That wasn't the real Kurt. We talked about how everything would go back to the way it was once he retired. Probably just a few years from now."

Yvette looks out at the sanctuary—*really* looks. Her lids flutter. She folds up her paper, mumbles "Thank you," and quickly returns to her seat.

Organ music starts. The pallbearers stand, proceed to the stage, and carry the coffin down the stairs. Dylan whimpers, rocking back and forth. I'm wary of Dylan after my conversation with Nikki and Jackson. But my heart also breaks for her, a child who lost her father and will face vicious gossip in a matter of minutes. Yvette drapes a protective arm around her daughter's shoulders. Dylan cries louder. The priest beckons the family to follow the coffin; Dylan attempts to stand, her legs buckle, and she falls back onto her seat, nearly hitting her head against the wooden back of the pew.

Yvette tells the priest that they need a few minutes.

Footsteps and muted whispers fill the church. Nikki and Jackson leave with the others, but Yvette, Kurt's parents, and I remain seated.

"Dylan, sweetheart, come here." Betty pulls her granddaughter into her thin arms.

Yvette thanks Betty and asks me to go with her to the ladies' room. She leads me through a back hallway and into the powder room. Instead of going to the bathroom stalls, she sits on the green-and-maroon-striped couch in a small lounge section.

"What happened?" Yvette asks.

I take a seat next to her and ask what she means. But I know what she means.

"In the middle of my eulogy . . . people were staring at their phones."

The overly sweet smell of potpourri makes my eyes water. The room feels drab, with peeling beige-on-beige wallpaper, a busy-patterned, thin granite counter, and a simple square mirror without a frame placed on the wall.

I tell her not to worry about it now, but she pushes.

"It was an article about Kurt's . . . mistress," I say reluctantly.

"What did it say?" She takes off her hat with the attached veil, and I stare into her swollen, watery eyes.

"Nonsense." A sound at the door stops our conversation. Yvette and I watch a tall, thin woman enter, wearing a black dress and carrying a large red bag.

"I'm sorry for your loss," she says, her voice a deep velvet, so familiar in its cadence that I wonder if I've heard her on a podcast.

"Thanks," Yvette says. "Do we know each other?"

"No," she says in that rich, deep tone. "I'm here with my sister." She raises her chin, and I notice an almond-shaped birthmark on her neck.

"Thanks for coming," Yvette says as the woman walks toward the stalls. Yvette turns her eyes back on me and sticks out her hand. "Let me have it."

I relent, handing over my phone.

"She's very pretty." Yvette studies the screen. I remain silent, watching the pain in Yvette's face as she studies the picture. Does she notice her Picasso in the background? "How can they publish such lies?" she asks as she stares at the peeling wallpaper.

"It's disgusting," I say.

The woman with the red bag reappears, keeping her head down, and shuffles by us. Yvette holds my phone in a death grip like she's trying to squeeze the words away. "I remember the community service project," she says more to herself than me. "I offered to help . . ."

Betty knocks on the door and tells us we need to leave for the cemetery.

Yvette and Betty join the rest of her family in the limousine. Clusters of people linger outside the church despite a bone-chilling drizzle—weather Nikki claims befits a burial. I sludge through puddles to my car, program the GPS for the cemetery, and turn on the radio news. What I'm really curious about is Gene. Did he get released on bail? He was a no-show at the service. The announcer hurries through weather and traffic before moving on to Kurt's funeral. After a commercial break, the announcer reports Gene Robbins made bail a few hours ago. *A few hours ago?* Was he at the funeral? Maybe hiding in the back?

I reach the cemetery and wonder if I'll see Gene here. I drive through the majestic gate into an area that looks more country club than graveyard, with rolling hills dotting picturesque vistas. I half expect someone to yell *fore* as I make my way to Yvette and her family under a sugar maple tree with bright-orange autumn leaves.

Mason Burke joins our group. My muscles stiffen as he gets close, but I hold my ground, refusing to move. I don't back down from bullies. Yvette tells the priest he can start, her voice catching. Does she know that Gene was released? Does she even want to see him?

"Now that you are away from the cameras and the crowd," the priest begins, "I hope you can allow your feelings an outlet. I wish I could supply you with reason for tragedy. God works in mysterious ways." He opens a prayer book and starts reciting from it.

Yvette grips Dylan's hand as she peers into the deep hole in the soft earth that will be Kurt's resting place. Someone set up two folding chairs for Betty and Gregory, who now sit side by side. Betty cries softly into a handkerchief as Gregory rocks his body back and forth. I feel Mason Burke's heavy breath behind me. Beyond the priest, a limousine engine backfires.

The priest talks over the noise. "And so . . . by whose mercy the faithful departed find rest. Send your holy angel to watch over this grave, through Christ, our Lord."

Gears grind as the coffin descends into the earth.

Dylan and Yvette whimper. Gregory and Betty clutch each other.

"May God bless you." The priest closes his Bible and reaches out to take Yvette's hand as a cold rain starts again.

I open my umbrella and hug Yvette. "I'm so sorry."

She hugs me back, and I lean against her ear. "I thought you should also know Gene was released on bail."

"Is he here?" she whispers.

"I didn't see him." I offer to escort her family back to their house, but she says they need time alone. Mason Burke approaches, and I step back. He puts an arm around Yvette and Dylan and guides them across the grass toward their limousine.

I take a last look into the grave, the shiny coffin now covered with a layer of earth. *Well, Kurt,* I think to myself. *This is goodbye.* His face surfaces in my mind, the one from the pictures in Yvette's home. The face of the man who loved his wife, laughed at their wedding, bought her the Picasso, and—despite affair after affair—always stayed. I also remember the fearless player. As an athlete, I will forever admire his incredible work ethic and competitive intensity. And his sense of humor and love of life.

The fog remains heavy as I drive home. I'm desperate to get out of my wet clothes and eat something. A siren sounds from behind. In my rearview mirror I see an unmarked vehicle motion me to pull over. Did I go through a stop sign? Red light? I pull to the side, wary of the request.

Then my anxiety turns to rage as Liam Murphy steps from the police car.

CHAPTER 24

I'm so angry and tired I consider driving off. He's halfway to my car, holding the top of his trench coat over his head against the rain, which picked up in the last minute. Karma. My opportunity to leave closes as he reaches my window, motioning for me to lower the glass. I reluctantly oblige. "This is rich," I say.

He rolls his eyes as if I were a child throwing a tantrum. "I didn't want to embarrass you at the funeral," he says. "I figured the kids don't know about me?"

Does Liam seriously want points for consideration? "What was wrong with talking yesterday at the police station?" I spit the words out. "Remember? *You* blew me off?"

Always on his schedule. A truck grinds past. I smile to myself when the tires spray water onto his legs.

"Whatever." He wipes the water from his pants with his hand. "It's silly to argue." He looks tired, circles under his bright eyes, and tells me he wanted to make sure I'm all right.

Should I tell him about the person I thought was following me last night in the park? Fool me once . . .

"If that's all . . ." I reach to roll up my window.

He puts his hand on the window to keep me from closing it. The rain changes direction, and drops fly against my cheek. He leans closer, and I smell coffee mixed with sweat. "I followed up on the ultrasound you gave me."

I remove my finger from the electric window switch. He gives me a half smile. "Now I have your attention," he says.

"We are on the side of a street. So maybe don't draw it out . . ."

"The baby is definitely Kurt's," he announces.

"That was really quick."

"We know what we're doing," he says. "We tracked down the doctor listed on the ultrasound and got a warrant for the material."

I let that information sink in. Mia Mars is pregnant with Kurt's child. Liam reaches for his scar as he watches me.

"Before you ask," he says, "Ms. Mars has an alibi for the time of the murder."

"What is it?"

He taps the side of my car like it's a horse he's encouraging to move along. I lean out the window as he turns away, ignoring the deluge now raining down on my head. "What is the alibi?" I yell but he's already halfway to his car. I roll my window up and drive home. Liam Murphy is the most frustrating person alive. And manipulative. He's leaving me dangling on purpose. He knows I'm going to want to hear about Mia's alibi. And to do that I'll need to communicate with him. *Damn him.*

Nikki greets me as I open the door. "God, Mom. You look awful."

"Thanks." I lean against the coatrack to pull off my wet boots, only to find my socks drenched too.

"Why don't you take a bath, change, and I'll make grilled cheese sandwiches for us."

"Really?"

"You sound so surprised." She feigns hurt. "I can be helpful, sometimes."

I don't question the offer, just run upstairs and rip off my wet clothing. I wrap myself in a towel and turn on the brass faucet, watching the water stream into the free-standing porcelain tub. I add some bath oils and adjust the temperature to hot, pull my hair into a ponytail, and examine the face staring back at me in the oval mirror above the sink. I look awful—my liner smudged and lips cracked. A proper mom monster. It could be my costume for Halloween tomorrow.

I scrub my face clean, but the person staring back remains scary—maybe more so. Without makeup, the lines by the corners of my eyes seem deeper and my skin looks ashen. Resigned to my present appearance, I turn off the tub, step into the warm water, and let the steam surround me.

This has been one hell of a day. There's the *regular* awful of it—the death and burial of my best friend's husband. And then there's the *extra* awful—Kurt was murdered, Gene is caught up in it, Dylan's mixed up with drugs, Burke and Yvette have some weird energy between them, and the other woman—that Mia Mars—looms over everything. And the icing on this horrible cake—Liam Murphy's audacity to pull me over on the side of the road. And then to leave before explaining Mia's supposed alibi. I squeeze my lids tight and try to clear my mind, breathing in the lavender and eucalyptus scents of my bath oils. I wet the loofah and rub the firm sponge against my skin, trying to scrape the day away, then lie back against the edge of the tub.

My mind wanders to Burke and the ease between him and Yvette. Does Burke have the capacity for kindness? I almost blanch at the thought. But I need to examine it. I know he feels a particular hatred toward female reporters; through the years, he's made his opinion abundantly clear. But he treats his teammates with respect, if not warmth. I would never have thought Burke would harm Kurt. Me, maybe. But Kurt? With all Kurt's affairs, I never considered whether Yvette would look elsewhere for affection. But why not? Still, connecting with Kurt's best friend? Then again, it's not like Yvette could just jump on Match.com.

I feel my body shiver and realize the water has turned cold.

I get out, towel off, and change into leggings and an oversize wool turtleneck. Hip-hop music blasts through the hallway, originating in

Jackson's room. I walk to his door, about to knock—and stop. I open my fist and place my hand on the outside of his door, feeling the vibrations from the music. Why do I need to check on him? I promised not to hover. He's fine. I turn and go downstairs.

"Voilà." Nikki places a grilled cheddar cheese sandwich in front of me on the counter and one at the seat in front of her. She pours me a cup of coffee and herself a green concoction.

"This is so good." I bite into the sandwich with gooey cheese and taste the richness of the cheddar. I take another bite, nibbling through the golden bread. The last five days have been such a nightmare, I've lost sight of the rhythm of everyday life.

She picks up her sandwich and starts eating. "Not bad, huh?"

"Excellent," I say. "What's the secret?"

"Extra grease." She laughs and takes a sip of her juice. I laugh. Even my health-freak daughter can't resist a good grilled cheese on occasion.

"Did you read the rest of that article? About that woman?" she asks.

So much for the regular rhythm of life. "Yes."

Nikki holds her glass in both hands. "Do you believe that Kurt was going to leave Yvette? Mia Mars says he was going to leave the day he was killed."

I take a sip of my coffee.

Nikki pulls out her phone. "Look. Kurt seems happy in this picture." She hands me her phone with that same picture of Kurt and Mia that I saw in Mia's office. "He was always scowling when I saw him."

"He does look happy."

"You know, everyone thinks Yvette is guilty," Nikki says. "What do you think? Do you think Yvette . . . could have killed him?"

I put my hand over Nikki's and find she's trembling. "I don't," I say. *I really don't.*

The grandfather clock in the hallway chimes its low, hollow gong, three times.

"God, it's all so morbid," I say. "Let's talk about something else. How was Starbucks? Did you have fun with your friends?"

"Yeah. It was fine. Zeke showed up with Madison from school. She's Christie Orlow's stepdaughter. It's weird he didn't go with Dylan to the cemetery."

Nikki stands, collects our plates, and takes them to the sink. "Maybe it was just for family. And you."

And Burke. "What are your plans for the rest of the day?" I ask, stifling a yawn.

Nikki grimaces. "Homework. How about you?"

"There are some calls I need to make. And some papers I should go through." I think about the pile of Gene's finances sitting on my bedroom floor.

Nikki laughs and suggests I take a nap.

"I must really look bad."

"Yeah," she says. "You do."

Upstairs in my bedroom, I step over the papers to sit on my cream comforter. I breathe in the lingering smell of lavender and look around my cozy room with its slanted cream walls, white wicker furniture, and velvet accents. I am exhausted. Maybe Nikki's right and I should take a short nap. I can return to my investigation after a little rest. A half hour, I tell myself. As I drift off to sleep, I remember my friend from Sarah Lawrence had left a message for me to call her back. She said something interesting turned up regarding Mia and her sister.

CHAPTER 25

I wake up with a jolt, completely disoriented. It's dark outside, and the house feels quiet. My phone shows 5:00 a.m. My half-hour nap turned into twelve hours. The cotton blanket from the foot of the bed covers me. Nikki's doing, no doubt. I smile, thinking of her kindness yesterday. How lucky am I to have caring kids?

The cold floorboards send a shiver through my body. I fumble for my UGGs and head down for much-needed coffee.

By my second cup, I'm back up in my room and have completed organizing Gene's papers. The first pile contains expenditures. Pretty much what one might expect, monthly utility bills, a cleaning service, electricity payments, garbage pickup, etc. I also find payments for equipment, some company dinners, and a weekly Sunday charge at Joe's Pizza in Greenwich. For Sunday football at Kurt's house? Gene likely stopped at Joe's the day of Kurt's murder. I make a mental note to swing by Joe's.

Next pile contains bank papers, including a stack of unopened certified letters from the Greenwich Bank. I open the most recent, dated two weeks ago, and read the document over twice. The letter is a notice of foreclosure. It states that the Robbins Brothers Corp. is in default on its mortgage and owes over a million dollars. I open the other letters—all variations of the same.

Yvette told me that Kurt had paid off the gym's mortgage last year. Gene must have taken out another mortgage and not told them. Why? I text Yvette to see if she's free for a visit. My phone rings immediately. Before she says anything, I hear shouting. It sounds like Dylan.

"Dylan refuses to open her door," Yvette says. "She's locked herself in her bedroom and won't leave or let anyone inside."

I offer to come over, but Yvette says she needs to get out of the house. "Somewhere . . . discreet." She suggests a local gourmet market with a few outdoor tables that are almost never used. We agree to meet in an hour.

It's nearly 9:00, and I hear the kids stir. After she spoiled me yesterday, I figure Nikki deserves a good Saturday-morning Halloween breakfast. As I put together a green concoction, my mind wanders to Gene's life choices. Yvette told me Gene came out of college a tech superstar, developing a popular music app. Then squandered his money until he went bankrupt. I know he married a Comets cheerleader five years ago, but divorced a year later. He barely dates and never had children. Gene seemed to exist in the shadows. Maybe he got resentful and snapped.

I hear the kids on the stairs, grab my Halloween gear—something I've done every October thirty-first morning since they were toddlers. "Happy Halloween!" I greet Jackson and Nikki as they saunter into the kitchen. Nikki holds up her hand to block the sun shining through the window.

"Mom," Jackson says. "Take that silly witch hat off your head. We're not twelve."

"Never!"

Jackson tries to stifle a grin, but I see it. Balancing the hat on my head, I put the finishing touches on the table and pour myself a third cup of coffee.

"This is really good," Nikki says, sipping her drink. "Especially for a witch."

"Thank you." I pantomime a bow, the witch's hat nearly falling onto the floor. I catch it and put it on the stool next to me and ask the kids their plans. They tell me the dance committee still has work to do for tonight's party.

"We figured we'd head over," Jackson says, glancing at Nikki, "unless you think it's weird to go to the dance?"

Nikki wipes some green foam off her lip with the back of her hand. "I mean, it does give us a good distraction. Do you think it's . . . insensitive?"

Outside, the garbage truck rumbles down our street for its Saturday-morning pickup. "I think it's fine. Christie has a reasonable point: that it is probably good for all of you to be together. And there's no reason you shouldn't have fun."

Jackson asks if I'm going tonight. I tell him I'm signed up for a late shift. "I think I'm working at one of the carnival games."

"You know Dad volunteered too." Nikki rolls her eyes in a very dramatic fashion.

"I can handle him."

"But can Nikki?" Jackson taps his sister on the head and jumps off the stool. "Going to get ready. Ten minutes, Nikki, and we've got to leave."

"Everything okay with you and your dad?"

"Yeah. Same as usual. You know, he's just . . ."

"Intense?"

"Yup." She hops off her chair, too, and heads after Jackson. "See you tonight."

"Have a *ghoo-ul* day."

Groans and giggles ring from the hallway.

I finish up the breakfast dishes, wondering if I should worry about Nikki and her dad. She usually takes his intensity in stride—but with the SATs and college around the corner, it makes sense she might feel pressure. It bothers me more that Tyler doesn't try with Jackson. Like he views our son as a lost cause because he's an average student. Still, I make a note to check in with Nikki after the weekend.

With that resolved, I call my friend from Sarah Lawrence, anxious to hear what she dug up. She says the rumor was that the mom drank too much at parents' day and was drunk when she drove home. She also tells me her freshman roommate didn't remember Mia but remembered her sister, Heather Mars. "They worked together at the school newspaper for a bit," she says. "Although Heather was more interested in radio. Apparently, she had a great voice."

My mind flashes back to the funeral and the woman with the velvety voice who interrupted me and Yvette in the bathroom. Could that have been Heather?

"Any chance your friend has a photo?" I ask.

"I'll check," she says and hangs up.

I feel unsettled that Heather Mars might have come into the bathroom while Yvette and I were talking after the funeral. It feels like an aggressive move. Like a peacock displaying its feathers in a show of dominance. I finish the breakfast dishes and leave to meet Yvette. With no sign of her in the parking lot, I head inside and purchase two five-dollar coffees and decadent lemon-ginger scones, also obscenely priced. As I return outside, I spot Yvette closing her car door, dressed in leggings, sneakers, and a full-length down jacket with the hood up. The outdoor seating area consists of two round metal tables overlooking the parking lot. Needless to say, it never sees much action.

She gives a little wave and climbs the steps to meet me at the far table. I sit, handing her a coffee and scone.

"I love these scones. Thanks." She keeps her hood up but removes large round sunglasses. Her eyes are still swollen and dull. "It's so strange to be out in the world."

I wrap both my hands around the warm coffee and rest it against my chin. Yvette nibbles at the pastry.

"How is Dylan? It sounded . . . *intense* . . . on the phone."

"My heart breaks for her," Yvette says, staring at her scone. "I know she's grieving, but I feel like something else is also going on."

Before I can ask her to elaborate, she switches topics and asks about Gene.

I tell her about the foreclosure notices on the gym.

"That can't be right," Yvette says, a bit too loudly, causing a customer to stare in our direction. She lowers her voice and tells me again that last year Kurt paid off the whole mortgage on the gym. "Gene wanted to buy a house and couldn't afford mortgage payments on the gym and a new place. So, Kurt helped him out. Again."

I break off a piece of my scone and take a bite. It's good. Very good. But not *priceless* good. "There were a lot of letters from the bank. It's hard to imagine they made a mistake. Is it possible they took out another mortgage on the gym?" I ask.

"I would have known if Kurt was involved in that . . ." She lets the words linger. The implication is clear. If there was another mortgage, Gene got it without telling his brother.

Yvette holds her coffee against her chin. "I guess none of it matters now."

"What do you mean?"

Yvette tells me they read the will last night and Gene gets 10 percent of Kurt's estate, which provides more than enough money to pay off any mortgage. "And, ironically, his jewelry," she says.

"You mean the jewelry Gene supposedly took off Kurt's body actually belongs to him?"

"Mm-hmm."

"Did the police drop the charges against Gene?"

"I'm not sure what's going to happen. He still messed with the crime scene. I didn't want him at the reading . . . after what he seems to have done. But Betty insisted. She doesn't believe Gene did anything wrong."

Yvette goes on to tell me that Kurt left another 10 percent to his parents and the rest to her and Dylan. "Which would be a good thing, but the police think it gives me even *more* of a motive."

A woman holding the hand of a small child walks out of the store and gawks at Yvette. I glare back, and she walks off. But Yvette looks shaken, gathers her coffee and scone, and tells me she's not ready to be out. That this was a mistake.

I follow Yvette to her car. There's still one more thing I need to ask her, even though I know she won't like it.

CHAPTER 26

As we approach Yvette's car, part of my brain tells me to let it go. But the other part pushes harder. She may not like the question, but it's relevant. If Yvette and Burke are in a relationship, Burke could have wanted Kurt out of the way.

"Are you and Burke having an affair?" I blurt out.

Her mouth gapes. "An affair? With Burke?"

Explanations pour from my mouth. *You wanted me to leave when he came to visit. He's very touchy feely. He was strangely absent the day Kurt died.*

Her eyes widen like those of a wounded animal. "Of all people, I never imagined you'd jump to such . . ." She searches for the words, and I brace myself against the sting. "Such salacious conclusions. I mean, Kate, after your thing."

"But is there any truth to it?" I ask, registering that her rebuff did not include a denial.

She shakes her head in disgust, gets in her car, and shuts the door.

I thought she might get annoyed, but her reaction feels extreme. And possibly like a deflection. She never answered my question. Still, I'm her friend, not her mom. I didn't intend to hurt her feelings. Guilt washes over me as she drives away. But the question still lingers. And I still believe it's relevant.

My phone immediately vibrates. I hope it's a text from Yvette. But it's a text from my friend from Sarah Lawrence. It's a photo of the staff from the Sarah Lawrence newspaper with a circle around Heather Mars. The woman resembles a younger version of the person from the bathroom. I study the image and notice a small almond-shaped birthmark on her neck. There's no question, it's the same person. Was Mia Mars at the funeral too? Lurking somewhere in the corner? I'm surprised she didn't announce herself in the middle of the whole service and add to the spectacle.

On the way home, I swing by Joe's Pizza at the bottom of Greenwich Avenue. As soon as I walk through the narrow cave-like entrance, a middle-aged woman with a tomato-stained apron greets me with a smile from behind the counter. "Trying to beat the lunch crowd?" she asks.

I explain I want to ask her a question, and she immediately asks if it's for television, telling me she recognizes me from TRP Sports. I don't want to lie, but I also don't feel compelled to dissuade her from making that assumption.

"You want to know if Gene Robbins got pizza here on Sunday?" she says, taking off her apron.

"How'd you know?"

"Police came by the day after the murder." She peers out the window onto the street and asks if I have a camera crew with me.

"I wanted to stop by on my own."

"Oh, like a pre-interview." She smiles, puts her apron back on, adds flour on the cutting board, and starts kneading a ball of dough. "Gene got his usual—two large pepperoni pies, extra cheese, and a bucket of chicken wings. I took the order."

My stomach rumbles at the smell of the homemade tomato sauce, sweet with basil. I might as well order a couple of slices since I'm here. I place my order and ask if she knows what time Gene came by.

"I do. I checked the credit card receipts. He paid at two sixteen."

Good to know it was two *six*teen.

If Gene left Joe's Pizza around 2:16, did he have enough time to get to the Robbinses' mansion, shoot his brother, and then call 911? I need to find out the exact time of the 911 call. And for that I might have to talk to the father who shall not be named.

"You coming back to do that interview on TV?" she asks, handing me the warm pizza box.

"I'll let you know if I can get a crew." I thank her again, get into my car, and drive home.

The afternoon comes quickly, bringing with it the first wave of trick-or-treaters. From my front window, I watch two little girls tumble out of a red wagon, wearing purple and pink taffeta dresses. They scramble up the brick path, swinging plastic pumpkins. How nice to be young and carefree. The little girls stop at the spider webbing on the porch, push their hands into the thread, laugh, and scamper up the stairs.

"Trick or treat!"

I open the front door and hold out a giant plastic pumpkin filled with Cookie Dough Bites and Muddy Bears.

"My favorite!" The girl in pink grabs a box of the Muddy Bears.

"Take two," I say.

She smiles and runs away with her friend.

A second group of youngsters approaches my walkway and crosses the porch.

"You guys are really scary," I say.

"Not me!" a brunette in a pumpkin costume shouts. "I'm a *vet-gab-bul.*"

"Yes, you are." I laugh. "You kids wouldn't want some candy, would you?"

"*Yessss!*" they yell, and I hold out the pumpkin. Across the street, I see a zebra, two kangaroos, and a pilot run to the Puke House. They grab boxes of candy and giggle as they cut across to my neighbors.

By 6:00 p.m., I am on my second grocery bag of candy and opening the door for scarier, older trick-or-treaters: glow-in-the-dark skeletons, bloody witches, and toothless zombies. Across the street, screams echo from the retired teacher's front porch.

"Careful of that house," I warn a werewolf. "It's a scary place."

"Awesome," the werewolf answers as he takes candy and runs into the night. Someone howls. More voices join in and then more—another silly tradition on the block, something like clinking silverware against a champagne glass at a wedding. Any time someone howls, everyone's expected to join. I let out a little baby howl.

A hulking figure walks toward my house. I recognize his gait immediately and consider shutting the door and hiding. But I have questions that only he can answer.

"I come bearing gifts." Liam holds up a little bakery box with red string as he closes the distance between us. He tells me he waited to make sure the kids weren't home before approaching. Add stalking and spying to my list of complaints. "Just five minutes," he says. "It's important." *It's always important when he wants something.* "I never got to tell you about Mia's alibi," he adds, giving me a half smile.

I step aside so he can enter. He walks into my hallway, filling the whole space.

"I need a drink . . . want something?" I say. He follows me to the kitchen, saying he wouldn't say no to a beer. He pulls out one of the kitchen stools, and I notice how rickety the three-legged blue wooden chair looks next to Liam's large frame. He sits down, the wood creaking under his weight.

I suddenly feel embarrassed by the papers and mail scattered on the butcher-block counter and fight the urge to straighten up. I get him a beer, me a glass of wine, and stand across from him.

"Your block goes all out for Halloween," he says, taking a long sip of beer.

"We have a good candy-to-walking ratio for this town."

He laughs. "Open the box." He gestures to the bakery box in front of me. "They used to be your favorite."

"When I was six?" I say.

"Just open it . . . I'm trying."

I pull off the red-and-white string and lift the cardboard lid. The smell of sugar and butter reaches my nostrils, and I hear my stomach grumble at the sight of the orange-frosted pumpkin cookies.

"They smell pretty good," I admit, picking up a cookie and taking a bite, savoring the vanilla and butter. "You used to get these from the bakery near the apartment, right?"

He smiles, a full-on grin. "Yes. Michelle's Bakery. It's still there. I live around the corner. A different building, though," he says, and I realize I know nothing about his life. I don't know what street he lives on, whether he's involved with someone, or anything. He gets up and walks to the refrigerator, where I have pictures in magnetic frames, and picks up the photo of Jackson, Nikki, and me from Great Adventure.

"Jackson looks so much like you," he says. "Your eyes are the same bright blue."

Like yours.

He puts the picture down and comes back to the kitchen counter, but remains standing. "I guess you want to know why I'm here." His tone turns serious. I nod my head. He tells me that the tech department finally fixed the security tape taken from outside the Robbins house. "They identified the car as Yvette's," he says, studying me.

"What time was the car at the house?" I ask.

"Why don't you seem surprised?" he asks.

I ignore his comment and ask again. "What time?"

"Yvette's car arrived at her house at one fifty and left at two oh two," he says.

"What time did Gene call nine one one?" I ask.

He shakes his head, clearly annoyed, but tells me the call came in at 2:26 p.m. I grab a piece of paper and pen and start writing.

1:50–2:02—Yvette (allegedly) at house
2:16—Gene leaves Joe's Pizza
2:26—911 call

I ask, "What did Gene do between the time he left Joe's and arrived at the mansion? It's only a five-minute drive. He had time to shoot Kurt and then pretend to find him." I tell Liam about the foreclosure notices I found.

"We already know about all that." He takes a sip of his beer. "The problem is Gene's car doesn't show up on the security footage until two twenty-four, two minutes before the nine one one call. So, it's more likely he found Kurt, performed CPR, and called nine one one. Don't forget, Yvette *lied* to us about going back to the house."

"You have to admit that Gene had time."

"It would have been tight. Really tight."

"I've been wondering about the security camera," I say to Liam as I bite into my second cookie. "Did the camera cover the west side of the lawn? Because someone could have parked down the block and gone around the back or something."

"Except they have that metal gate all around their property."

"But does the camera capture the west side of the lawn? You haven't answered the question."

"It's irrelevant."

"I'll take that as a no," I say, then ask him about Burke. He tells me the doorman at Burke's building never saw him leave and there's no sign of him coming or going on the building's security footage.

"What about Mia? What's her lame alibi?"

"You are obstinate." He shakes his head, not amused, and tells me that Mia was in the Bronx at the apartment she shares with her sister.

"I thought relatives weren't great alibis."

"We prefer people who aren't relatives. Neighbors also heard Mia and her sister in the apartment, apparently having a bit of a fight. And

Mia filed a story on the Comets website from the IP address at her house ten minutes before the murder."

"Couldn't her sister have filed it for her?"

"Give it a break, Kate. And watch your back. I'm worried your stubbornness is going to get you hurt." He gets up to go, and I follow him to the front door and pull it open.

The cold air rushes inside, but he remains standing in the doorway, seeming to debate something. "Kate," he finally speaks. "This is almost over. You know that, right?" He leans down to try and give me that awkward half hug, but I step away and shut the door before he has a chance.

CHAPTER 27

The block remains packed with kids as I leave for my shift at the Greenwich Lake Halloween dance. I dump all the remaining candy into three large bowls, place them on my porch, and get into my car.

Between the crush of trick-or-treaters and a light mist, navigating a departure proves tough. By the time I reach Greenwich Avenue, I'm already late for my shift. Of course, the lower lot by the school is completely full, including the illegal spot behind the dumpster. The mist thickens, and I turn on fog lights as I drive to the far lot behind the admissions building, where I find a spot next to a school van. As I turn my car off, I realize all the exterior lights back here are out. I turn on my phone's flashlight. The light beam diffuses in the mist, creating the illusion of lotion rubbed across a lens. It appears a figure looms beyond the bushes at the edge of the lot.

"Hello?" I say. No answer. *Probably my imagination,* I tell myself.

A gust of wind blows hair across my face, giving me a start. I tuck the strands behind my ears and pick up the pace. As I pass by the Roman columns of the admissions building, a shadow catches my attention—a darkness against the white column. Hesitantly, I move my flashlight from the pavement to the column. I reach up and feel something sticky on my fingers, like paint. Maroon or burnt red.

I raise the beam higher and hear myself scream.

Calm down, I tell myself, and force my eyes back onto the column. There's a rustling behind me. I turn quickly, the light on my phone skimming the brush behind the cars. The bush in the far corner sways, as if someone or something skittered past.

Turning back to the column, I study the red substance splattered over a photo of Dylan Robbins. The photo, which looks like a blown-up yearbook picture, based on the deliberate pose and forced smile, is tacked on the column of the building. Dylan's face is smeared with angry brushstrokes in what I *hope* is red paint. Even more disturbing than the vicious red defacement of the image are the words below: *Beware Dylan—you are next.* The word *next* is painted in large jagged letters.

I force myself to snap a picture with my phone. The image comes out blurry. *Steady,* I tell myself and try again. This time the picture is clear. I hear a noise behind me. My back tenses, and I stifle a scream. Don't look; just move. *Walk,* I tell myself, and set off on the path that leads to the gym.

As soon as my hands stop shaking, I dial Liam Murphy.

"He—o." His voice comes through in bits.

"It's Kate—there's a—um. A threat—picture . . ."

"Kate? Is—you?"

"Yes. Can you hear me?"

"Ka—I can't—"

I check the bars on my phone: just one. Damn. Deep breaths. This is probably just a twisted prank. The call goes dead. I pick up my pace; my boots click against the walkway and echo in the starless sky. I dial again.

"Kate." Liam sounds clearer. "Are you okay?"

"Can you hear me now?"

"Yes."

"I'm at Greenwich Lake School. Dylan. There's this picture . . . it's covered in paint or red something, I don't know. They're threatening her—it says she's next!" A car engine roars to life by the front of the gym. Headlights turn on, blinding me. I shield my eyes with my empty hand. Liam's voice is loud. "Speak up."

I push the phone tighter against my ear.

"Are you alone? Inside?" he asks.

"Right outside the school gym," I say.

"Are there people around?"

"Not out here, but inside—there's a party."

"Go inside. I'll stay on the phone till you're there."

I'm about to tell him he's being ridiculous, but I find myself relieved to have him on the other end of the line. The car in front of the gym revs its engine again and screeches onto the road, coming at me. I jump to the grass as the car zips close to the curb. My heart speeds up.

Liam yells, "Kate? Kate! *Kate?* Are you okay?"

The car screeches past and speeds away.

"I'm fine. Just a crazy driver." I look behind and see taillights disappear. "Probably kids." I reach the gym door. "I'm here."

"Go inside. I'll call the local police. Don't leave until I get back in touch, do you understand? Stay there."

I yank the door open to strobe lights bouncing off the ceiling and music screaming across the gym. I feel a flood of relief at all the bodies; sort of a safety in numbers thing. "Da—wait!" I yell into the phone. "I took a picture of the sign. I'll text it to you."

"You should have just gotten the hell out of there!"

"What about Dylan? She might not be safe."

"We'll send police over to the house right now."

He hangs up, and I look around. The relief I felt a second ago drains from my body with the realization that the perpetrator could be someone here. Is it the girl next to me, dressed as a dragon? Or that boy in the zombie costume? Hundreds of kids churn about, laughing and smiling. And one of them might very well be a killer.

I scan the gym for Nikki and Jackson. A large crowd of teens gyrates to music on the dance floor in the center of the gym. Orange and black strobe lights make it impossible to distinguish one teen from the other. I scan the fake cemetery, carnival games, and haunted maze. But the only figure I can distinguish is Frankenstein's monster looming over bundles of hay. I step toward the crowd, hoping for a better view.

"Kate." Christie stops me in my tracks. I would ignore her, but maybe she's seen the twins. She's waving me over to a table with black cloth and spider webbing. I step past a carnival-style cotton candy cart, where volunteers twirl spun sugar onto orange paper cones. Normally, I love cotton candy, but the overly sweet smell makes my stomach turn.

Christie wears a full princess outfit, yellow taffeta, sparkling tiara, and all. She looks a mix of regal and ridiculous with her hair matching the buttercup color of her dress, cheeks flushed and hazel eyes washed out under purple glitter eye shadow.

"Sorry I'm late."

"Very late." She studies my plain black leggings and sweater as I ask her if she's seen the twins. She tells me Nikki is on the dance floor and Jackson just swung by for cotton candy. Relief floods my body. My kids are safe. I debate grabbing them and leaving, but Liam said to stay put, and my gut says to listen to him. Besides, the sign is probably just some stupid Halloween prank. A stupid, awful prank.

Christie folds her arms over her chest and gives me the once-over. "No costume? And why is your hand red?"

I look down at my hand and realize the paint from the sign is all over my palm. Christie pulls a few wipes from her purse and hands them to me. "Where's your costume?"

I scrub the paint from my palm and tell her I'm dressed as a party pooper.

She doesn't laugh. "Here, put these on." She hands me a headband with little green spiral wires with googly eyes on the ends. It must be an attempt at a sci-fi creature. "Come on. For the kids."

"For the kids." I place the headband on, as if the kids care what I'm wearing. She consults a clipboard and tells me I'm assigned to the pumpkin pitch at the cauldron carnival games. She reaches into a jar and pulls out a ticket. "This is to vote for your favorite jack-o'-lantern. It's on the way to your spot. And remember, my stepdaughter, Madison, carved one of them."

I take the ticket and walk toward the jack-o'-lanterns displayed on black tables in the back of the gym. The innocuous orange vegetables from Sunday sneer up at me with hollow eyes, pointy teeth, and misshapen noses. I stop in front of Madison's ghoul, with its translucent skin and jeering scowl. Even without Christie's prompting, I would vote for Madison's creation. It's terrifying in a Tim Burton–movie way. I put my ticket in the jar and walk to the pumpkin pitch.

"Kate." Gloria peers at me with one surprised eye; the other is hidden by a black patch, part of a pirate costume, along with a fake sword and black hat with a feather stuck in it.

"Hi." I adjust my googly eyes.

She blushes. "I didn't know we were at the same station. I hope you don't mind. They asked me to help since so many parents canceled."

"Of course not." Gloria gets so uncomfortable whenever she does anything relating to the twins, as if she's an impostor because she's only a stepmom. Hell, has she met Christie?

"Have you seen the twins?"

"Yes. Nikki seems to be having a good time dancing." She points to the middle of the dance floor, where the strobes now pulsate yellow and blue. Nikki bounces to the music in a gold-sequined beret, gold jumpsuit, and funky silver sunglasses. "Is she dressed as a disco dancer?"

"Yeah. Believe it or not, that outfit is from my closet," I laugh. "Part of my metallic phase. Have you seen Jackson?"

"He's over there." She points to the bleachers. Jackson sits with two other boys, eating cotton candy. He's wearing one of those non-costume costumes: a black-and-red flannel shirt and a bandanna around his head. He could be a hiker or lumberjack, or something like that.

A phone rings, a low beeping tone from Gloria's bag, but she doesn't move.

"Sounds like you're getting a call."

"It's not my phone," she says. "It's Tyler's. I'm holding it for him."

I stare into her worn leather tote, lying open at our feet. Every muscle in my body tingles with the urge to grab Tyler's phone. It might tell me what was so critical that Tyler missed Dr. Michelson's appointment on Sunday. I know it's not necessarily important for me to know, but something feels fishy.

Gloria watches me. "Are you okay?"

I give her a smile and ask how the game works. She picks up the orange Hula-Hoops and explains that for each ticket, you get three tries. The more Hula-Hoops that land around a pumpkin, the bigger the stuffed animal prize. Two ghosts come over. I collect their tickets, and Gloria hands them the Hula-Hoops. They miss each time. I hand each of them small stuffed goblins anyway.

"Christie would be mad." Gloria smiles.

"Who cares?" I laugh, wanting to tell Gloria not to worry so much.

For the next half hour, a few stragglers wander over, but we clearly don't rate high for attractions. I keep hoping Gloria will run to the bathroom so I can fish around for Tyler's phone. I even buy her a large soda, hoping to help the process along.

Meanwhile, I haven't heard anything from Liam. I text him, asking for an update.

He doesn't respond. Part of me wonders if I should call Yvette and warn her myself about the threat against Dylan. I'm not even sure she'd answer. So far, she's ignored all my attempts to talk after I asked about Burke. And Liam promised to send police right over to the Robbins mansion. The music stops, the lights go dark, and screams fill the gym. I feel myself grab Gloria's arm. Is she laughing?

"Don't worry." She pats my hand. "They've been doing it all night. A bit of a fright for the kids."

I let go.

She giggles. "Now a scary voice will come on."

Just as Gloria predicted, a voice sounds across the loudspeaker.

"Doooon't fooorget tooo visit theeee haunted maze. We're going bat-ty here . . . ooooooohhhhhhh." There's a pause and then a piercing scream.

Gloria giggles again. "That's Tyler."

"Tyler? On the loudspeaker?"

She nods her head and explains that he put his voice through some app that makes it sound spooky. The strobe lights start flashing again, the music returns, and the kids start dancing.

"I thought he hates Halloween."

"He seems to be enjoying it this year." She points to the haunted maze, where Tyler stands in a full vampire costume, including red lipstick and black eye shadow. In all the years we were married, he hardly acknowledged the day. I ask Gloria if she'd mind if I go talk to Tyler.

I walk past the dance floor as the music slows and the lights change to a soft red. Groups of kids stream off the floor as couples sway to the song. Nikki stands with a curly-haired boy I don't recognize. It's hard to tell if they're friends or more since they remain about a foot apart, close but not *too* close. I approach Tyler, who stands at the far corner of the maze, hiding behind a mechanical skeleton. Each time someone passes by, he presses a gadget that makes the skeleton shake, and the kids scream.

"Tyler." He turns around, and I stare into his heavily made-up face. "I thought you hate Halloween?"

"I'm trying to be more involved," he says. "For the kids." That's the second time in the last hour I've heard that dressing up is *for the kids.* He could have just opted for a googly-eyed headband.

"Can we talk for a second?"

He looks around at the approaching teens, waits for them to get close, and presses the button, shooting the skeleton forward.

The girls squeal and run off. "What do you want now?"

"Do we need to talk here?"

"Yes. I have a job to do." He points to the skeleton.

I clear my throat. "Promise me you will go to Jackson's next appointment with Dr. Michelson."

He breathes in deeply and lets it out. "Seriously, Kate? That's what you want to talk about?"

"We missed the warning signs once. We need to do everything it takes now. We might not be so lucky again." I squeeze my eyes closed against the image of Jackson at the hospital, his heart flatlining.

Tyler frowns with his red reptilelike lips, exposing plastic fangs. "You act like I don't care about my own son. Something came up Sunday. I will be at the next appointment." He hits the button, and two boys jump.

"Just, please go Tuesday," I say.

"For God's sake, I will," he says and turns his back to me.

I return to the pumpkin pitch feeling anxious. *Something came up Sunday.* Those were Tyler's words. Evasive. Usually, he's very detailed with his explanations. It's just not sitting right with me.

Zeke approaches with Christie's stepdaughter, Madison. She wears the same googly eyes as mine but sports a matching green jumpsuit and green eye makeup.

"I like your costume," I say to her, eyeing Zeke as he puts his hand on Madison's back. I remember Nikki said Zeke showed up at Starbucks with Madison after the funeral. The last thing I want is to immerse myself in teen drama—but something strange seems afoot. "Zeke, how's Dylan holding up?"

His face turns beet red, and he tells me they didn't connect today. Madison jumps in, explaining to me that she and I are dressed as creatures from the cantina in the old *Star Wars* movie.

"I was wondering," I say.

Zeke tugs at his Nirvana T-shirt. "I'm a groupie."

"Ready to play?" Gloria returns and hands Madison three Hula-Hoops. She takes the hoops and swings the first one into the air, missing the front pumpkin. She tries again. Misses. Then she picks up the third hoop. This time the hoop ricochets off one pumpkin and lands over another.

"Yes!" Zeke pumps his fist. Madison screeches and grabs his arm. Gloria hands her a small stuffed goblin, and the two walk off laughing.

"Is that the boy who's dating Dylan Robbins?" Gloria asks.

"That's what I thought," I say.

"Hey, ladies." Christie appears in all her buttercup glory. "Can I borrow one of you to help me with the cotton candy machine?" She looks right at me, but I'm hoping Gloria will offer.

Gloria agrees and reaches for her bag. I offer to watch it for her. "It might get sticky over there."

"Oh, yes, thanks." Gloria walks off with Christie, leaving her bag with Tyler's phone at my feet.

CHAPTER 28

I watch Gloria cross through the papier-mâché tombstones to reach the cotton candy cart on the other side of the gym. Lucky for me, Gloria's purse is one of those totes without a zipper, making it easy for a thief—or ex-wife—to rummage through the contents. I crouch down, stick my hand into the bag, and feel around for a cell phone.

Two girls step over. "Can we play?"

I straighten up, thwarted in my mission, and hand the Hula-Hoops to a small, heavyset brunette who takes them, walks up to the line, and swings the Hula-Hoop back and forth but doesn't throw.

"Go ahead," her friend urges.

She puts one foot in front of the other and swings the hoop like she's pitching a softball. It lands around the middle pumpkin. "Yes!" She jumps up and down.

The other girl, slender with black hair, looks up from her phone, only mildly interested.

"Hey!" Tyler approaches out of nowhere. "Why are you jumpy?" he asks me, squinting his eye. I notice the vampire makeup cracking around the corners of his mouth.

"You startled me."

"Where's Gloria? She has my phone."

The two girls come over, pushing past Tyler. "Did we win anything?" the smaller one asks.

"You did." I grab a stuffed goblin and hand it to her. "Congrats."

"Where's Gloria?" Tyler asks again. "I thought she was working here."

"She went to help with the cotton candy. It's by the entrance."

He turns away and strides across the gym, his vampire cape bouncing behind him. My body tenses. I need to hurry. I plunge my hand into Gloria's bag and pull out two iPhones: one wrapped in a pink sparkly case, the other in a sleek silver one. I toss the pink phone back into Gloria's tote and try entering Tyler's birthday to unlock the other phone's screen.

"Hi, Mom." Nikki appears in front of me. I put the phone behind my back, but I think she saw. She's standing with the tall curly-haired boy she was with a little while ago. Nikki's face looks flushed. She hands me a ticket, and I point to the Hula-Hoops with my right hand, my left still behind my back. Nikki walks up to the line and throws her first Hula-Hoop, which hits the ridge of a lopsided pumpkin and bounces off.

I return my attention to the phone and try Nikki's birthday and then Jackson's. The screen remains locked. I glance up as Nikki tosses her second hoop. It hits the outside of a fat pumpkin and rolls toward the witches' toss.

"I'll get it." The boy walks over to the other carnival game.

Nikki approaches me and asks why I have her dad's phone behind my back.

"How did you know?" I ask.

"You're not as stealth as you think," she replies.

"I just need to check something."

She stares at me with her big hazel eyes. "And you say I'm nosy." Nikki laughs. "It's your birthday." She goes to take the hoop. Tyler used my birthday as his code?

Super strange. I punch the numbers 1204. The screen opens to a picture of Nikki and Jackson as toddlers. I open the phone app and scroll to Tyler's calls from Sunday. There are two. One at 2:01 p.m. and one at 2:05 p.m. Jackson's appointment with Dr. Michelson was for 2:30.

I hear Nikki giggle as I copy down the phone numbers from the two calls—both start with the local 203 area code. At the cotton candy machine, Tyler stands facing Gloria.

"We lost." Nikki walks over to the table. "This is Adison, by the way. We're in English together."

"Hi."

"Hi." He smiles, and I notice the freckles across his cheeks. I take one of the little stuffed goblins and hand it to Nikki. "For playing."

She smiles, and they walk away. I glance back at the cotton candy machine. No Tyler. He must be on his way here to get his phone. I scroll through his voice mails. Only the first caller left a message. I hit play. *Tyler, this is Kurt. I've changed my mind. Keep the ten mil in the investment. Will explain tomorrow.*

My breath catches. Kurt Robbins left Tyler a message just before the murder. Has Tyler told the police? I feel my heart race. Does this have to do with Kurt's death?

I look up and see Tyler by the dance floor, the green strobe lights casting a ghoulish hue over his skin. He's glaring at me. Does he know I'm listening to his message? I fumble in my pocket and take out my phone, hit record, and replay the voice mail from Kurt.

Tyler moves within yards of me, sweat on his neck, melting more of the vampire makeup. I feel something I've never felt around him: fear. I fumble with his phone, gripping it in my left hand and positioning my arm just above Gloria's bag.

"Why didn't you tell me Gloria's purse was here?" He pinches his lips into a frown.

"Hello to you too." I open my fingers and hope the phone falls inside Gloria's tote.

He folds his arms over his chest. "Can you please give me Gloria's bag?" He says each word slowly, as if speaking to a belligerent child.

I bend down and grab the strap of her bag. "Here you go."

Before he can look inside, the lights turn on and music stops. Another prank?

"Can I have everyone's attention, please?" The principal's nasal voice echoes through the gym.

I look toward the DJ booth and see Liam and Detective Bernard standing next to the principal. This is no prank.

CHAPTER 29

Everyone is instructed to quickly take seats on the bleachers. I squeeze next to Nikki and Jackson in the second-to-last row as Tyler joins Gloria in front of us.

"File in. File in." The principal's voice reverberates through the gym. Jackson lifts his arm, and I see cotton candy stuck to the black-and-red flannel sleeve. He seems nervous. Everyone does. A low buzz of speculation circulates through the gym. *Is someone hurt? Another murder? Does this have to do with the Robbins family?* Nikki pushes her silver sunglasses onto the top of her head to hold back her hair. A child's eyes filled with innocence and fear stare back at me.

"If we could have quiet, please." The microphone moans with feedback. "There's been an . . . *incident*." At the word *incident* the buzz gets louder. She says something about the police speaking to us, but most of her words get drowned out by anxious parents and students. I hardly recognize Detective Bernard, who looks like he's just rolled out of bed in a wrinkled sweater, jeans, and a Yankees baseball cap pulled down to his wire-rimmed glasses. I doubt he had time for face powder.

He takes the microphone and yells into the mic, causing a crackle that's painful to the ear but gets everyone's attention. After introducing himself, he explains that one or more *perpetrators* defaced a school building and made a serious threat against a student.

"It is important we determine whether this was an ill-advised prank or something more . . . sinister. If you are the responsible party, you must turn yourself in immediately. If you come forward, we will hand the problem over to the principal. If you don't come forward, it *will* be a police matter." He scans the bleachers, as if to suggest he possesses a superpower that can determine who among us is hiding information.

Nikki leans toward me, the gold material from her spandex jumpsuit moving with her. "There's the guy who was staring at us at the funeral." She points to the floor at the base of the bleachers, and reluctantly I look down at Liam, whose large body dwarfs Bernard. He's scanning the bleachers, probably searching for us. I glance away.

"I noticed him too. He looks familiar," Jackson says. I ignore them, pretending to give Bernard my undivided attention.

Tyler stands up and waves his hand, which makes his black cape bounce. "Excuse me."

Detective Bernard looks in Tyler's direction.

"I'm one of the parents here," Tyler states. I notice he's holding the plastic vampire teeth in his right hand. "Are our children in danger?"

"No one is in danger," Bernard says. "Trust me when I say that we are doing everything possible to protect them."

"Oh no," Nikki whispers. "Dad's going to go ballist—"

Before Nikki can finish, Tyler erupts. "Excuse me if your word isn't quite enough to comfort us. We *need* information." Scattered applause rises from the bleachers. Detective Bernard might be out of his league. A big part of me enjoys seeing Bernard squirm, even if it's at the hands of my ex. Especially because I now know he's responsible for falsely prosecuting an innocent man from Queens. And is probably preparing to do the same to Yvette.

Bernard coughs, stalling for time. "Parents. I appreciate that you have questions. I'm going to have to ask you to trust me. Trust *us*. The police have good reasons for not sharing the details of the situation."

Tyler's neck muscles tighten as his skin reddens in the spots no longer covered in makeup. "That's not acceptable. You need to tell us who the threat was made against. We can't feel comfortable any other way."

"You are being ridiculous," Bernard shouts.

Stunned silence follows. Then yelling. Everyone appears shocked by Detective Bernard's outburst. Even the principal looks astounded.

"I'm sorry for that," Bernard stammers. "What I mean is, we can't share any more information at this moment."

"Can't or won't?" Christie jumps up, her tiara toppling from her head and falling through a crack in the bleachers. "We have a right to know if our children are in danger."

Madison, who's seated near us, snorts at her stepmother's comment. The parents get louder.

I text Liam. You need to give the parents more information.

"We are doing—" Bernard tries again, but his words get drowned out by more angry parents. I watch Liam reach into the pocket of his jeans and pull out his phone. He reads the text and once again scans the bleachers. I continue to keep my body low. Frustration flickers across his face as he leans over and whispers into Bernard's ear. Bernard's body stiffens, but he surrenders the microphone.

Liam flashes his half smile as he takes the microphone. "Ladies and gentlemen, my name is Liam Murphy, and I am a detective with the NYPD assisting the Greenwich Police in some of their ongoing investigations." He specifically avoids mentioning the Robbins murder.

I watch my father and wonder if anyone will realize our connection. I took my stepfather's last name when I was a kid. But Tyler might recognize Murphy. Liam didn't come to our small wedding, but I did show Tyler some photos of Liam in his police uniform. Will Tyler connect the dots? I casually glance at him. Tyler's face gives nothing away.

Despite the pinball jitters racing through my body, I force myself to remain still. Liam continues speaking in his raspy voice. "We understand you're nervous. That's why we want to resolve this issue as quickly as possible. While I can't tell you the nature of the threat, what I can tell you is that I truly believe there is no reason for anyone here to be nervous. And that the threat was not made against anyone in this room. Unfortunately, that is all we can say at the moment."

There's something about Liam's manner that calms the crowd. Probably his authoritative air.

He keeps going. "We made sure there is a strong police presence outside. You have nothing to worry about walking to your cars. Please contact the police if you have any concerns. And we will do everything we can to provide an update tomorrow."

"This is bullshit," Tyler grumbles under his breath, but lets it go.

The principal takes the microphone back and thanks Liam before she announces that she will be dismissing the crowd by sections. "Please provide your names to the officers standing by the exits as you leave. Let's start with section . . ."

I tune out as she starts calling rows. A couple of janitors, along with some staff, enter the gym to break down the decorations. One crew walks to the haunted maze and hoists the giant Frankenstein's monster off the ground, with two women holding the feet and two holding the green head. On the other side of the gym, three male janitors start stacking the jack-o'-lanterns onto a large metal cart. The students and parents in the front sections clamber down the stairs to form two lines, winding all the way around the back wall to the exits.

"Kate." Tyler turns his sweaty face toward me. "Can you find out what's going on?"

"Me?"

Tyler folds his arms over his chest and suggests that I must have some connections to the police. Does he mean Liam? Nikki and Jackson look at me with new interest. The principal's voice interrupts, calling the next three sections.

A new group of students and parents scramble down the bleachers. Tyler raises his voice to be heard over the noise. "You must know someone." He leans his broad shoulders forward. "What about that Greenwich detective, Bernard. Didn't he interview you earlier this week?"

I search for malice in Tyler's face. Does he really wonder if I can ask Bernard, or is this about Liam? His narrow brown eyes don't give anything away.

"I doubt it," I tell Tyler, explaining Bernard was pretty rude to me when we *talked*.

Nikki exchanges a glance with Jackson, who slumps next to her.

"You don't usually give up so easily." Tyler raises a brow, hostility in his tone. But is there something else? How far would Tyler go if threatened? I reach my hand into my back pocket to make sure my phone is still there with the recording of Kurt's words.

Our section is called. Jackson stands, and we follow him down the bleacher stairs. Tyler and Gloria walk toward one line, and I pull Nikki and Jackson over to the other. In the center of the gym, by the papier-mâché tombstones, Liam catches my gaze. Our eyes meet for a second before I look away.

"Name?" a young female officer asks as we step up to the door.

"Kate Green. These are my kids, Jackson and Nikki Edison."

She scans her clipboard and checks off our names.

Outside, the damp, cold air cuts through my thin jacket. A beam of light flashes in our direction, and I raise my hand against the glare. I explain to the kids that my car is in the back lot.

Nikki wraps her arms around her chest as we trudge past three cop cars in the school driveway, their red siren lights casting shadows on the sidewalk.

At the crosswalk, most people veer off to the left and to the closer lot. An older officer at the intersection notices us and asks where we parked. I point to the back parking area by the admissions office. He offers to walk us to our car, an offer I gladly accept. We follow him along the path, Nikki's gold platform clogs clip-clopping against the ground.

Jackson stops at the admissions building. "Is this where—"

"Can't talk about it," the officer says. But it's obvious. Half a dozen forensic experts are busily working in the area where the poster hung just a short time ago.

"Is that blood?" Nikki gasps, pointing to the red stains on the closer column.

"Might just be paint," I suggest, knowing that what got on my hands was definitely not blood.

We reach my Beamer and thank the officer. To our right, another police team walks the perimeter of the bushes. They stop near the spot where I thought someone stood watching me. One investigator moves the beam of her light down, pointing to an area on the ground.

"In the car," I bark. The kids climb inside; I turn on the engine and put the car in drive, realizing my hands are trembling.

"Mom, it's going to be fine," Jackson says. "Don't worry."

"Shouldn't I be telling you that?"

I pull out of the spot and head home. On Greenwich Avenue, I brake at a walkway to let a young couple cross. They weave back and forth, like they've had a little too much alcohol.

"Tell me about that boy you were with." I look at Nikki in the rearview mirror.

She pulls her legs up on the seat and shrugs as I turn onto our cul-de-sac.

"Mom wants to know if he's your *boyfriend*."

Nikki's cheeks redden. "He's nice. He's on the soccer team. We're . . ." She doesn't finish her sentence. Her words morph into a scream as I slam on the brakes.

CHAPTER 30

I tell the kids to wait in the car as I get out and walk up the driveway. The smell of sulfur stings my nostrils. Rotten eggs drip from our windows, yellow globs streaking the glass.

But the worst sits under the large oak tree where I had hung the new shimmering ghosts. The heads bob from the branches—their bodies lie on the grass. Someone decapitated the ghosts. I feel an overwhelming sense of violation. And a little fear.

I lead the kids up the walkway and into the house, shutting and locking the front door. Jackson pulls open the curtain in the family room, and we examine the rest of the cul-de-sac to see if anyone else's homes got hit. Everything looks normal, from the blow-up ghost in front of the Puke House to our neighbor's lit-up pumpkins, still twinkling in the night. As awful as it sounds, I'd feel more comfortable if another house on the block showed signs of vandals. Could this incident be related to what just happened at the school?

I pick up my phone. *Do I call Liam? Detective Bernard? The rude Greenwich desk sergeant?*

Nikki watches, her face ashen. I dial the main number for the police. "Hi. My house has been egged and . . . well, vandalized." I'm aware that I'm rambling, but can't quite pull myself together.

"Ms. Green?" the female voice asks.

"Yes."

"It's Diane." I search my memory for a police officer I know named Diane, but nothing comes to mind. "Your *friendly* officer from the waiting room at the police station."

Just my luck, I'm talking to the condescending desk sergeant.

"You were hoping for someone else." She practically laughs, while assuring me I shouldn't worry. "First, is the damage only on the outside? Or does it look like anyone went inside?"

"I had put the house alarm on," I say, something I only started doing a week ago.

"Good," she says but urges me to check the rest of the house anyway while she remains on the line. I scan the wood-paneled family room. The embroidered chair faces the leather couch, the wooden coffee table between them. Everything looks in place. I motion for the kids to sit down in the family room as I step on the wooden planks, which creak below my feet, familiar but unnerving. "The kitchen also looks normal. Messy. But normal."

She tells me to check the bedrooms. I walk upstairs and do a sweep of the second floor. Nothing appears disturbed. She instructs me to lock all our windows and doors and turn on our alarm. "But don't worry," she says. "We've had a lot of vandalism this Halloween. More than usual. Kids egging homes and destroying decorations. Sounds like you got hit by the same thing." She tells me an officer will swing by as soon as possible—probably in the morning. "If you notice anything else, call me back. Okay?"

I thank her, hang up, and tell the kids that a lot of houses had similar vandalism. That doesn't seem to ease Nikki's fear. I suggest they get ready for bed and offer to bring them some hot chocolate, as chocolate tends to be my go-to beverage remedy for things.

Jackson extends a hand to his sister. She stands and follows him to the stairs. I smile at him and mouth a silent thank-you.

In the kitchen, I put the kettle on and double-check the kitchen windows are locked as I wait for the water to boil. I pour two packets of hot chocolate into cups, add a little milk, and then the hot water. I turn the house alarm back on and head upstairs with the steaming cups of cocoa. Just the smell of the sweet chocolate makes me feel a tiny bit better.

The light under Nikki's door is off. I put the mugs down and turn the handle, push the door open, and peek in. She's lying on her side and tells me she's going to skip the drink and try to fall asleep. I shut her door and go into Jackson's room. "Doing work?" I put the hot chocolate on the desk, next to where he sits.

He closes the screen of his laptop. "Nah." He picks up the mug. "Thanks for the cocoa."

I thank him for his help tonight and head to my room to get ready for bed. Jackson seems to have come such a long way—so calm tonight. Stepping up. Comforting his sister. I'm glad the attack didn't throw him.

Thinking about Jackson brings me back to Tyler's phone. Besides the call from Kurt at 2:01 p.m., there was a call at 2:05. The second call coincided with the time Tyler picked Jackson up for his appointment. I don't recognize the phone number, but it could have been a work call. The timing fits. I also didn't recognize the number Kurt called from. Another burner, perhaps? If it was a phone registered to Kurt, the police would have tracked it down by now. I make a mental note to look into the calls tomorrow.

In my dream, I see Mia Mars rest her strong back against the grand oak front door of the Robbins mansion. Is she waiting for someone? My fingers grasp the gold-tipped iron posts of the front gate. I shake to try and get in. Mia doesn't move, but I sense she hears me. Her lips turn up in a smile. She opens her mouth and bellows in laughter.

My hands squeeze into fists and bang the metal posts. "Let me in. Let me in." Adrenaline rushes through my veins. I hear a noise. A scream. When I look up, I see Yvette's face pressing against the glass of the third-floor arched window under the spire. She mouths, "Help me. Help me . . ."

"Mom," a soft voice beckons from afar. "Mom! Wake up." Between sleep and dream, I register Nikki and open my eyes, squinting to focus in the dark. She's shaking my arm, her oversize pink T-shirt hanging from her slender frame. "Wake up, Mom."

I flip on the nightstand lamp; yellow light floods the dark, attic-like bedroom. Something must be wrong if she's waking me while it's still dark outside.

I blink Nikki into focus. Her brows squeeze together as if trying to keep herself from crying. She tells me some people *claiming* to be the police are at the door. "That's what they said. I didn't let them in." She rubs her eyes with the back of her hands. "It's so early . . . and I was worried. Maybe they're pretending?"

I tell her she did the right thing as I jump out of bed and grab my sweatshirt and leggings. I tell her to go to her room. Her lip quivers. She doesn't move.

"Please, Nikki. Go to your room." My phone shows 5:45 a.m. I pull Liam's number up in case I need to quickly dial it, and walk downstairs, thumb hovering over the call button.

"Who's there?" I yell through the door.

"The Greenwich Police—it's me, the desk sergeant. Diane." I peek through the curtains and see the wrinkled face of the Greenwich Police desk sergeant. She smiles, creating even deeper craters in her ruddy skin. I put my phone down and open the door. She strides past me, and I'm surprised to see we're the same height. From behind her desk at the police station, she seemed smaller.

Another officer stands behind her, but Diane doesn't bother to introduce him.

I close the door against the cool dawn air. "Is this about the vandalism?"

The officer with Diane tells me that the *sarge* doesn't usually go out in the field these days. "But she insisted on coming here, seeing as you're friends and all."

I study his wide eyes for signs of sarcasm and don't find any.

"Well, I appreciate that. Do you want some coffee?"

My new best friend tells me she takes her coffee black, while her partner likes milk and sugar. Then they inform me that they will start looking around outside. In the kitchen, I put up the coffee as a suggestion of sun glimmers through the window, casting shadows across the room.

Nikki pads into the kitchen and sits on a stool, resting her elbows on the butcher-block island. I pour coffee for the officers and offer Nikki some. To my surprise, she says yes. "With lots of almond milk." She puts her head down into her arms, honey hair flowing over her.

I make her coffee and then head outside. Sergeant Diane and her companion stand by the oak tree, studying the beheaded ghosts' bodies on the ground. I hand them each a yellow-flowered mug. I can't take my eyes off the decapitated heads bouncing eerily from the branches.

"Did you see this?" Diane points to the bark of the tree with one hand, holding her coffee with the other. My breath catches. The feeling of being violated returns, mixed with something else. Anger. Terror. I stare at letters written across the upper trunk of the tree, just below where the branches jut out. Is that spray paint? Or blood? The first words are easy to decipher—*Stay away*. The next I can't make out. There's a *t* . . . an *h*; maybe an *e* or a *y*. And then a warning: *or suffer the consequences.*

What is wrong with people? The anger trumping fear.

Sarge Diane points to the unintelligible word. "It looks like the paint ran out on that word—the shade of red appears different than the following words."

"So, you do think it's paint and not . . . blood?"

"Too early to say for sure," Diane says as the other officer snaps a few photos of the graffiti. "But probably."

I look closer at the unreadable word. Is that *ther? Thy?* "The person spelled *consequences* wrong," I say, aware that's the least of the issues. "Did the other houses that were vandalized have writing like this?" I ask, but I already know the answer. This is connected to the attack on the school last night.

Diane and the other officer brush off my question and walk to look around the backyard.

I return to the kitchen, where Nikki and I sit in silence, sipping our drinks. Outside the window, the husband from the Puke House opens his door and starts cleaning up candy wrappers and bottles from the lawn. His wife appears on the porch, holding a mug.

"I hope they don't cancel the soccer game today," Nikki says out of the blue. "It's an important game."

"Quite the new interest in my sport." I attempt a smile as she makes a gagging face. I assume it would be better for the kids to be out of the house. And the school will surely have a large police presence after last night's threat.

Through the window, I watch the sergeant and her partner in our backyard. The wife from the Puke House motions her husband, pointing toward the action. He puts down the garbage bag and stares. Nikki stretches her slender arms over her head and yawns. I suggest that she go back to sleep.

"Yeah. I think the coffee made me tired."

"It must have been the warm almond milk that made you tired."

She shrugs and walks down the hall, her steps soft against the floor. Sarge Diane appears at my back door and tells me they're finished. I take their empty coffee cups and ask if they found anything else.

Diane holds up a plastic evidence bag with a can of spray paint. "Maybe we'll get some fingerprints."

She tells me they will be in touch. "In the meantime, keep your alarm on and the doors and windows locked."

As their car disappears, I pull out my phone and swipe to the picture of last night's graffiti at the school. *Beware Dylan—you are next.* I study the large jagged letters in the word *next*. There's no question the letters share the same spiky edges as the warning on my tree. The person who attacked the school is the same person who decapitated my ghosts and defaced my oak tree. But why go after us?

CHAPTER 31

I walk through my house, making sure every door and window is locked. Too amped up to go back to bed, I grab a bucket filled with warm, soapy water, a sponge, and head outside. The splattered egg comes off the windows easily, but the yolk on the siding proves more stubborn. I rub until my shoulders ache.

Inside the kitchen, I find Jackson dressed in jeans and a hoodie, taking eggs, milk, and butter out of the refrigerator. Nikki appears in the doorway, also in jeans and a thick sweater.

"I'm making eggs. Scrambled. Anyone want?" Jackson takes out the frying pan and places it on the stove top.

"Who are you? And what did you do with my son?"

"Ha ha." He cracks eggs into a bowl and starts whisking.

Nikki asks for eggs.

My stomach turns at the smell, and I opt for something small, putting a piece of bread in the toaster and taking out raspberry jam. Jackson places plates of scrambled eggs in front of himself and Nikki. I bring my toast to the counter, and we chomp in silence. Nikki finishes first and clears her plate.

"Jackson—have you heard anything about last night?" She turns on the sink.

"Only that they'll cancel the soccer game unless someone either turns themselves in or is caught." He picks up his plate.

"They didn't cancel yet. Maybe that means they have a suspect?" Nikki sounds more interested in going to the game than catching the perp. *Ah, puppy love.*

Jackson puts the milk away as we negotiate the rest of the day. They want to get a ride from friends, assuming the game doesn't get canceled. But I'm not even comfortable with letting them out of my sight. At the very least, I'd like to evaluate the school security myself. I insist on dropping them off but agree they can get a ride home. Reluctantly, they relent to my demand.

Still on edge, I shrug on my coat and head back outside to finish cleaning. Too sore to continue scrubbing the siding, I move on to the ghosts. The sparkly heads bob on the trees, their silent screams mournful as if they understand what happened to them. I cut the ravaged ghosts from the tree and throw the remnants into a garbage bag. My rage mixes with sadness as I bend to collect the fabric bodies scattered like dead leaves across the lawn. Sometimes people just suck.

As I finish, Nikki pokes her head from her window to tell me the game is on. I finish up, shower, pull on jeans and a black sweater, and meet the kids in the car. From one crime scene to another.

"If the game is on, that means they caught the vandals. Right?" I ask.

"It does. But no one knows who they are." Nikki stares at her phone, as if willing the information to appear.

"It's going to be cold watching the game," I say.

Nikki holds up a big duffel so I can see it in the rearview mirror, telling me they brought blankets. I remember playing in brisk weather like this. The cold wrapping around my legs, my breath frosty, fingers raw. All during warm-ups, I'd wonder how I was going to get my body to function, feeling like the Tin Man from *The Wizard of Oz.* Then the referee whistled the start of play. Muscle memory mixed with adrenaline took hold, and the chill evaporated.

Those were great days, I think, pulling onto the street. My smile fades as I catch Jackson staring at what's left of the eggs on our siding.

"Mom," Jackson says. "Maybe you shouldn't be home alone. You know, until they catch the people who did this to our house."

"You can go to Yve—" Nikki begins to say.

"Not Yvette's." Jackson turns on Nikki. "She's, like, the main suspect."

"God, Jackson. You sound like your father." I regret the words as soon as I say them. On so many levels, it's a terrible comparison to make for him. Tyler's been such a disappointment to Jackson. "I'm sorry. I just mean your dad said the same thing to me. About Yvette."

"Whatever," Jackson mumbles. My stomach turns. I hope I didn't send Jackson into a spiral. My words were so insensitive. Nikki tries to lighten the mood by suggesting I join them at the game.

"Nothing like Mom to cramp your style, Nikki." Jackson smiles, and I feel the knot loosen a tiny bit. I turn onto Greenwich Avenue and pass residents bundled up in down coats and pushing jogging strollers.

"Why don't you go to Starbucks or something," Nikki says. "Or go to Dad's house. It's not like he's dangerous."

"Just a bit of a jerk," Jackson adds. I hope Jackson is right about Tyler and that their father is *just* a jerk. After listening to the voice mail Kurt left on Tyler's phone, I'm not sure. The message itself seemed innocuous enough: *I've changed my mind,* Kurt had said. *Keep the ten mil in the investment.* Tyler is—was—Kurt's money manager. But the timing stinks. Within an hour of Kurt's murder. I glance into the rearview mirror and see Nikki, feet tucked under herself, staring out the window. She may belittle her dad, but she loves him. They both do. If Tyler did something *really* bad, it would shatter them.

I turn on the radio. "More trouble at the exclusive Greenwich private school where Kurt Robbins's daughter attends—"

Jackson changes the station, and hip-hop pounds through the car.

"I love this song," Nikki says and leans forward, and I smell her bubble gum lip gloss. "Turn it up."

On a regular day, I'd insist on my news station, but we can all do with a distraction this morning—even a loud one. Jackson turns up the volume as I take a right onto Lake Drive and stop at the line of cars by the gatehouse at the entrance of Greenwich Lake School.

I pull behind a sleek metallic sports car. Up front, police stand by the gate.

Nikki whispers something about Madison.

"She's been arrested. And Zeke!" Nikki hands her phone to Jackson. He gasps.

"Someone tell me what's going on, please," I say.

Jackson hands me the phone, and I stare at a photo of Madison and Zeke in handcuffs. Christie's stepdaughter was arrested with Zeke. I remember last night at the dance: they were hanging out together. But threatening Dylan? Where did that level of rage come from? Or did they just think that was *funny*? And why would they target my family? Unless the attack at my house really wasn't connected?

A car horn startles me. I inch forward.

Jackson turns to Nikki. "Zeke I can see. He and Dylan haven't been . . . you know, so tight lately. And he has a temper. He screamed at me one day, thought I was moving in on Dylan."

"Which you were," Nikki says.

"Whatever," Jackson says. "But Madison? She's like—like a—"

"Mouse," Nikki chimes in.

Madison may be like a mouse, I think to myself, but her stepmom resembles a lion. I almost feel sorry for Madison; whatever trouble she's in with the school or police will seem like a picnic compared to the hell Christie Orlow will unleash on the child.

The driver behind me honks. I inch up, then put the gear in park, and look again at the photo. Madison and Zeke stand side by side on the stairs of the police station. The streetlights are on, so they must have been arrested last night or very early this morning. That means my new friend Sarge Diane knew that suspects were already in custody. How very coy of her not to mention it. I study the picture further. Madison's head tilts up toward Zeke, who is being escorted by Detective Bernard. In the corner of the frame, with most of his body cut off, I recognize Liam's profile. I feel my blood boil. He should have told me about the arrest.

"This is crazy." Nikki leans back in her seat. "Dylan's dad is murdered, Madison and Zeke arrested, our house vandalized . . ." She freezes. Her eyes widen. "Do you think Madison and Zeke vandalized *our house?*"

"Why would they do that?" Jackson asks. Why, indeed?

The car in front moves forward. I quickly put my car in drive and step on the gas so the person behind me doesn't honk again. A police officer motions me to stop, walks over to my window, and asks for identification.

He looks inside. "Ms. Green."

I recognize the young officer's face but can't quite place it. He takes off his sunglasses, and I see the wide eyes of the young cop who stopped Yvette and me outside the mansion the night of Kurt's murder.

"From one good assignment to the next." I hand him my ID.

"Been a hell of a tough week." He signals to the officer at the gate as I comment on the large police presence. He tells me it's more for the parents than anything else—so they don't worry. "Safest place in Greenwich today. That's for sure."

As we pass the admissions building, I can't help but slow down. A tarp blankets the ground around the defaced column, and someone is already painting over the vandalism.

At the soccer field, Nikki leans forward and tells me again not to go home. I remind her and Jackson that I'm the parent—it's my job to worry about them, not the other way around. I watch Nikki and Jackson join the other kids walking toward the bleachers. Again,

I'm overcome with gratitude for the wonderful kids they have become. Despite their father.

Für Elise interrupts my thoughts, and I click the phone on. Liam's voice sounds through my speaker. "Your timing is good," I say, explaining the kids literally just got out of the car.

He tells me to turn around. Through the rear window, I see crowds of teens streaming into the stands and uniformed officers by the entrance to the field. "To your right," he tells me. Past the crowd, near the field house, stands Liam. He raises a gloved hand. "See me?"

I tell him that I do and remind him that his grandchildren still don't know about our relationship. "I'd like to be the one to share that information."

"Hopefully soon," he says. I don't answer but watch as Bernard huddles with the school principal and a few other staff members. Liam scolds me for not calling him last night about my decapitated ghosts.

"I called the police. I thought you would be tied up with the stuff at school."

"You should have called *me*." He keeps his tone steady, but anger seeps into his words. "I stationed an officer at your house."

"What?" I'm stunned.

He tells me it's just a precaution. It feels like an invasion. I ask if he thinks Zeke and Madison are responsible for what happened at my house. He feigns surprise when I mention their names. More games. "It's all over social media. Stop with the lying," I say.

He rubs his nose with his gloved thumb. "I didn't know it was public."

"It doesn't matter. You should have told me." I throw his words back at him.

"I need to go," he says. "Stuff is moving fast."

"What stuff?" All I get is a click. What does he mean? An arrest? A new suspect? I dial Liam back. He looks at his phone and sends my call to voice mail. What a jerk.

I try Yvette; hers also goes straight to voice mail. My head spins with different scenarios, all of them bad.

I pull away from the curb as a silver garbage truck rumbles down the road, turning into the parking lot and up to the dumpster. A fork-like metal arm reaches toward the dumpster, secures it, and then flips the metal bin into the air. Cardboard boxes, dark-green plastic bags, squashed pumpkins fly through the air and into the cargo box. I drive past the admissions building, where the painters shift the ladder to the back of the column. A first coat of paint obscures the graffiti, but doesn't completely hide it. I pass the gatehouse and turn onto Lake Drive.

I tell Siri to call Yvette's mobile again. The phone rings and rings. I cut it off before it hits voice mail. Next, I try her landline.

"Hello. Robbins residence."

"Betty? It's Kate."

She doesn't speak. Yvette must have told her about our fight. I don't care if Yvette doesn't want to see me. She needs me right now. "Can you tell Yvette that I'm going to swing by?" I ask.

"She's busy." Betty's tone sounds strained. I turn right and merge onto Greenwich Avenue, where a line of people, bundled up in navy and camel cashmere coats, stand outside the Greenwich Muffin Shop. Traffic slows.

"I can come later then," I say.

"Don't come at all." Betty clicks off. I'm shocked. Betty is always so sweet. I wonder what Yvette said to her. Or is her reaction about something completely different? I have a really bad feeling, but I will give Yvette a few hours. If I don't get a return call, I'll head over. Whether they want me there or not.

CHAPTER 32

Just as promised, a patrol car idles outside my house. Complete overkill. No doubt the rumor mill is already in full swing on my little cul-de-sac. First, the police this morning, and now a marked car parked on the street. I pull alongside the vehicle. The officer from this morning rolls down his window.

I stick out my head. "You should have told me about Zeke and Madison being arrested," I say.

"Sorry. Following orders." He shrugs. The idea of going inside my house suddenly feels oppressive. And there's someone I need a straight answer from. Now seems as good a time as any. I put my car in reverse as the officer asks me where I'm going.

"I forgot to stop at the grocery store." He scowls; it's obvious he doesn't believe me. What's he going to do? Charge me with pretending to buy cereal?

I head toward the southern part of Greenwich, where Tyler and Gloria live. It's time Tyler and I had a serious conversation. Halfway to Tyler's neighborhood, the landscape shifts from flat, grassy lawns to jagged inclines. In case visitors miss the transformation, the street names provide a not-so-subtle hint. Names like Mountain View, Peaks Lane, Hilltop, and my favorite, Summit, where Tyler resides. At Tyler's gate, I press the buzzer. Nothing. I try again. And again.

I examine the keypad. Could the code be my birthday, the same as on his phone? I try 1204 and wish the steel-and-iron-slatted panels apart. They remain shut. I try Nikki's birthday, Jackson's, and then Tyler's. The panels click and slide open, slowly revealing the steep charcoal pavers leading up to the house.

The modern rectangular glass-and-birchwood structure looks more LA than Greenwich, with sharp angles and floor-to-ceiling windows. I never much liked it, but today there's an upside to the design. I clearly spot Tyler through the window as he scurries up the stairs. A terrible house for hide-and-seek.

I ring the bell. And ring and ring. "Tyler, I know you're there. I saw you!" I shout, knocking on the glass. I ring. And knock. "I'm not leaving until we talk."

Tyler finally reappears in the hallway, pulling on a starched T-shirt. He tucks the shirt into ironed jeans, opens the door, and asks whether I've been waiting long.

"Are you kidding? You saw me through the window."

"I just got out of the shower." He opens the door and runs his hand through his short dyed hair to show me it's wet; so, therefore, he's right and I'm wrong. "What are you doing here?"

"We need to talk." I push past him and step onto the white bleached plank floors. "Do you have any coffee?" Without waiting for an answer, I stride through the open living room with its white-on-white furniture and into what I know to be the kitchen.

A half-full coffeepot rests on the sleek black counter. He's redone the kitchen. For the life of me, I can't figure out how to open the red lacquered cabinets that are missing handles.

He reaches over me and presses the cabinet, which swings open. He grabs a square glass mug and hands it to me. I step back to put a little distance between us and pour coffee into the cup, watching as steam rises over the rim. He takes down another cup, fills it with coffee, presses on a panel below the counter, and out pops a refrigerated drawer with milk.

He puts the milk back, bumps the drawer closed with his hip, and tells me to come into the living room. I follow him into the main room, where he sits on an oblong chaise in front of a floor-to-ceiling window and points for me to settle on the couch across from him. I drop onto the low, wide cushions, which feel more like cardboard or concrete.

"So?" Tyler rubs his chin. "What did I do now?"

"Where's Gloria?"

"At the grocery store." He crosses his legs. *Grocery store*—same excuse I just gave that officer.

"Well? What do you want?" His narrow eyes flash irritation.

I put the coffee mug on the bamboo-and-glass table between us.

"Is this about last night?" he asks. "I heard they caught the kids who spray-painted the school. Hard to believe Christie's daughter would do something like that. She's such a shy girl. That Zeke kid must have put her up to it. Wasn't he Dylan's boyfriend?"

"I'm not here about that. Or our kids." I stare into his hard eyes. "I know Kurt left you a voice mail right before he died."

Tyler's cheeks flush. "Excuse me?"

"I know Kurt Robbins left a voice mail on your phone. Right before he died. Tyler, did you—"

He slams his coffee cup down on the table with such force that liquid splashes over the rim. "Excuse me?" He stands, hands balled into tight fists at his side. "Did you go through my phone?"

"That's not the point. Why did Kurt leave you that message?"

He takes a step around the coffee table. And another, stopping right in front of me. Sometimes I forget how muscular Tyler is. As he's standing over me, I realize that despite my strength, he'd beat me in a fight. That is, if he could catch me. I force myself to stand too.

He leans down so his face is inches from mine. My pulse quickens. He keeps his voice low, but that doesn't disguise his disgust. "That's why you sent me on the wild-goose chase in search of my phone last night. You had it all along, but you wanted to stall me," he says.

"Why did Kurt leave you a voice mail just minutes before he died?"

"It *is* the point." His breath feels hot on my cheeks. "You spied on me."

His face turns even redder. He grits his teeth, lips tightening into a sneer. Every part of me wants to run, and I realize what a stupid mistake it was to come here, father of my children or not. Did he kill Kurt? I hadn't thought it could be true. Not really.

He raises his hand, and again I tell myself to run. But my feet fail me. The vein in his neck pulsates. I take a step backward. But Tyler does something that surprises me. He collapses onto the couch, his shoulders slumping over his frame. I'm shocked. What do I do? Make a quick getaway?

He puts his hands over his face and takes a deep breath; his shoulders rise, then fall. "What exactly do you think you heard?" Tyler whispers. "On the voice mail."

"I heard Kurt tell you to keep ten million dollars in his account."

Tyler takes his hands from his face but keeps his head down. "What's suspicious about that?" He looks up at me. "He was going to pull money out of his account and then decided against it."

I'm sensing the moment of danger has passed. I perch on the edge of the couch, far enough to make a getaway if I need to. "The call was right before he died."

"So?" His voice remains flat.

"If there was nothing to it, why didn't you tell the police?"

"Who says I didn't?"

"Did you?" I whisper.

Tyler gets up and walks to the floor-to-ceiling windows, staring at the woodlands at the edge of his property. The tall trees stand bare and gray, with naked limbs reaching upward.

"Did you tell the police about the voice mail?" I walk over to the window. He remains there, staring outside as he explains he didn't see the point in telling the cops because it had nothing to do with the murder.

I feel the cold through the glass, even though the room itself is warm. "Be honest," I say. "You didn't tell the police because you didn't want to become a suspect."

"Do you see the bulges on that tree?" He points to a thin, tall trunk on the edge of the woods. "Those are old wasps' nests. The insects are long gone, but the nests rot the tree, slowly killing it."

I stare at the bulging, mossy-brown growths on the bare limbs. Since when does Tyler know anything about nature?

"Will you always think the worst of me?" he asks. "My God, we were married."

I don't answer. He turns and looks at me. I meet his gaze, which is pained and hurt. "You want to know if I killed Kurt?"

"Yes."

"And you have no problem thinking it's me, even though all the evidence points to your BFF."

"You're twisting things, Tyler. There's a voice mail. And you didn't tell the police."

He shakes his head. "Why would I want to kill Kurt if he decided *not* to take money out of my fund? What's the motive?"

I don't answer.

"You think I held a gun to his head and forced him to make the call before I shot him dead. Is that it?"

"Did you?"

He doesn't answer, just turns his back toward me to look out the window once again.

"It wasn't him." A female voice interrupts from behind us. We both turn to stare at Gloria, whose usually sweet smile is pulled in a tight grimace.

"Gloria! When did you get here?" Tyler takes a step toward her.

"Don't come any closer!" She puts her hand up.

"Why?"

"Don't!" she growls. "Don't come near me." She moves her gaze from Tyler to me. "He didn't kill Kurt," she says with such disgust that it sounds like she almost wishes he had.

"What's behind your back?" I notice her other hand behind her. Nothing about what I'm seeing makes sense.

"Gloria?" I keep my voice even. "How do you know Tyler didn't—wasn't—involved with Kurt's murder?"

She pulls her hand forward, and I start to duck, scared she has a gun. I hear a thud. Gloria's thrown a thick manila envelope at us that's landed on the floor.

"Because he was screwing around when Kurt was shot," Gloria says. "And if he told the police about Kurt's call, he'd have to tell them his alibi is his mistress." Her features are twisted in anger. "I want you out of the house, Tyler. And don't forget that stupid prenup you made me sign. It's void if either of us cheats. And look who cheated." She storms out of the room and up the stairs.

"You signed a prenup promising not to cheat?" I say, bending down to pick up the envelope.

"I thought this time was different."

Across the top of the envelope are black letters spelling out *Greenwich Private Investigators*. I open the flap and pull out a stack of pictures. The first shows Tyler opening the door to a motel room, holding the hand of a woman whose back is to the camera. The time stamp shows 2:22 p.m., Sunday, October 25, the day of Kurt's murder. If Tyler checked in to a hotel at 2:22 p.m., he must have left immediately after he'd dropped off Jackson at the psychiatrist. I study the woman's image. There's something familiar about her frame. Or her hair. I can't place it. I pull out the next photo and hear my breath catch. He's having an affair with her?

CHAPTER 33

"Oh my God." I feel my jaw drop in shock. "How could you?"

He stares into his hands.

"With *her*?"

Tyler shrugs. "It just sort of happened. Christie and I bumped into each other at lunch. One thing led to another . . ."

I look back at the photo and see his arms wrapped around Christie Orlow's waist. She's smiling at him, their foreheads touching. *Christie Orlow.*

"Do the kids know?"

"Of course not!" he says. "I was careful."

"Clearly not as careful as you thought." I study the photos. "Was *she* careful? Does her stepdaughter know?"

"Madison?" He looks at me. "I can't imagine she knows."

But we're both thinking the same thing. It's out of character for shy Madison to vandalize school property. Did something send her over the edge? Like learning her stepmom was cheating on her dad? And all of a sudden it hits me, the word I couldn't read on our tree. It spelled—*Tyler. Stay away, Tyler, or suffer the consequences.* But why write it at my house and not here?

"I'll end it," Tyler says. "I promise."

"It's not me you need to make amends with." I stand up. "So, you didn't tell the police about the call from Kurt because you didn't want people to learn about the affair?"

He nods as everything clicks into place. The second call on Tyler's phone must have been from Christie. I pull out the next photo with an image of Tyler and Christie under the neon sign reading GREENWICH MOTEL, which is just down the street from Dr. Michelson's office. So, Tyler dropped off Jackson and then drove to the hotel. I think back to Sunday at Greenwich Lake School. Christie left shortly after Jackson— telling me a client wanted to see a house, unexpectedly.

Tyler keeps staring out the window. "Did you know I love the woods? Sometimes I go hiking out there. Especially this time of year, when it smells like pine and moss. We should have gone on some hikes."

He walks across the floor and sits down on the couch. I almost feel sorry for him. Almost. Tyler starts losing focus; his eyes are getting cloudy. But I need more information from him.

"Tyler, do you know why Kurt originally wanted ten million in cash?"

"I do," he says. "Kurt was renting a house near his home. He and Mia would . . . spend time. I think he planned to buy it. And just before he died, he changed his mind."

"Let me get this straight," I say, processing the information. "You're saying Kurt rented a home for him and Mia to meet at?"

He nods his head.

"And this home was near his and Yvette's mansion?"

Tyler nods again.

This information has profound implications. Right before Kurt got shot, he nixed buying a house for himself and Mia. That must have enraged Mia.

"If Kurt decided not to buy the house, it means he decided to stay with Yvette. You need to tell the police. That's extremely important."

He leans down and grabs his coffee cup, holding it between his thick fingers. "I considered that. But Kurt almost bought three houses over the past month. Then, another home on North Street. Then this one."

"Do you know the address of the house they were renting?"

He shakes his head *no*.

"You know more than you're telling me."

"Nothing for sure . . ."

"But?"

"He once asked me for a recommendation for a rental agent. And . . . well, I—"

"You recommended Christie."

He nods his head and takes a large gulp from his mug. The more I learn, the crazier and crazier this becomes. Kurt rented a *love nest* somewhere in Greenwich where he and Mia would meet. And they considered buying. Maybe Kurt did intend to leave Yvette? Although, if he canceled his plan the day of the murder, it appears he decided to stay with Yvette after all. Yet, the murder could have had nothing to do with a lover spurned, but drugs. Or money.

A crash on the floor above startles me. It sounds like a volcano erupted upstairs. I ask Tyler what he thinks Gloria is doing. Tyler turns his face toward me, mouth slack and eyelids drooping. "I think she's gathering my things to either pack in a suitcase or toss out the window."

"I never pegged Gloria as someone with a temper." I imagine the scene above the ceiling, an avalanche of ties and suits and watches.

"She's the most even-keeled person in the world," he says. "Until she's not. And then, well . . ." He motions to the ceiling. "Then she gives a tsunami a run for its money."

I ask Tyler what he plans to do. He takes another gulp from his square glass coffee cup and tells me he'll get a room at the Harbor Inn. "Unless you want to take me in?"

"Nice try." I stand and straighten my sweater. "Let me know where you end up, though."

He gives a tired smile. "Do I detect concern?"

"So the kids can reach you." I step around the couch in the direction of the front door. "Hey. One last question." He turns to face me.

"What phone did Kurt call you from? I didn't recognize the number," I say. "I assume it was a burner?"

"Yeah. He had a lot of them," he replies.

I remember Yvette mentioning the police confiscated burner phones from the mansion, but they must've missed this one. Otherwise, they would have already spoken to Tyler.

"You know you're going to have to talk to the police," I tell him.

He looks down at the scattered photos on the table. "No reason not to now." I watch as he stares at the photographic evidence of his lies and infidelity.

"There was no reason before," I say. Then walk out of the room and to my car.

Next stop, Yvette. I need to get to the bottom of what's going on with her and Betty.

CHAPTER 34

The inside of my car feels as cold as outside. I turn the key and shiver at the puff of cool air from the heater, waiting for the engine to warm up.

Through the wide glass windows of the house, I spot Gloria descending the stairs and striding toward the living room, her cashmere dress hugging her slender frame. She jabs the air with pointed fingers. Tyler remains still with his mouth closed. That seems to infuriate Gloria, who picks up the half-empty coffee cup, dangles it with one finger, the dark liquid dripping onto the white shag rug. Time slows as she lifts her arm, the glass cup behind her back, and hurls it at Tyler. The mug sails beyond his head and crashes against the window. It's like I'm watching a silent movie. I feel the tension without hearing the words.

Tyler bends to clean up as Gloria storms from the room. I put the gear in reverse and back down the driveway. At the bottom, I turn onto Summit and wind my way through the Greenwich hills and to the Robbinses' mansion.

I don't care what Betty said, I need to talk to Yvette, now.

Meanwhile, Liam needs to know about Tyler. "Siri—call Liam."

It goes to voice mail. "Hello. This is Detective Murphy of the NYPD. Please leave a message, and I'll get back to you a-sap."

"Hey—it's Kate. This is *really* important. My ex-husband has information about the case that changes everything. Call me right away. Or, better yet, go talk to him!"

The car in front stops short, and I slam on my brakes, screeching to a halt, inches from smashing into the other vehicle. My body snaps forward, then back. *Focus, Kate.* I ease off the brakes, eyes pinned to the road, as I instruct Siri to connect me with Christie Orlow.

Another call sent to voice mail. I leave her a stern message, saying we need to speak right away. Once again, I turn onto North Street, passing under the imposing oak trees, where only a scattering of autumn leaves still clings to the branches. On the right, I pass the Georgian colonial near Yvette's house. Gardeners, bundled up in scarves and wool hats, rake fallen foliage into bags.

I pull up to Yvette's mansion and stop at the closed wrought iron gate. The locked gate draws me back to this morning's dream: me, trying to get into Yvette's house as Mia Mars stands laughing from the front door. I glance toward the entrance, half expecting to see Mia Mars. No surprise—Mia isn't standing in the front, but what I see is equally disturbing. I enter the code and drive to the front, where Betty is scolding Yvette as Gene carries two large suitcases to his blue Mercedes.

I walk toward them, shivering against the bitter cold, my eyes trained on Betty and Yvette. Betty raises her hand and slaps Yvette across the face. I hear myself gasp and rush to Yvette as she crumples on the driveway, holding her red cheek. Her body shakes under the thin silk shirt.

"Yvette," I say, reaching for her.

She turns away from me, telling me to leave her alone. The front door slams as Dylan runs inside. I approach Gene and ask what's going on. He pushes past me and lifts the suitcases into the trunk.

"Gene?" I try again. He looks at me but doesn't utter a word.

"I'll tell you what's going on." Betty steps forward, her small frame hidden under a heavy tweed coat. "Yvette killed my son. My baby." Her voice cracks. "All these years, I've loved her like my own daughter, and then she kills my baby."

An animal-like cry erupts from Yvette. Betty turns to face Yvette, disgust in her eyes. "Like the scripture says, 'The Lord weighs the heart.'"

Gregory Robbins puts his large hands over his chest. He's bent at the waist, like a broken tree. He looks at his wife, confused and scared. Betty takes his arm and encourages him into the car. Gene opens the door as his mother and father slide into the back seat.

"Betty." I reach for her arm. "Surely, you can't think—"

She shakes me off. "Wake up. Wake up!"

The anger in her eyes clouds over with something else. Fear? Gene shuts the car door and turns to me. "Tell Yvette that Dylan can always stay with me," Gene says. "This has nothing to do with my niece."

He gets into the car and drives off. Yvette lets out a wail that echoes across the chilled air and through the trees. She remains on the ground, teeth chattering, lips blue. I open the front door and urge her inside. She refuses to move.

"You're freezing." I take her hands. "You need to get out of the cold."

I would pull her into the house, but I'm worried I'll hurt her. "Come inside. For Dylan. You won't be any good to her if you freeze to death."

"On the contrary. It could be the best thing for everyone," she says.

A gust of wind cuts through my leather jacket, sending icicle-like chills shooting through my torso. If I'm bundled up and freezing, Yvette must be near hypothermia. "If you won't come inside for yourself or Dylan, come inside for me. Because I'm about to freeze to death. And I'm not moving if you're not."

She looks at me with flat eyes, but finally steps into the house. I follow and close the thick wooden door against the cold. Under the yellow light of the grand crystal chandelier, Yvette's skin looks sallow. I ease her onto the ivory marble floor, aware she won't make it to a chair.

She grabs my hands. "I shouldn't have snapped at you about Mason Burke. I don't know why I did. Nothing was even going on. We're just friends. I mean, he might have a little crush on me. He did try to kiss me once, a week before Kurt died. But I made it clear we were just friends." She puts her hands over her face. "Although, I'll admit, the attention was nice. But I swear, nothing else happened."

Tears pour from her eyes. I pat her back as she heaves under the weight of despair.

I don't even care about Burke at this point. I mean, he's a horrible, lying jerk. But, whatever.

"Yvette," I say. "Don't give up. This will sort itself out." I think of the new evidence Tyler revealed. It gives Mia Mars an even stronger motive. The police *must* investigate it.

"What's the point? If Betty thinks I killed him, everyone will." She lowers her chin, tears dripping from her eyes.

"Look at me," I say. "What triggered Betty's reaction?"

She raises her face, and I see the handprint where Betty slapped her turning an angry reddish blue. She tells me the police plan to arrest her this afternoon. "I'm so tired, I could sleep for a week."

She sags against me. I urge her upstairs. She no longer fights me, and we walk slowly up the steps and across the lush crimson carpet into the immense bedroom she shared with Kurt. I escort Yvette across the muted beige carpet to the king-size bed with a tufted taupe headboard. I remove her shoes and tuck her under the cream duvet.

"Can you stay with me?" she murmurs as I pull the blanket over her. "I don't want to be alone."

I agree and walk to a velvet chaise longue by the far window and lower my body onto the cushions. I close my eyes and feel my fatigued muscles melt against soft fabric. *Don't fall asleep,* I tell myself. *Just a short rest. Five minutes.*

The sound of a siren startles me awake, and for a second, I'm not sure where I am. The siren fades in the distance, and the memory of resting on Yvette's chaise returns. I swing my legs to the floor and listen to Yvette's breathing—soft and even. This could be the last good rest she gets in a long time.

Carefully, I put one foot down on the carpet and then another. She doesn't move. I walk toward the door, think better of it, and turn around, my eyes landing on Kurt's wooden nightstand. The police clearly missed at least one burner phone—maybe I can find it.

I tiptoe across the carpet to his side of the bed, bend down, grab the handle of the top drawer, and pull. The drawer squeaks. Yvette turns over and mumbles. I freeze. She turns again. My legs cramp, but I maintain a squat position. Her breath settles. I pull the drawer again. It slides quietly open. I turn on the flashlight from my phone and peer inside. The contents prove highly disappointing: a few sports magazines, pens, and some matchboxes. It was silly to even look.

I close the drawer and start to leave when I spot the closet open on my left. Something draws me to it, and I step inside, close the door, and click the light on. The closet is double the size of my bedroom. Hell, it might be the size of my whole house. I could happily live in here.

I walk down the aisle of clothing. Yvette's silk blouses and wool pants hang on the right, while Kurt's suits, starched shirts, and khakis are on the left. I stop at the dressing area with large floor-to-ceiling mirrors and banks of drawers. I open one of Kurt's drawers and pull out a tray of cuff links. The next drawer contains perfectly folded white undershirts. The third drawer holds photos and mementos. I pick up an album labeled *High School* and sit on the chair at the dressing table, flipping through the first pages—action shots of Kurt playing basketball in a poorly lit cinder block gym with a packed crowd seated on wooden bleachers. Kurt's grinning. I turn the page and see a young Yvette smiling wide, Kurt's arm wrapped around her shoulder. They look so happy and carefree.

"Mom?" Dylan's voice echoes into the closet. "Mom?"

I shoot up, my foot kicking the edge of the chair. Did Dylan or Yvette hear?

"*Dylan,*" Yvette's voice whispers.

"Are you all right? Don't let Grandma upset you," Dylan says. "She'll come around. She's just confused."

Yvette scoffs and tells Dylan there are more important issues at hand. I hear her whispering with her daughter, but can't make out the words until I hear my name. Yvette says something about me being in the room. Dylan confirms I'm not.

"Yes, she is. Look on the chaise."

I feel silly hiding in the closet. But also, too tired to explain what I'm doing here. Outside the closet, soft steps approach. Dylan asks Yvette why the closet light is on.

I scan the room. My eyes stop on a mirrored panel. Is that a doorknob? I rush to it, turn the knob. The door clicks. I push it open and peek inside, hoping it leads anywhere but back into the bedroom. I hear Dylan's hand on the closet door. The door squeaks open.

I slide into the next room and find myself in Yvette's marbled bathroom. I flush the toilet and turn on the faucet. Next to the sink sits Yvette's bag. I look inside, finding a wallet, brush, makeup bag, and a pill bottle. It's OxyContin, prescribed to Yvette Robbins in the summer of this year. The strongest thing I've ever known Yvette to take is a glass of wine or an occasional sleeping pill. I put the bottle down and open the door that leads back into the bedroom.

Dylan turns to me with distrust in her eyes.

"You're awake," I say to Yvette, trying to act normal. As normal as things get when you're in a friend's bedroom minutes before she's about to be arrested for murder. Dylan folds her arms across her chest. Her head tilts in question, but I can't read her expression in the darkness.

"Why don't we let your mom sleep some more," I say and start toward the door. Dylan watches me, but doesn't move. Yvette always bragged that nothing got past Dylan. I hope that in this one instance, she's wrong.

Dylan follows me from Yvette's room and stops on the landing. She stares at me under her long lashes. She looks deep in thought, pulling at her cropped oatmeal sweater.

"Were you in my parents' closet?" she asks.

"Why would I be there?" I reply.

She studies me for what feels like minutes. I suggest we go downstairs. I ask her what happened with her grandparents, hoping to change the subject and figure out what got Betty so worked up.

"Gene said something to them. Then Grandma Betty went crazy—screaming and yelling," she says, tears sprouting from her eyes.

I suggest we get coffee. She follows me across the marble tiles and down the hallway with the family photos displayed on the sideboard. "I remember that day." She stops and points to the picture where she's on Kurt's shoulders, arms wrapped around his head. She tells me she had just turned six and Kurt bought her a shiny red two-wheeler for her birthday.

"Look at this picture." She picks up the wedding photo of Yvette and Kurt, both beaming, Yvette's smile bright and full, and tells me it's her favorite picture of them.

"You know, they really got along better than most people realized." Dylan puts the picture down. "My dad always said he loved my mom, no matter what. And I should never worry about what I read or saw—that he'd never leave her. He had promised." She turns to me. "That's why I don't believe the stories that he was leaving my mom for that person. She's awful, anyway."

"Have you ever met her?"

"I saw her once." She puts the wedding picture down and looks at me with pain in her eyes. "They didn't know I was home, but I saw her sneak into the house through the woods."

"Dylan, she *snuck* into your house?" I knew from the picture I discovered in Mia's office that she was inside the mansion, but it never occurred to me Mia didn't enter through the front door.

CHAPTER 35

I follow Dylan to the glass windows in the kitchen. The sunlight outside glimmers over the sizable infinity pool. The whole backyard looks like an ad for an exclusive Caribbean resort: teak decking, a spacious hot tub, woven wicker lounge chairs—more like outdoor beds—and a bar and cabana. Behind the pool sits a well-manicured tennis court that backs up against perfectly symmetrical pine trees.

Dylan points to the area past the court and explains that there's a spot where the fence is broken. "Zeke used to sneak across our neighbor's yard, and then climb through the opening." Her voice hitches. "Dad caught him once. He was so mad. I thought Dad fixed the fence. But he had Mia use it instead."

I stare outside where Dylan is gazing. I can make out some details of the fence, strong iron slats running vertically and horizontally.

"Did you tell the police about the broken fence?" I keep my voice soft.

"No." She hangs her head.

I put my hand on her back as I consider Dylan's revelation and all its implications. First and foremost, there was a way onto the Robbinses' estate that the police weren't aware of. That's huge. It increases the suspect pool immediately, answering the question of *how* someone could access the property.

They'd also have to *know* about the broken fence. I look at Dylan, trying to gauge how much I can push her. I want to know *when* she saw Mia Mars use it. And was she aware of anyone else sneaking onto the property?

Under my hand, I feel her shaking. "Let's sit down." I lead her to the stools at the kitchen island and offer to make coffee.

She slumps into the seat, like a rag doll, and rests her head on her hands. I walk to the Nespresso machine, pop one pod and then another into the compartment, and then listen to the familiar hiss of espresso and steam. I add milk to hers and carry the two white china mugs back to the counter. She wraps her hands around her cup but doesn't drink. Or speak.

I sit down on the hard metal stool next to her and stare outside. I wonder what is on the other side of these woods. Perhaps another home? Could it possibly be the rental that Mia and Kurt met at? The thought of that feels both logical and crazy. I check my phone to see if Christie called back yet. Nothing. I send her another text, stressing the urgency of our need to speak.

"You know, I had a big fight with my dad the night before he died." Dylan breaks the silence. She keeps her head down as she tells me Kurt died thinking she hated him. "That's what I said: 'I hate you.'"

"Oh, honey." I put my arm around her. "Every kid says that to their parents at some point."

Dylan slumps her body against my shoulder. I want to ask her why she was so angry with her father. But I sense if I push too hard, she'll clam up.

I keep my arm around her, staring outside, trying to visualize the woods behind the fence. Greenwich is known to have old hunting trails in the woods. Could one of those paths be behind the Robbinses' property? And where does it lead?

"I think my dad wanted a do-over," she mumbles. "He was going to leave us."

I turn to her, pulling her away and holding her shoulders so I can look into her eyes. "Why do you think your dad was going to leave?" I ask, keeping my voice even.

"I heard them," she says, rubbing her swollen lids.

"What do you mean?" I ask. "You heard who?"

Yvette? Mia?

Her lips tremble.

"Dylan," I stare into her eyes, trying hard to keep impatience from my voice. "It's important you tell me."

She sighs and gets up, walking to the sliding doors by the patio, arms folded across her chest. She mumbles something and points outside, but I can't hear.

I approach Dylan, standing very still, and ask her to repeat what she said. She opens her mouth to speak. I bend down so I can hear, when a loud angry buzz rings through the mansion.

CHAPTER 36

The buzz is accompanied by police sirens, so loud it sounds like every cop car in Greenwich is speeding down North Street.

The buzz, which turns out to be the intercom, rings again. Angry and loud. Dylan shows me the intercom. I tell her to call her mom's attorney. She nods her head like she understands but remains planted in front of me. I take her hands in mine.

"You can do this," I say. "Call the attorney. Get your mom. Now go. Fast."

She reaches into her jeans pocket, pulls out her cell, and walks away from the noise. I press the silver button, my mind still on my unfinished conversation with Dylan.

"Hello," I say distractedly into the intercom.

"This is Detective Bernard of the Greenwich Police Department. Please let us inside. We have a warrant for your arrest."

I steady myself. I need to focus on what's happening in this moment.

"Mrs. Robbins. Open the gate." Bernard's voice booms through the intercom.

I push down the button. "This is Yvette's friend, Kate Green. Yvette is calling her lawyer. We'd like to wait for her attorney's instructions before opening the gate."

Muffled sounds follow. Whispers and conversations that I can't make out.

"Ms. Green," Detective Bernard says. "Mrs. Robbins's attorney can meet her at the station. I must warn you that if you don't open the gate, we will break it down. You have one more minute."

Dylan runs up to me and throws the phone in my hand and then runs upstairs to be with Yvette.

I put the phone to my ear.

"Thirty seconds," Detective Bernard's voice warns.

"Is that the police in the background?" Yvette's attorney asks me over the phone.

"Yes," I tell her.

She tells me to let them in and to remind Yvette not to say anything until she gets to her at the police station.

I press the unlock button and look up the stairs to see if Yvette has woken up. I don't see any sign of her.

The police cars speed into the driveway, sirens screeching. Red and blue lights flash through the rotunda, making it feel like a dizzying disco. I stare through the glass as police car after police car arrives. Why so many vehicles? Do they think Yvette's going to make a run for it? Pull an O. J. Simpson? Officers get out, leaving their car lights blazing. Shouldn't the police have asked Yvette to voluntarily surrender? She would have done that. No need for a spectacle.

And then I spot the news vans just outside the gate. This whole performance is for the press. Of course. Another photo op for Detective Bernard. I'm furious. Where is his compassion? Or humanity? A knock bursts from outside of the door. Loud. Powerful. Detective Bernard announces himself and orders the door open.

I unlock the door and turn the handle. Before I can even pull the door open, bodies push through. Detective Bernard steps in front of me; clean shaven, hair gelled, dressed in a suit and tie. Face powder applied. Half a dozen officers surround him. "Where is Mrs. Robbins?"

"She's upstairs," I say.

He nods to a few officers. They rush the steps. I yell after them, urging that they be gentle—that her daughter is upstairs too. The officers reach the landing and disappear down the hallway.

I feel a hand on my arm and look up into Liam's unshaven face. "What are you doing here?" he asks.

I pull my arm away. "What are *you* doing here? Want to be part of the spectacle?"

He gives a tired half frown and asks if we can talk in private. Without waiting for my response, he starts down the hallway toward the kitchen. Behind me, I hear a female police officer yell from the top of the stairs that Yvette is getting changed.

"Five minutes. But no more," Detective Bernard barks.

Liam enters the kitchen and leans his heavy body against the counter.

"Guess you didn't get the memo about the photo op?" I say. Under his leather jacket, he's wearing a T-shirt. He grimaces but doesn't respond.

"Why are they putting her through this circus? She could have turned herself in, quietly."

"Wasn't my call," he says.

"Did you get my message? You should have called me back. There's at least one more burner phone out there. And you need to talk to my ex . . ."

Liam stops me midsentence, telling me all the evidence points to Yvette.

"But you're missing important new evidence. You need to speak with Tyler!"

Just then, Dylan runs into the room, eyes wild, and grabs my hand, pulling me back into the rotunda. Liam stops me as Dylan runs to Yvette, who is now flanked by two officers.

"They should have let Yvette turn herself in," Liam says. "I agree, this spectacle is wrong. That doesn't make Yvette Robbins less guilty.

This case has more evidence than almost any other I've investigated. And it all points to her. You need to let it go. For your sake."

"For my sake? You are ignoring important developments. Dylan just told me there's a hole in the gate where Mia would sneak . . ."

"Kate," he interrupts. "Just stop already."

I stare at him. This is the Liam I remember from my past—harsh, dismissive.

Fool me once. My brother's words return to me again.

Anger pulses through my veins. "Unlike you, I don't abandon people!"

He flinches.

"Help!" Dylan yells from the hallway. I bolt toward the front.

"Wait—please!" Dylan cries as Detective Bernard places silver handcuffs around Yvette's thin wrists.

"Mrs. Robbins," he says. "You have the right to remain silent. Anything you say can and will . . ."

Yvette stares beyond him, her eyes searching the air as if trying to spot a ghost. Her blouse hangs loose over wool pants. Her hair is neatly pulled back by a headband.

"You have the right to speak to an attorney," Bernard goes on, "and to have an attorney present during any questioning . . ."

Dylan squeezes my hand.

"Do you understand?" Detective Bernard asks. Yvette just nods her head.

"Let's go," Detective Bernard says. Police officers gather in front of and behind Bernard, as if lining up for a parade.

Liam pushes past the rear line. "One second, Peter." He leans down and whispers close to Bernard's ear, holding out his jacket. Bernard's face reddens. He shakes his head. Liam whispers again, continuing to hold out the jacket. Bernard relents, and Liam drapes the jacket over Yvette's wrists to cover the handcuffs, saving her a tiny bit of dignity.

My eyes find Liam, and I whisper, "Thank you."

"Open the door," Detective Bernard orders one of the officers. He leads Yvette forward. I step in front of the entrance. Bernard tells me to move aside. We've done this dance before—outside this house the evening Kurt was murdered, when Detective Bernard whisked Yvette away. I brace my legs and whisper to Yvette not to speak to anyone until the attorney arrives. Then, I feel someone grab my arm and yank me back.

"Let her go," Liam yells. Immediately, the officer releases me.

Outside, reporters holler from behind the gate:

"Yvette—over here!"

"What were his last words?"

"Why did you do it?"

Next to the reporters stand camera crews on ladders. With zoom lenses, no doubt, capturing a cruel portrait of Yvette.

Jacket covering handcuffs or not, the image will plague Yvette for the rest of her life.

CHAPTER 37

From the window, Dylan and I watch Bernard lead Yvette to the back seat of a marked vehicle. Bernard takes his time opening the door, milking his show for the media. Sirens blare. Lights flash. The vehicles proceed slowly out of the driveway onto North Street, like part of a parade.

"Who is the cop who put the jacket over Mom's handcuffs?" Dylan asks.

"It's a long story," I tell her.

She stares at me with swollen, red eyes. "Should we go to the station?"

"We won't be able to see her until tomorrow's arraignment. I'm sorry."

Dylan looks down at her toes, which are painted a hunter green. This poor girl—father murdered, mother arrested, uncle a jerk. I still have a lot of questions for Dylan, but at this moment, I need to get her out of the mansion and somewhere away from prying eyes. I instruct Dylan to pack a bag and tell her we'll go to my house. She pads up the stairs as my phone vibrates. It better be Christie.

The text is not from Christie but Nikki. Everytphing good. We won. Jackson and I going 2 celebrate w/team. Be home 4 dinner.

I respond with celebratory emojis before letting her know about Yvette's arrest and that Dylan will be staying with us tonight. Dylan calls from the hallway that she's ready. I put my phone away as Dylan lugs a Comets gym bag over one shoulder and tucks a daisy-print pillow under her arm.

As we get ready to leave, she drops her bag and pillow on the ground, runs down the hallway in pink high-tops, and returns with the wedding picture of her parents. She opens the gym bag and tucks it inside. I ask her if she wants to set the alarm. She shrugs.

"Do you usually use it?" I ask.

"Not really," she says. I tell her she should set it, just to be safe.

We walk quickly across the pavers to my car. I unlock her door and usher her inside. Wind whistles through the bare tree limbs as I walk around the other side and hop into the driver's seat.

"All right, let's get this over with." I put the gear in drive, press the gas, and pull up to the gate. The gates swing open. I turn onto North Street and hear the din of the generators that power the news trucks. Reporters swarm my car. I tell Dylan to keep her head down and not to make eye contact, no matter what.

A knock on my window startles me. I turn, ignoring my own advice, and see Cal Callahan motion for me to roll down my window. Instead, I honk and step on the gas, the reporters dispersing. God, what monsters.

"Holding up okay?" I look at Dylan. She nods, but doesn't speak. "You should probably avoid social media for a few days," I say.

We drive past the terra-cotta roofs and Palladian windows and onto Greenwich Avenue, where, even after 2:00, a late lunch crowd is still lining up in front of the creperie. A group of high school students waits on the sidewalk. I recognize some faces from Greenwich Lake. A few turn toward my car. Dylan slinks down in her seat.

A traffic officer blows his high-pitched whistle, forcing me to stop. Dressed in a bright-yellow vest, he holds one arm out at me, signaling that I remain stopped as he swings his other arm in circles for the teenagers to cross. They stroll past, whispering and pointing. One takes out their phone and snaps a picture. It takes all my restraint not to plow forward.

The traffic cop blows his whistle again and points for me to go. I drive, turn at the bottom of the Avenue, and wind my way onto my street.

"Why are the cops here?" Dylan's voice cracks as she stares with horror at the vehicle parked in front of my house.

I explain that the house was vandalized, and the police are being extra careful. "It's nothing to do with your mom," I say.

She nods her head, but I'm not sure she fully believes me. I pull into the driveway and turn off the engine. I usher Dylan up the walkway and into the house, settling her on my sofa. I sit next to her, prepared to finish our conversation from earlier. I take her hand. "I'm sorry to have to ask you some more questions right now. But it's important." I look into her eyes. "You understand that, right?"

She nods her head.

"You said you thought your dad was going to leave your mom because you heard them talking. Who was your dad talking to?"

She bites her lip and looks away from me. I stay very still even though I want to shake the information from her.

She looks back at me and whispers the word *Mia*. "I heard Mia tell my dad she was . . . pregnant." She spits the word *pregnant* out with disgust, her whole body shaking.

"Where were you?"

She explains she came down to the kitchen for a snack and stopped when she heard voices. "My dad must have thought I was out." She looks at her hands.

"Mia told Dad she was pregnant. I thought he'd be angry. But he was excited. He picked her up and spun her around."

Outside, I hear the Mister Softee truck coming down our street. He must be in his final week, as the weather is not conducive to ice cream anymore. If anything, we need a Mister Hot Chocolate truck.

I turn back to Dylan. "Did your dad *say* he was going to leave you and your mother? All I'm hearing is that he seemed happy about Mia's pregnancy."

"It's obvious," she says, as if I'm missing the clearest of facts. "I was a disappointment." She sniffs back tears. "He wanted a do-over with a good kid."

The minds of teens. I take her hand in both of mine, and she lifts her head to look at me. "Dylan," I say, staring into her watery eyes. "Your dad loved you unconditionally. That's just how parents are. Even if he and your mom divorced."

Dylan flinches at the mention of Yvette. I stare at her, but she avoids my eyes. "I need to ask you another question," I say. "When did Mia tell your father about the pregnancy?"

"A little over a week before his murder. But I didn't say anything to my dad until the night before he died. That's what I fought with him about that night." That's interesting. Yvette told me Dylan and Kurt fought about Zeke. Either Yvette didn't know the real reason her daughter and husband fought. Or she lied. Again.

Just then my phone rings, and I see it's Christie. I tell Dylan I need to take this call and that I will be right back.

"Christie?" I step into my hallway.

"Please . . . Madison didn't mean to vandalize . . ."

"I didn't reach out about that. We need to talk ASAP. I want to . . ."

There's yelling in the background. Probably her husband. "Not over the phone," she whispers.

"Fine." I instruct her to meet me at the Greenwich Diner in twenty minutes, and hang up.

I return to the family room, where Dylan is lying in a fetal position, eyes closed. I debate shaking her but decide to give her a few minutes. I go into the kitchen and pull out my laptop. Should I look at the news? With my finger hovering over Google, I stare out the window. My cul-de-sac sits quiet right now. Hints of Halloween remain on only a few of the houses. Ignoring my advice to Dylan, I type *Robbins murder* into the search bar and brace myself.

YVETTE ROBBINS CHARGED WITH MURDER

LOVE TRIANGLE TURNS DEADLY

WIFE SHOOTS KURT ROBBINS—"HE'S NOT LEAVING ME
FOR ANOTHER WOMAN."

The headlines are accompanied by photos of Detective Bernard walking a handcuffed Yvette into the police station. What a jerk! He removed Liam's jacket at the station to reveal the cuffs. Enough of this.

I type *Mia Mars* into the search bar. Scrolling through the sensational headlines, I stop at a blog on the Comets website called *Fan News*, by Mia Mars, with a profile picture of Mia, icy-blonde hair framing her face.

I browse those headlines too: COMETS BID FAREWELL TO THEIR STAR; COMETS SALUTE KURT ROBBINS; TEAM PLANS TO RETIRE KURT'S NUMBER. I go back further, to the day of the murder. Liam claimed Mia had posted an article right around the time of Kurt's murder.

Sure enough, a post pops up. Liam said the IP address showed Mia had written it from the apartment she shares with her sister in the Bronx, giving her even more of an alibi than just her sister's word. I read through the text.

> The Comets held a productive practice at the Greenwich Training Center. They were gearing up for their first week of the regular season. Star forward Kurt Robbins said he thinks the Comets are on track for another championship. Coach Seb ran the team through a bunch of drills . . .

I click on another article, this one from the day before the murder.

> The Comets predict another great season. Players ex-
> press excitement talking about the upcoming games.
> Mason Burke, the team's point guard, says this will be
> the most exciting season yet. "We have a great team . . ."

Something doesn't sit right with me, but I can't place it. I stand up,
fill a glass with water, and then sit back down.

Grudgingly, I must admit that Mia's a decent writer. Her stories are
snappy, rah-rah kind of pieces that fans love to read. I study the text
again from both articles before closing my computer. I need to wake
Dylan up. I need to get the answer to my last question, and I can't wait
any longer.

CHAPTER 38

"Dylan," I whisper. She remains curled up in a ball, facing the cushions on the couch. I put my hand on her shoulder and gently shake her. She turns toward me and pushes herself into an upright position.

I sit down next to her. "There's just one more question I need to ask you. Okay?"

She nods her head, nibbling at her lips.

"I know you confronted your father about the pregnancy. Did you tell your mother?"

Dylan's very quiet, which leads me to believe she did.

"Dylan, did you tell your mom that Mia was pregnant?" I ask again.

She nods her head.

"When?"

"She heard me and Dad fighting about it. The night before he died. That's when I told her."

"The night before he died?" I repeat, just to make sure. She nods her head. I squeeze her arm. "You did good. I need to go out and meet someone. Will you be all right?"

She nods again and curls back into the couch. I put on my leather coat and throw my bag over my arm, aware of how much new information I need to process. And that what I learned does not necessarily look good for Yvette. I'm about to leave when Dylan calls my name.

"I owe you an apology." She sits up and looks toward me. "I'm the one who gave Jackson the drugs." She starts to cry. "It's not an excuse, but Zeke kept pressuring me to . . . *help* him. Zeke even made me hide his stash, which I gave to Jackson because I was scared my dad would find it. That's why I searched Jackson's room." She lowers her head.

The image of Jackson in the hospital flashes through my brain, along with the utter terror I felt when I thought he might not survive. But he did survive, and Dylan needs my empathy. I give her a nod. "I appreciate your honesty," I say. "Zeke sounds like bad news."

"Yeah. My dad was right about that. It doesn't matter now. Zeke broke up with me," she says, sounding more sad than relieved.

"Are you sure you will be all right?" I say, having second thoughts about leaving.

"I'm sure," she says. "I'm going to take a nap. I'm feeling very tired." She turns on her side, and I cover her with the throw blanket.

The officer flags me down as I pull beside him. He's irritated and asks where I'm going.

"More cereal." I smile.

"What about the girl you came with? Isn't that Dylan Robbins?"

"It is."

He's about to say something else, but I pull away before he has the chance.

I turn toward the diner without even thinking, my mind replaying my conversation with Dylan and all the implications. Yvette knew about the pregnancy. Mia Mars snuck into the mansion the week before the murder and told Kurt she was pregnant. Yvette sent me to search for Mia's identity, but she clearly already knew who she was. I feel so angry at being played the fool.

Before I realize it, I'm at the Greenwich City Diner, the neon lights shining from atop the silver roof, illuminating the many empty spots in the lot at this postlunch and predinner hour. Inside, the place smells like coffee and french fries.

"Back for more pancakes?" Jo, the waitress from earlier in the week, walks up with a big smile plastered on her plump face. "That handsome boy of yours joining you again?"

I smile at her description of Jackson and tell her I'm meeting a woman with a blonde bob.

"Haven't seen anyone like that. Just Gus." She motions at a lone man perched on a stool, eating a piece of pie. "And a bunch of teens in the back. Sit anywhere you like while you wait."

I thank her and walk across the checkered floor and slide into a booth by the window. Above me hangs a poster of James Dean.

"Try today's muffin: banana chocolate chip. On the house." She puts down the pastry. I thank her and take a bite of the muffin, which tastes amazing. Jo nods knowingly and tells me she'll be back with a fresh pot of coffee. A bell sounds, and I see a middle-aged man lumber in. He rubs his hands together as he takes a seat at the counter.

Jo pours him a cup of coffee, and the two begin to chitchat. Above the counter, the flat-screen is tuned to the local News 12 station, where video shows cop cars arriving at the Greenwich police station. Detective Bernard appears from the passenger side of the car and opens the rear door. I avert my eyes, not wanting to see any more.

"I can't believe it was her." Jo sets coffee in front of me. "No milk or sugar, right?"

"Huh?"

"The coffee. You don't put anything in it?"

"Right," I say.

She looks at the screen. "That Yvette Robbins must be a coldhearted broad." Jo turns back to me. I'm about to defend Yvette, but I stop. I'm starting to wonder if I missed something. Was I so desperate for a friend in Greenwich that I overlooked warning signs?

Jo motions to the front door and says, "Is that lady your friend?"

I spot Christie, who's wearing a crazy outfit. She's sporting a rain-coat, large round sunglasses, and a scarf tied under her chin. Talk about a drama queen.

Christie sees me and moves quickly to the booth. She removes her sunglasses and scarf while explaining she doesn't want to see anyone right now. Her usually well-sprayed hair looks frizzy and unkempt. I might feel bad for her, except she cheated with Tyler. And her stepdaughter decapitated my sparkly ghosts and egged my house. Jo approaches us. Christie just orders coffee, and I request another muffin.

"What do you want . . . ," Christie says once Jo steps away. I wait to see what she'll say next. Some people hate silence so much they'll start talking just to fill the space. Christie strikes me as that kind of person.

"You know none of this was Madison's fault," Christie says, picking up her paper napkin and ripping a corner. "Zeke manipulated her."

"As much as I'm angry about Madison and Zeke," I say, "that's not why I asked you to meet."

She doesn't seem to hear me, continuing to explain that Madison spray-painted my house because she was mad about Christie's affair with Tyler. Christie keeps her head down as she talks. The door opens, and a young mother and two little girls step into the diner. The mother helps remove the girls' coats. Underneath, they wear matching pink ballerina costumes with tulle skirts. "If you don't press charges, they'll let Madison off with a lighter sentence," Christie goes on. "It may not seem like it, but I really do care about her."

So that's her angle. She doesn't want me to punish her stepdaughter. "Why my house and not Tyler's house?"

"I guess it wasn't just about Tyler . . . apparently Zeke and Jackson have had some—issues." She gazes into her coffee. "Besides—Tyler's house is a fortress . . . guess yours was the next best thing. But Madison only wrote the Tyler message. She swears she didn't do any of the other stuff."

"Like decapitating the ghosts?"

Christie flinches and insists Zeke is to blame. "He's bad news," she says.

Jo comes over to check on us. I wait till she's out of earshot before telling Christie that the police don't need me to press charges. She explains her lawyer says the police won't make a big deal of it if I don't. I take a sip of coffee and study Christie, who continues to rip her napkin into smaller and smaller pieces.

"I need to ask you something," I say. "Did you rent a house to Mia Mars or Kurt Robbins?"

"What does that have to do with Madison?" she asks.

"This has nothing to do with Madison. But you're asking me for my help. Now I want yours. Did you rent a house to Mia Mars or Kurt Robbins?"

"No. If I had, I would have told the police."

"Because you believe in being completely honest."

"That's not fair!" She leans back and folds her arms across her chest.

"Did you rent anyone a house near the Robbins mansion? Maybe within a mile radius or so?"

"There is one home," she says slowly. "But it wasn't to Kurt, or anyone associated with him. I rented it to a middle-aged woman."

"Had she offered to buy the home recently?" I ask, remembering the money Tyler mentioned. Kurt was going to take $10 million to buy a house but changed his mind right before the murder.

"Buy it? No."

"Are you sure? Maybe she didn't go through you?"

"I'm positive. The home belongs to a banker and her husband. They were in London for a two-year stint, but they are coming back. Can I go now?"

"What did the woman look like? The one who rented the house?"

"Middle aged. Tall," Christie says. "She had a beautiful voice, deep . . ."

"Oh my God," I say.

"What?" Christie looks confused.

I grab my cell phone and pull up the picture my friend sent of the newspaper staff from Sarah Lawrence. "Is this her?" I ask Christie, pointing at the tall woman with the frown. "Look closely. It's an old picture. But it's extremely important."

Christie takes the phone from me and stares at the screen. "Yes. It's definitely her." She hands me back the phone. "I never forget a face."

"That's Mia Mars's sister."

"Are you sure?" Christie asks. "Her last name was different . . . Smith or Stern, I believe."

"Whatever last name she used, it's definitely Mia's sister, Heather," I repeat, blood pounding through my body. "What's the address of that house?"

"I don't understand," she says.

"Tell me the address," I say, aware of the manic tone in my voice.

Christie rubs her hands together. I can't tell if she's thinking about whether she'll give me the answer or she's trying to remember it.

"Please," I say.

"It's—the house is on Chester Street," she says. "Twenty-five? No. No, it's twenty-three. Twenty-three Chester Street." She looks at me and frowns. "Kate, you aren't thinking of going to the house by yourself, are you?"

I don't want to lie, so I don't answer.

She stares at me, weighing her words. She picks up her coffee and then puts it back on the table without taking a sip. "Listen, about Tyler . . ."

"It's none of my business," I say.

"Let me finish. My marriage hasn't been great. And . . . well, Ty is sort of charming." Her cheeks redden. "What I'm trying to say is that I'm sorry if I hurt you or your kids or anything. I realize how much damage I did to Madison." Christie looks contrite. She opens her small clutch and pulls out a wallet.

"It's on me," I say.

She puts her wallet back and slides out of the booth. "Thanks, Kate. Please, think about what I said about Madison. She's a good girl."

"I'll think about it," I say.

She nods, gets up, and walks away. I immediately pick up my phone and google Chester Street, which is in the general direction of Yvette's mansion.

I widen the map and see that the streets are parallel to one another—which means that Mia could have cut through the woods to the broken gate behind the Robbinses' tennis court and snuck into Kurt's house without being caught on the security camera. It's a lot of ifs, but it's also a lot of coincidences. I don't trust Detective Bernard with this information, so I call Liam. The phone rings and rings. Then voice mail.

"Call me," I say and hang up. Would Liam even care at this point? He didn't seem interested in following up with Tyler. And now, even I'm wondering if pursuing Mia is a wild-goose chase. Maybe my judgment about Yvette has been off the whole time. I get up. Whatever the truth, I need to know. And I need to know—now.

CHAPTER 39

It's not even 4:00 p.m. and already starting to get dark. The GPS winds me around the traffic on the Post Road through dark side streets until I reach Yvette's street for the second time today. The naked branches of the large oak trees arch toward one another like limbs of skeletons holding hands.

Up ahead, traffic slows. The young police officer from this morning stands in the middle of the street, directing traffic around news vans parked in front of the iron fence protecting the Robbinses' mansion. I pull next to him and roll down my window.

He peers into the car. "No one's in the house," he says and motions with his chin toward the mansion.

"I'm heading to see someone on Chester Street," I say as nonchalantly as I can.

He waves me through without hesitation.

I wind past the media circus now transplanted back in front of Yvette's home. *What hate are they spewing now?* I wonder to myself, feeling a mix of sadness and anger. North Street widens as the lights from the media fade. A car behind me turns onto a side street. The last bit of sunlight disappears beyond the horizon, and darkness descends over my car. I flick on the brights and study my surroundings.

I've never journeyed this far down North Street. Unlike Yvette's section of the street, this area doesn't even hint at the hidden mansions; these estates rest far beyond walls and gates.

Turn right, my GPS directs. I turn and stop at two wide stone columns. A bronze-plated plaque reads PRIVATE COMMUNITY. RESIDENTS ONLY. I press the gas and continue forward. Once again, the neighborhood transforms. These mansions are traditional colonials, close to the road and within sight of one another.

Turn right onto Chester Street. Destination is half a mile on the right. I drive slowly down the road, reading the numbers on the mailboxes. Forty-three Chester Street is a large white colonial that's completely lit up. From the road, I see the television screen in the kitchen. I continue slowly down the street: 41, 39 . . . 25. And 23. My breath catches. I stare at the yellow house with flowerpots filled with orange mums set on either side of the front door.

A warm light shines from the entrance, but other than that, the house sits in darkness. I peer up the driveway and don't see any cars.

I back my car up and park in front of the white house, just in case someone shows up. I get out and wrap my arms around my chest against the cold. My breath fogs up in the icy air as I walk to number 23. A dog barks, making me start. I look into the window of the house across the street and see a white labradoodle in the window. *Jumpy much?*

I stop at the mailbox of number 23 and study the property. There's a wide blacktop driveway that leads to a two-car garage on the side of the house. In the back of the home, past a flat grass lawn, are thick pine trees. If there's a cut through, it would be beyond the pines. Along the perimeter of the property is a low white fence. I can follow the fence to the pines and search for a path. I decide against using my flashlight, so I don't draw any attention.

I walk over to the fence and place one hand on the slats and creep farther and farther from the road. I can hardly make out the lines of the deck at the far end of the back. And the wide, flat grass lawn looks like a pool of lava. A bird hoots above me, and I start. *Calm down. Calm down,* I tell myself again. The air grows colder. I realize my teeth are chattering. *One foot in front of the other.* The wooden fence feels damp and cold, but I maintain the connection even though the moisture is making the tips of my fingers throb. With each step, my boots sink a little deeper into the soft ground, creating a squishing sound.

I'm moving so slowly; I feel like each step takes an hour. The labradoodle barks. And barks. And barks. Will the neighbor come out and investigate? For a little fluffy dog, its bark is fierce and incessant. I inch toward the pines, ignoring the animal.

About ten steps from the edge of the trees, I turn on my flashlight and study the woods. The trees seem thick, almost impenetrable. I hear a crackle behind me and turn. A deer flits through the neighbor's yard. With the light pointed against the tree trunks, I step away from the fence and walk along the line of pine trees, searching for an opening. The thick smell of Christmas is fierce, too much of a good thing. At the edge of the trees, I spot a slight clearing. It's hardly a trail, more like a foot-wide gap between branches and pine needles.

I turn my body sideways, cover my eyes, and step into the thicket. Pine needles scratch my hands. I take another step and open my eyes. I hold up the light from my phone and examine the surroundings. On my left, the trees are thick and close together. I take a step forward, crunching down on brown pine needles. The trees on my right are maples or oaks. Their dead leaves, large like open palms, are scattered in piles around their trunks. I move toward the nearest trunk and shine my light across the ground. Straight ahead appears to be a dirt path, maybe two feet wide. It's covered in leaves, but they seem packed together as if stomped on by feet.

I step forward along the path. Is this the route that Mia took to visit Kurt—sneaking through the damp, dark woods to be with him? I imagine Mia, tall and slender, winding her way along this path. Maybe she saw it as an adventure. I bet Kurt did. Anything to raise the stakes—a man turned on by adrenaline. Affair after affair splattered all over the tabloids. Maybe that wasn't enough. Maybe he was looking for something more audacious, like housing his mistress behind his home.

There's a rustling behind me.

"Hello?" I say.

I hear thinness in my voice. Turning, I brace myself as if I'd just jumped into a *Friday the 13th* movie. I look right, then left, but I only see leaves swirling in the wind. I force my gaze forward and continue along the path of dead leaves, the smell of decay pungent. One foot in front of the other. A few yards ahead, the path widens and becomes more distinct, packed dirt and small rocks. This could be an old hunting trail.

Do I follow this new trail? The path below me seems to dead-end into it. I shine the light two feet in front of my ankles and make a slow circle to confirm there is no other option. An owl hoots overhead, and I look toward the sky. The branches are so thick, I can no longer spot the moon. I feel myself shiver, and it occurs to me that it might have been a bit foolhardy to come out here on my own. I check the service on my phone. Only one bar. Typical spotty Greenwich service. I try to dial Liam. The call doesn't go through.

An overwhelming surge of fear grips my body, and I want nothing more than to run to my car, drive home, and lock my doors.

I consider turning back, but Yvette's handcuffed figure flashes in my brain. I can't let her down. With new determination, I forge ahead, winding my way left, then right. A few hundred yards later, I emerge from the trees into a clearing with low brush. The smell of burning firewood wafts through the air, and I breathe it in. From the clearing, I can once again see a sliver of moon. I trudge over the decay and reach pine trees planted in a neat row, suggesting the work of a gardener. I squeeze past the uniform pines; a hum of conversation reaches me, low and without form, but definitely human.

I press my face against the slats of the tall fence. With the help of outside lights, I can make out the framework of a tennis court, pool, and cabana. There's no question this is Yvette and Kurt's home. I know this is what I was looking for—but now that I'm here, I can't believe it.

I take my phone out again. Now there are no bars. I turn on the camera and snap shots of the path and the fence.

The voices rise again from beyond the house. I can't see the journalists, but I'm sure they are the source of the noise—reporting from the street about Yvette's arrest. Part of me wants to run across the backyard and share my discovery. But there's a final piece to find—the break in the fence. I turn my attention back to the structure. There are tall, thick stakes and thin metal rods running horizontally about a foot from one another. The material looks so strong that I don't even think a sledgehammer could damage it. I walk along the back to the area behind the tennis court, where Dylan claimed there were loose rods.

I reach down to the bottom rod and shake it. Nothing. No give at all. I put my hand around the next rod and shake hard. It vibrates. I put my hand around the rod again, but this time move it side to side to see if there is any give. The rod squeaks and falls loose. I move the rod to the ground and try the one just above it. The same thing happens. The opening is too narrow for an adult. I try the third rod, and it comes loose. Now the opening is about three feet wide, definitely large enough for a thin person to get through.

This is it. This is what Mia did to visit Kurt! *And kill him?* The only issue is the IP address. She'd logged onto her computer, filing a story for the Comets right around when Kurt was killed. But couldn't her sister have sent the story?

There was something that bothered me about that writing, but I still can't put my finger on it. Something about the style. It was written differently from the other stories. I need to get back on the computer and reread the copy.

I put the top rod back, twisting it into the hole. I do the same with the second. I pick up the third rod and push it into the right post and then try to attach it to the left post. It falls out, clanks against the other slat, and bounces against a rock. Did someone hear? The only noise remains the voices from across the mansion. I catch my breath and step to the rock, where the rod landed. I reach down to get it and notice a piece of fabric caught between two rocks.

It's zebra patterned and appears thin and pointed, about an inch in length. I pick it up and freeze. I know this shoe. I wore mine just like it into the city this week. This must be from the matching pair Yvette bought when we were on our girls' trip. Silly zebra-patterned shoes. Mine are intact in my closet—so this heel clearly belongs to her.

I think back to the day of the murder: Yvette returned to the gym wearing sneakers. She never wore sneakers. A feeling of nausea overwhelms me, and I sit down on the rock. It must have been Yvette all along.

CHAPTER 40

I emerge on the other side and start to run across the yard, but stop, quickly stepping back into the shadows. Yellow light pours from the first-floor windows. I fight the urge to bolt across the lawn and instead force myself to walk along the edge of the fence, remaining in the cover of dark.

A bright outside light shines across the paved driveway, where a large suitcase sits next to a sedan. Have the owners returned from London? Or does the suitcase belong to Mia? I scan the area. No one is in the driveway, and I can't see the front of the house from my vantage point. If I run across the yard, I can hide at the back of the house. From there it's only about forty yards to the street. Once again, I scan the yard to confirm no one is visible. I take a deep breath and run onto the grass, my bag flapping against my hip. I'm halfway across the lawn when a figure steps onto the pavement. I stop. *Do I go backward or forward?*

A voice travels across the air—a velvety, deep voice I recognize as Heather Mars's. I leap forward, sprinting to the rear of the house, slamming into the cedar siding, the hard material cutting into my shoulder blades.

"This nightmare is almost over," Heather Mars says, her beautiful voice traveling through the air.

I see a flash of Mia's white-blonde hair. "Thank God they arrested her. I was getting nervous."

"The sooner we get out of here, the better," Heather says. "I can't believe how out of control—"

"Sh," Mia says. "We have to be careful." Mia looks around. "We're so close to getting away." I hear a grunt and a thud, which I assume is the suitcase getting loaded into the trunk.

I process Mia's last sentence. *We're so close to getting away.* It was them, all along. I was right about Yvette. I'm so relieved, I want to jump up and down for joy. But I will need proof. I reach into my pocket, take out my phone, and hit record.

"You really outdid yourself this time," Heather says, her voice filled with disgust.

"What choice did I have?" Mia says. "He promised to be there for me. He promised. And then at the last second, he changed his mind."

"You didn't have to shoot him," Heather snaps. *She said it.* I look down at my phone to confirm it's recording.

An engine starts, and a car door opens.

"I didn't mean it," Mia replies and opens the passenger-side door. "I just wanted to scare him. He laughed at me. And the gun was sitting right there. I didn't think it would go off so easily."

My phone still only shows one bar. I try Liam. It doesn't go through. Damn. As soon as Mia and Heather leave, I'll find Liam. Just one more second. I start toward the edge of the house, thinking they should be pulling out now. I realize my mistake immediately. Mia is out of the car and staring at me from the edge of the driveway.

She screams.

Run, I tell myself. *Run.* I make a wide circle around Mia, ready to sprint into the street, when, out of the corner of my eye, I glimpse Heather reversing her car right toward me. I'm fast but not fast enough to outrun a car. The back fender smashes into my hip. Pain explodes through my side as I feel my body fly through the air and slam onto concrete. My face ricochets against the ground. Pain shoots through my jaw. In my peripheral vision, I watch Mia's sister, Heather, step out of the car, and everything goes black.

My body is lifted, but I can't place where I am. I try to open an eye, but the throbbing in my head stops me.

"She heard us," Mia says. "What are we going to do?"

"I don't know." The velvety voice floats over me.

I feel my body hoisted into the air, then dumped onto a hard floor. Darkness swallows me. Pain pulsates through my flesh. The bouncing makes it worse. I feel around. There's something above me. I hear a car. Where's the car? It's loud. Is it getting closer? I'm thrown forward and back. A car isn't nearby. I am *in* the car. In the trunk. Hard metal smashes against my shoulder, and I realize I'm jammed against a suitcase. I reach my hand up. The trunk inches above. I sense myself panicking. *Calm down, Kate. Breathe.*

I force my eyes open despite the pain. It's completely dark. I reach into my pocket for my phone. It's not there. I grope around for my bag but can't find it. I hear Mia and Heather talking, but I can't make out their words. My mind flashes back to the Comets articles, and I realize what was off about the writing. The article filed on the day of Kurt's murder was in the past tense. All the rest were written in the present. It was a different style. And a different author. Heather must have written the one from last Sunday. The car swerves, and I'm thrown against the side, pain shooting through my back.

I feel a curved shape by my head. Space for the tire? There's a damp blanket or towel too. The liquid feels sticky. I bring the fabric closer. It smells of blood. My blood? I'm woozy and adrift. *Kate, stay in the moment. Stay focused.* The car jolts. My head knocks against the side, and pain shoots through my brain again. There's not enough air. I'm suffocating. I clench my hand into a fist and bang against the hood.

"She's awake." I hear Heather's beautiful voice. "What are we going to do?"

"Heather." Mia sounds calm. Too calm. "There's really no choice . . . she knows too much."

"I didn't sign up for this shit," Heather says. "Let me think . . . just let me think."

"Fine. But you know we don't have a choice," Mia says.

The weight of their words washes over me, replacing the pain I felt a second ago with terror. They are planning to kill me. Why did I go on this wild-goose chase? What was I thinking? What will happen to Jackson and Nikki? I feel tears on my cheeks. I need to do something. I start pounding on the trunk with my fist. Louder and louder.

"Shut her up," Heather yells.

"How?"

Their words are drowned out by a sound. A gong? No. A siren. Lots of sirens, getting louder and louder. The police. Are they here for me? But how could they have known? The car swerves. I smash against metal; something pierces my ribs. A crowbar. *Help. I'm in here,* I say. Or do I only think the words? Everything goes dark. I wake up to a shooting pain in my side. I reach for the spot to feel for blood. It's wet. Maybe my ribs? I take a breath, but there's no air. I'm aware that the car is stopped. How long have I been unconscious?

"Help. Help." I force my fingers into a fist and bang. And bang again.

"In here!" a voice yells. "Hold on, we're coming. Someone's in the trunk. Come on. Get it open."

The trunk opens, and a beam of light flashes in my eyes.

"Are you okay?" A police officer shines his light at me. I squint against the brightness. "We found her," he says over his shoulder. "Over here. Get a medic and a stretcher."

I hear steps. A medic. I'm loaded onto a stretcher. "Phone—my—"

"Don't speak," the medic says. "Save your strength."

My—phone—find it—I recorded her . . . listen to the recording.

"She keeps mumbling," one medic says. "Give her something to calm her down."

No. Wait. The phone.

I feel my body lifted into the ambulance, and a warm sensation washes over me.

CHAPTER 41

I open my eyes to bright lights. Beeping. Needles in my arm. I smell Lysol.

"She's awake." Jackson's voice calls through the fog. Nikki leans over, a small smile on her face. But her eyes are flooded with worry.

"Mom," she says. "You're in the hospital. Try not to move."

Too late. I attempt to shift as pain shoots through my right side. Nikki's talking again, something about my spleen and a rupture. An operation. Broken ribs.

"What . . ." The pain in my throat stops me from speaking more. "Wha—" I whisper, but that burns too.

Jackson's now on the other side of the bed.

"Don't move," he says. "There's a tube down your throat, so you can't really talk. Just rest."

I'm aware of someone else in the room. A nurse, I think. "Welcome back, Ms. Green," he says. "I'm just going to give you something to help you rest."

I want to tell him not to, but my mind goes fuzzy as I feel myself drifting off.

I hear beeping and feel something squeezing my arm. Am I still in the trunk? Did they bury me?

Open your eyes, Kate. Open your eyes.

"Wake up, Kate," a familiar raspy voice is saying from afar. "You're in the hospital. Everything is all right. You're having a bad dream."

I blink my eyes open and try to turn my head toward the voice; a piercing pain erupts in my head.

"Don't move. You still have a bad concussion. You need to rest."

"But—I—what happened with Mia?" I whisper against the burn in my throat. It hurts, but I think the tube is gone. I try to blink Liam into focus, but his image looks hazy. "Where are Jackson and Nikki?"

Liam tells me he's been stopping by before visiting hours to avoid any awkward situations with the kids and my mom and stepdad. *My mom and dad are here.* I feel that squeezing on my arm again. Liam says something about a blood pressure cuff.

"You're lucky to be alive," he says, and I sense anger in his voice.

"Everything hurts." I reach my hand down to my ribs.

"Not surprising." Did he laugh?

"Did you find the phone?" I manage.

"Yes. The medic told us you kept mumbling about a recording."

I wasn't sure if I'd said it or dreamed it. "How? How did you find me?" I mumble.

Liam rubs his face, and I notice the salt-and-pepper stubble on his chin and under his lip.

"Your friend Christie called the police."

"I don't understand," I say, trying to think why Christie, of all people, would call the police. I think back to my last conversation with her. We were at the Greenwich Diner, and she told me about the house she rented to Mia's sister on Chester Street. Christie told me not to go there. But how would she have known I wouldn't listen?

Liam must guess what I'm wondering because he explains that Christie tried to call me after we talked at the diner. "Christie told the police she tried you half a dozen times and every call went straight to voice mail."

"Bad cell service," I manage to say.

"She called Jackson and Nikki," Liam continues. "When no one could locate you, she had this feeling you might have gone to Chester Street." He sighs, and I hear the irritation in his voice.

"And?" I say.

"Christie drove to Chester Street, spotted your car parked there, and then when she couldn't find you, she called the police." He shakes his head. "She saved your life."

I run Liam's words around my brain. *Christie Orlow saved my life.*

A nurse comes through the door. He's wearing a colorful bandanna over his head and says something about how I need to rest.

"Feel better, Kate." Liam leans down and gives me a kiss on the forehead. "Next time," he says, "I'll listen."

CHAPTER 42

The sound of the television reaches my brain. I recognize the voice of TRP's main anchor. Is he here? I try to focus on his words.

"Amid great tragedy . . . Comets . . . first game tonight . . ." I force my eyes open. Yvette sits next to me, wearing a silk blouse and twisted pearl necklace. She's changed her hair; it's short auburn beach waves. Dylan is with her, holding a small orchid plant.

"Hi?" I whisper, the pain in my throat still intense.

"Stay still," Yvette says as Dylan brings me the flower.

"It's so pretty." I thank her and suggest she place it on the windowsill.

"You're free," I whisper.

"Thanks to you." Yvette smiles. "You saved me, Kate. The police arrested Mia Mars. Her sister, Heather, made a deal with the prosecutors. So, between that and your recording, Mia's going to pay for what she did to Kurt."

On the screen, someone sings "The Star-Spangled Banner."

"It's the memorial for Kurt," she tells me. "They're retiring his number before tonight's game."

"What day is it?"

"It's Thursday. You've been in the hospital for four days now."

"You're not at the game?"

"Dylan and I wanted to be here with you," she says. "We don't know how to thank you."

Dylan smiles and grips her mom's hand. "You saved my mom." She leans over and kisses me on the cheek. "Thank you."

"We're so grateful," Yvette says, and I see the light back in her copper eyes. On the television, the camera scans the crowd, a sea of fans wearing Comets blue. The camera zooms in on a group of young girls with the number 25 written on their cheeks. Their eyes full of tears.

"It looks like a beautiful ceremony," I whisper.

On screen, the stadium goes dark and thousands of flashlights turn on from the stands. The words to "Amazing Grace" rise in the arena.

"Knock, knock—lunch." A hospital aide appears at the door, brings a tray over, and places it on a small table. She adjusts the table toward me. "Let's try to sit you up a little." She presses a button; I hear a whirring sound and feel my upper body rise. Pain reverberates in my side, and I must make a noise, because the bed stops moving.

The nurse says she'll bring me more pain medication after lunch. "I'm afraid all you can eat right now are soft foods. Can I help you with this?"

"We can help her." Yvette smiles at the nurse.

I watch the nurse pad out of the room. Yvette pulls the lid off the applesauce and dips the spoon into it.

"I'm not hungry."

"At least try." Yvette spoons a little applesauce up and holds it to my lips. "Remember, you made us eat to keep up our strength." Dylan giggles, resting her hand on her mom's shoulder as Yvette continues to encourage me. "You need to build your strength now."

I swallow against the pain in my throat. "A few more bites," she says.

I force another spoonful down and study Dylan. Her face glows. Her big smile reminds me of Kurt's. Mia's confession must have freed Dylan of all her anguish and guilt. That and the knowledge her dad decided in the end not to leave.

Yvette lifts another serving of applesauce to my lips, but I push it away and tell her I'm tired.

"Then rest," Yvette says. "We'll stay here with you."

She sits back in the chair next to the bed as I feel myself drift off to sleep. In my dream, I'm back in the woods behind Yvette's mansion. I find the hole in the fence. But I find something else—Yvette's broken shoe. Why is it there? Now, I'm in the trunk of Mia's car.

Mia shot Kurt. She admits it. She's trying to escape. She wants to kill me. She's hitting me over the head . . . with the heel. Yvette's zebra-patterned heel.

Something is squeezing my arm. It hurts. It's buzzing. I open my eyes . . . and try to scream.

"Kate. Kate." Yvette leans over me. "Wake up."

"I—" My head throbs, and my abdomen burns. The pain around my arm releases. It was the blood pressure cuff again.

I look around the room. It's dark now, the only light coming from the hallway and the television. I focus on the screen; the game must be over because an old movie is playing.

"Was the rest of the ceremony nice?" I ask.

Yvette clicks the TV off. "It was fine."

I can see some of the medical staff at computers in the hallway.

"Were you having a nightmare?" Yvette says.

"Where's Dylan?" I look around the room.

"She went down to the cafeteria to get a snack," Yvette says.

"I found your zebra-patterned heel in the woods by the gate," I whisper. "You went back to the mansion a second time, didn't you?"

Yvette folds her arms over her chest. The beeping from the EKG fills the room. "Yvette." I put my hands on the bed rails and try to sit up. Pain thwarts my attempt. "Did you go back a second time?"

Yvette walks over to the window and pulls the shade down, then turns to face me. "I wasn't planning to." She leans against the windowsill.

"Kurt rushed me out of the house so quickly. I had this feeling in my gut that his mistress was coming over to the house again. *My* house. She'd been there the week before. Well, you know that. Dylan told you.

"I drove the car down the block and sat there. Then I remembered Zeke used to sneak into our house by cutting across our neighbor's yard and climbing through the loose slats in the fence."

There's something about Yvette's manner that's unnerving—so matter of fact and devoid of emotion. Her voice is flat as she speaks. "I just needed to know," she continues.

Yvette walks away from the window, her heels clip-clopping as she approaches the bed. She puts her tote on the foot of the mattress, bouncing the blanket, which feels like a gut punch. Yvette either doesn't notice or doesn't care.

"Why didn't the neighbor's security footage show you?"

"The camera must not have extended to the west lawn." She shrugs. "I got lucky."

The blood pressure cuff squeezes my arm and then hisses as it releases. "Did you see Mia shoot him?" I ask.

She shakes her head. "I had no idea who killed him. You're the one who discovered that."

"What did you see?" I whisper.

"By the time I got there, I saw Kurt on the ground. I was confused. I thought he had a heart attack."

"Was he dead?" I ask.

The beeping of the EKG sounds so loud that I wonder if Yvette answered and I didn't hear her. Or maybe she didn't hear me. I try again. "Yvette, was he dead when you went back?"

Slowly, she turns to face me, leaning her head close to mine. Her eyes fierce.

"I went inside. He called to me to help. I froze. There was a pool of blood under him. He raised his hand toward me. *'Yvette,'* he said, relief flooding his face. But my feet wouldn't move. I was in shock. I just stared at him."

She pauses, looking off into the distance. "He looked confused. Then scared. I'd never seen him scared."

The coldness breaks, and I see sadness cross her face. Real or staged?

"Don't you see?" she continues, staring down at me. "I put up with the hurt and humiliation, but this time Kurt went too far. He planned to break our agreement. Dylan told me Kurt was going to leave me. Leave *us*." Yvette searches my face for understanding. "After everything I put up with, I only asked one thing of him—to stay."

Her lips tighten into a frown, maybe not finding the sympathy in my expression that she wanted. She turns her back to me and steps to the foot of the bed, picking up her bag and causing the mattress to bounce a second time. I wince against the pain.

She stands a few feet away, her arms folded across her chest.

"Kate," she says, her voice pleading. "The world gave me a way out. Don't you see—it was handed to me on a silver platter. If I just walked away, I'd be the widow and not the ex-wife. In that moment, I took it and ran."

"Yvette," I whisper, trying to square the coldhearted woman before me with the person I considered my best friend. "You know he decided to stay."

"Yes," she sighs. "Every time I look at Dylan, I remember that."

She takes a step toward me, and I feel myself flinch. She leans down, and I smell her floral perfume. "Kate," she whispers. "You're supposed to be my friend. At least keep it to yourself. If not for me, then for Dylan."

As if on cue, Dylan appears in the doorway. She's carrying a soda and smiling. And in that moment, I realize as much as I will want to report Yvette, I won't say anything. I can't.

———

Sunday comes, and I still can't get over what Yvette told me. The woman I considered my best friend let her husband die. A person she could have saved. How could I have been friends with Yvette for so long? Trusted her? I keep racking my brain for signs of this side of Yvette and realize there were moments I missed.

The most vivid was two years ago, during game seven of the Comets Eastern Conference Championship against Miami. I came over to her house to watch the game on television. I was already feeling sour that someone else had gotten the assignment.

The Comets were up two points with sixty seconds to go when Miami's center body-slammed Kurt. The hit was hard, and Kurt fell headfirst against the hardwood. The impact reverberated over the television. It was one of those awful moments in sports when everyone knows the injury is bad. It's just a matter of whether the player survives.

I got up and went to sit next to Yvette, holding her hand. She stayed very still, features not moving. At the time, I thought how stoic and strong she was. Now I believe her reaction was cold and unfeeling. The memory makes me shiver.

The nurse comes in carrying a large bouquet of flowers. Since Yvette's confession, she has sent a bouquet every day with the same message.

Friendship is forgiveness.

And every day I instruct the nurse to take the flowers to the children's ward. I may have misread her in the past. But I will never forgive her, even if she sends every single flower in the world.

"Before you tell me to take them away"—the nurse brings the flowers to me—"these are from someone else . . . a David Lopez."

"Really?" I take the card from the nurse as she puts the two dozen pink roses on the windowsill. I open the card and stare at the message.

Dear Kate,
    Wishing you a speedy recovery.

    P.S. I feel as if so much has gone unsaid between us. I never meant to give you the impression I was uninterested. I was trying to be a gentleman. Please forgive me and agree to let me take you to dinner when you feel better.
    David

I reread the card. David *is* interested. God knows, my people-reading radar is seriously out of whack. I fold up the card and decide, what the hell, maybe I will say yes. What's a dinner? And, if nothing else, Nikki will be happy to see me get out there. God knows, I could use a little normalcy in my life. Not to mention, a good meal.

CHAPTER 43

It's the day before I can leave the hospital, and I'm trying to focus on getting better. I'm receiving a lot of attention from the staff now that I've been moved into a private VIP suite on the upper level of the hospital. Yvette's flowers still arrive every day, but the nurses send them straight to the children's ward.

Shocker of shockers, TRP insisted on paying for the room. Not only that, but Charlie also offered me my job back. When I'm feeling better. *No rush. Take all the time you need to heal,* he said. The offer didn't come out of kindness or concern. Since my near-death experience, my stock has skyrocketed in the press. These days, even the *NY Post* sings my praises. *Soccer star turned hero.* Or something like that.

Live and die by the news cycle. But I'm not complaining. I'll be happy to return to work. Now more than ever, I need a distraction. And what's even better, I won't need to apologize to Burke again. Hell, it was almost worth dying just to avoid that.

I pack up the few belongings I have accumulated. A bathrobe. Sweats. A picture of Jackson and Nikki. The kids have been great. They visit me every day. At first, they were shaken, understandably. But now that I'm on the mend, they seem good. Nikki says Tyler is even tolerable, although she hates staying at the hotel he's moved into. It appears

Gloria will not take him back, so Tyler is looking at divorce number three.

It's wonderful to listen to Jackson. The sparkle has returned to his eyes, and he goes on and on about a creative writing class he's enjoying.

"I heard someone got cleared to go home in the morning." Liam pops his head in and flashes his half smile. He's also been visiting every day, and he makes a point to swing by when he knows the twins are busy. I haven't told him yet, but I think it's time Liam meets his grandkids.

Today, he's brought me a treat from Michelle's Bakery. I pull off the red-and-white string and open the box to find frosted sugar cookies. "These are so good," I say as I devour one.

Liam sits in the chair next to me and tells me about his newest case. We've found an easy rhythm over the last few weeks.

"You still seem troubled." He gives his half frown, studying me.

"I can't stop thinking about Kurt's last moments and the fact that Yvette could have saved him." I look down at my hands.

"Don't beat yourself up. It happens to the best of us," he says. "Have you given more thought to whether you want to go to the police? At the very least, she is guilty of obstruction of justice."

I lean back in the hospital bed and sigh. "I really want to go to the police. I don't want her to get away with it."

"But . . ." He tilts his head, and I can see he already knows what I'm going to say.

"But . . . if I report Yvette, then Dylan will know that she is the reason her father is dead."

"Because if Dylan hadn't told Yvette about the baby and her belief that her dad was leaving, then Yvette wouldn't have let Kurt die."

"Exactly." I hang my head. "I just can't do that to Dylan. As much as Yvette disgusts me."

Liam takes my hand and holds it in both of his. I raise my chin to look at him. "Kate, you are making the right decision. You are protecting Dylan. Sometimes we make tough decisions to protect our children." He lets my hand drop, stands up, and walks to the window.

"I guess. I mean, yes, there's really no choice." I look past him, out the window at the trees, which have now lost all their leaves and stand naked in the chill.

He returns to his seat, fidgety to the last.

"I also can't get over how badly I misread Yvette. How stupid I was."

"Like I've been telling you, it happens to the best of us," Liam says, giving me a sad half smile. "It happened to me and cost me dearly."

I study him and wonder what he means.

Liam sighs. "Next time, you'll be more careful," he says.

"Next time?"

"Kate, you did a darn good job with this case. You were right that Yvette didn't shoot Kurt. You found evidence no one else did. You should be proud of yourself. Like it or not, you're good at investigating."

I take another cookie and eat it. "When I was little, I wanted to be a detective, like you. Mom was so happy when I started focusing on soccer and stopped talking about investigating."

"It's in your blood." He flashes a rare full smile, his eyes sparkling. "Now you realize you actually enjoy it."

"I did like the challenge of figuring out what happened," I admit to him.

Liam says goodbye and walks into the hall. I move to the window and stare outside. One more night, then I can finally go home. I can't wait. Liam appears on the sidewalk and looks up. I raise my hand in a greeting, and he waves back.

Something he said rushes through my brain.

Sometimes we make tough decisions to protect our children.

I was talking about Dylan. But was he talking about my brother and me? And who did Liam mistakenly trust? I can't help feeling both those things are tied together and have a direct bearing on my child-hood. If I'm as good an investigator as Liam says, then I should be able to untangle that secret. I stare outside, and in this moment, I know with every fiber of my being that I will find out what Liam Murphy has been hiding for all these decades. And why.

ACKNOWLEDGMENTS

So many people have helped me on my journey here. Liza Fleissig of Liza Royce Agency—you changed my life! I love you and thank you for your support, confidence, and tireless work on my behalf. And to Ginger Harris-Dontzin and the rest of the LRA team, I'm so appreciative of everything you do to support me. To fellow sports lover and editor extraordinaire Liz Pearsons—working with you is a dream come true! Thank you for all your incredible guidance and for championing my work. Thanks to Grace Doyle, Sarah Shaw, Tamara Arellano, Jarrod Taylor, Alicia Lea, Jenna Justice, and all the amazing people at Thomas & Mercer for their support and guidance. A special shout-out to developmental editor Andrea Hurst, who challenged me in all the right ways.

There have been many iterations of *Lights Out* and a special group of friends who have read every single version. Linda Coppola, Tracy Kellaher, Gigi Georges—I would not have gotten here without your sharp eyes and sound advice. Thank you to all my beta readers: Pam Gerla, Michelle and Greg Marrinan, Cindy and Gregg Schwartz, Rachel Sherman, Risa Raich, Rachel and Everest Gray, Keshet Starr, Barbara and Michael Kalvert, and Sara Burns. Thanks to Kash Singhal and Cristian Mendez. In addition to your notes on the manuscript, a huge thank-you for your help with all things social media.

To those who got me over the finish line—Tessa Wegert and Naana Obeng-Marnu. Thanks for being trusted beta readers, advisers, and incredible friends. Thank you to my mentors—Pat Dunn, Carole Bugge, and Alan Turkus. You guys rock! Thank you to legal expert Audrey Felsen, police expert Greg Saroka, counseling expert Jen Gold, and Greenwich expert Luisa Viladas for invaluable advice. And thanks to Scott Soshnick, who has been my go-to person for everything sports since my first assignment, covering the 1999 NBA lockout.

Thank you to all my new author friends—your warmth and encouragement means the world to me. I can't imagine a more supportive group of people. I'm also incredibly grateful to the communities I've found through Sisters in Crime, Sisters in Crime Connecticut, and International Thriller Writers.

To my extraordinary extended family—Hartsteins, Kipnesses, Kalverts. Thanks for your constant encouragement, love, and support. To my "sister" Michelle Zelin—no one has my back like you. Love you. Thanks, Dorothy Kipness and Larry Broder, for your support. And to Irwin Kipness, for your love. To my aunt Sylvia Moss, for being my fierce cheerleader. I'm so glad I got to tell you about the book deal. I miss you terribly.

To my parents, Joyce and Marvin: without your love and support, this book would never have happened. I'm eternally grateful. To my kids, Justin and Ryan, who constantly cheer me on. I love you guys. To my husband, Rob, who read more drafts, talked me off more ledges, and fixed more embarrassing spelling mistakes than anyone. You are my rock. Love you. Always.

ABOUT THE AUTHOR

Photo © 2018 Adam Regan

Elise Hart Kipness is a former television sports reporter turned thriller writer. *Lights Out* is based on her experience in the high-pressure, adrenaline-pumping world of live TV. Like her protagonist, she chased marquee athletes through the tunnels of Madison Square Garden and stood before glaring lights, reporting to national audiences.

In addition to reporting for Fox Sports Network, Elise was a news reporter at New York's WNBC-TV, News 12 Long Island, and the Associated Press. She is currently co-president of Sisters in Crime Connecticut, as well as a member of Mystery Writers of America and International Thriller Writers. A graduate of Brown University, Kipness lives on a hobby farm in Stamford, Connecticut, with her family, three labradoodles, chickens, ducks, and one very cantankerous turkey.